The Kingdom of Quail

The Kingdom of Quail

Harris Strickland

Prologue

The Red Hills Region begins in Georgia and extends south into North Florida. This wedge-shaped parcel of land located between the Ochlocknee River and the Aucilla River is rich in wildlife. William Bartram, an early explorer, once described it as "a forest of great long-leaved pine, the earth covered with grass interspersed with an infinite variety of herbaceous plants and embellished with extensive savannas."

Set in the middle of the Red Hills is a small town in Georgia called Thomasville. During the Gilded Age, Thomasville was a vibrant resort town for affluent northerners who traveled by train for extravagant entertainment and an escape from cold winter weather. They came from New York City. They came from Philadelphia, Pennsylvania. They came from places like Cleveland, Ohio, and Newark, New Jersey. They came in private railcars with names like *Shining Star, Savannah Rose,* and *Lady Anastasia.*

There are thousands of quail in the Red Hills. Maybe millions. And lots of plantations surround Thomasville. Not cotton plantations, but quail plantations. The quail gather in coveys and scratch the ground for food in the grasses beneath tall pines. Hunting quail is much more than hunting quail. There is a certain mystique when done properly. But this story is not about quail. Quail don't change. This story is about people.

CHAPTER 1

Thomasville, Georgia

It was the summer of 1983. Ronald Reagan was president. Gas prices were just over a dollar a gallon. And a July heatwave had a stranglehold on South Georgia.

Angus Parker pulled his Ford truck into the parking lot of Grady's Gas and Grocery located one mile south of the Horseshoe Hill gate. It was noon and the sun glared from the tin roof of the country store. Dust rose from the gravel drive when Angus stopped his truck next to the lone gas pump. A handsome sunburned woman sat on the wooden bench by the door and a young boy sat next to her. The woman wore a blue denim shirt and a white skirt with purple flowers that matched the bruise on her cheek. The boy, maybe eight years old, sat beside her and used his hand to shade his eyes from the sun. Two canvas sneakers were tucked under the bench and the boy's blistered feet rested on a tattered suitcase. He wore faded shorts and a dirty white undershirt, both worn thin from too many washings.

Angus Parker walked inside, took two quarts of oil and a box of soda crackers from the shelf, and placed them on the check-out counter. He looked out the window at the woman and boy, then turned to the clerk. "How long have they been here?"

"They came walking down the road a couple of hours ago." The clerk took a ten-dollar bill from Angus and handed him change. "The lady went to the bathroom and filled up a jar with water. They've been sitting there ever since."

Angus took two pieces of bubblegum from a box near the register and laid his change on the counter. "Keep the change," he said. He pushed open the door and walked outside. "How about a piece of bubblegum?" Angus asked the boy. The boy looked down and shook his head. Angus turned to the woman. "Do you need a ride someplace?" he asked. "You look like you're waiting for a bus, but there's no bus here."

"No, thank you," the woman said. "I know there's no bus. My sister is on her way to take us to town."

"Do you live in Thomasville?" Angus asked.

"No, we live out here in the country," the woman said. "We're going into town so I can apply for a job."

Angus held his hand out to the boy again. "You sure you don't want this bubblegum?" Again, the boy shook his head. "What kind of job are you looking for?" Angus asked the woman.

"Brinkley's Diner needs help in the kitchen, and my sister knows the cook. I'm going to see if I can get on there."

"I know Brinkley's. It's one of my favorite restaurants. Good ol' family diner. If you get the job, maybe I'll see you there." Angus opened the door of his truck, hesitated, then turned around and walked back to the woman. "Listen, we need kitchen help at my place. If things don't work out at Brinkley's, give me a call. It could be the kind of job you're looking for." He reached into his shirt pocket and handed her a plain white card with simple writing. It read:

Angus Parker
Horseshoe Hill Plantation
(912) 272-5409

She took the card. "Thank you."

Angus climbed into the truck and started toward the highway. He glanced in the rearview mirror and saw the woman read the card and tuck it into her skirt pocket. Angus stopped, rolled the window down, and shouted, "We pay pretty good wages."

The woman nodded her head and Angus Parker left the dusty lot and turned south on the paved highway.

Two days after the encounter, the attractive woman with a bruise on her cheek called Angus Parker. Her name was Grace, and her boy's name was Luke. She said that Brinkley had offered her a job as night waitress, but the job was part-time, and she could not support her family on part-time wages. There was a note of desperation in her voice, so Angus Parker wasted no time. He drove his Jeep Wagoneer to town and brought Grace, her son, and the battered suitcase to Horseshoe Hill.

Thirty-eight oak trees lined each side of the long driveway from the front gate of Horseshoe Hill to the main house. Workers used the back gate. It was plain yet pretty enough for most people to admire. But the main drive was magnificent. The oaks reached across the drive and formed a green canopy that filtered sunlight through crooked branches and Spanish moss. The grass on each side of the drive was cut and edged sharp and straight. Outside the oaks, tall pines were scattered on rolling hills of wiregrass and broom sedge. Grace and Luke looked from side to side and rode in silence.

"My grandfather bought this place in 1905," Angus said. "He was one of the first industrialists to buy land here. Of course, in those days there were lots of northerners vacationing in Thomasville because this is as far south as the railroad came. That's when my grandfather and a few of his associates realized how cheap the land was back then."

Grace nodded and clutched her purse. Gravel crunched beneath the tires as they continued down the drive. In the distance, a box-shaped white house with columns grew closer.

"It might seem a bit extravagant now," Angus said, "but when my grandfather purchased this place, it was an abandoned cotton plantation with a dozen struggling sharecroppers. Land was cheap back then. Cotton had played out and nobody planted cotton anymore. Landowners couldn't pay the taxes. If not for the bobwhite quail...well, I don't know what would have happened here." Angus hesitated. "And even that may change someday."

Grace looked at Luke. "Do you have children, Mr. Parker?" she asked.

"I have a daughter," he said. "About the same age as Luke I would guess. My wife Catherine was raised in New York, and she places a high value on social etiquette. She dresses Annabelle like a young lady and tries to teach her to act like a lady. But I'm afraid she's a bit of a tomboy. I've seen her stare out the window during piano lessons and tea parties because she has more interest in hunting and riding her pony than piano lessons and tea parties."

Grace nodded.

"She's visiting relatives in Connecticut this summer," Angus added. He gazed out the window. "We don't have as many workers as we once did," he said. "When my grandfather was alive, the plantation was a community. There were rows of houses, a dairy, a school for the children, and a church. Every family had a small garden, but there was a big community garden, as well. Most of the workers were former sharecroppers, so they knew how to grow vegetables and tend to livestock."

Grace took Luke's hand and held it in hers.

"I think you will do fine here," Angus said.

They arrived at the big house, and Angus introduced Grace to Catherine. He left them in the library while Luke sat in the kitchen. Catherine asked Grace about her kitchen experience and questioned her about her housing needs. She made the decision quickly and by midafternoon that very day, Grace had a full-time job with the kitchen staff at Horseshoe Hill Plantation. The pay was good, and benefits included the key to a one-bedroom cottage behind the main house. The cottage was made of wood with whitewashed siding and green trim that matched barns, kennels, and equipment sheds located throughout Horseshoe Hill.

Catherine walked Grace to the kitchen and introduced her to Lula, a wiry black woman with gray hair. Catherine left, and Lula took a long look at Grace. "I sure am glad they hired some help for this kitchen," Lula said. "Miss Catherine's been having a party every night and it's 'bout worn all us down."

Grace nodded, smiled, and said nothing in return.

"You got a husband?" Lula asked.

"We're…I guess…" Grace searched for the words. "Yes, I guess so. But we're separated."

"Is he the one who put that bruise on your face?"

Grace looked at the floor. "I wasn't truthful about the job at Brinkley's. I didn't take the job because my husband found out about it. He would have come for us, and he would have caused trouble." She started to cry. "I don't want him to find us here."

Lula took Grace by the arm. "Don't you worry about that. We take care of our people around here. There's aprons in the pantry over there," Lula said. "Pick out one of the pretty ones, and you can help me roll out some biscuits. We've got party guests coming for dinner tonight."

Late that evening, long after the dinner guests had gone and after the staff had cleaned the kitchen and put away the dishes, Lula noticed a light in the kitchen. She opened the door, and there was Grace with a mop and bucket of hot water.

"We swept that floor good, Grace. And we're going to mop it in the morning. You don't need to be up working this time of night."

"I want to do everything right," Grace said. "I never imagined I would find something like this for me and Luke and I'm too anxious to sleep because I want to be sure I'm useful here."

Lula touched Grace's shoulder. "You'll be just fine. Now you go take care of that boy and get yourself some sleep. Miss Catherine's got another big party coming up this weekend, and tomorrow you can help me polish the silver. You'll wish you never saw such a place as this when you see all that silver that needs polishing. Now you go get some sleep, and I'll see you around sunrise in the morning."

"Okay, Lula." Grace placed the mop in the bucket and swept a strand of hair from her face. "I'm about done anyway."

The following morning Grace swept the porch on their cottage while Luke stood in the doorway and watched. Inside the big house, Lula and Roosevelt watched the newcomers through the kitchen window.

Roosevelt was the wagon driver. He was a large black man who had been born on Horseshoe Hill. Every morning, he had coffee in the kitchen with Lula.

"What's the boy's name?" Roosevelt asked.

"The boy's name is Luke," Lula replied.

"Luke." Roosevelt took a drink from his coffee and slowly nodded his head. "The Lord sent him."

Grace proved to be a valued addition to the staff on Horseshoe Hill. She was quiet, she worked hard, and she wore a simple smile throughout the day. Her body was lean, with a long back, and she had strong hands that were useful for polishing silver, kneading dough, and rolling biscuits.

One day, Catherine entered the kitchen with a notebook and two hardcover books in her hand. "I've got a fabulous plan for the kitchen," Catherine said. "Lula, do you remember when Angus offered to take me to France, and I ordered clothes and wine and food and pastries shipped from Paris?"

"I sure do remember. You were so excited about that trip, but Mr. Angus kept putting it off until another year," Lula said.

"Well, if he doesn't want to take me to France, I'll bring France right here to Horseshoe Hill. We'll start by learning how to prepare French food in our very own kitchen. Everyone in the Red Hills cooks wild game and some cook more beef, chicken and pork if they grow it on their property. But we can cook French cuisine. I know we can. Horseshoe Hill will be the place where our guests enjoy the finest French cuisine. It will be fabulous. You ladies are the best cooks I have ever seen. I know you can cook French."

Lula and Grace exchanged looks, but Catherine continued, "I have all the recipes in these two books." She showed them the green book, then placed it on the counter, and showed the brown one. "Can you read French, Grace?"

Grace looked at Lula for help. "I had two years of French in school, but I'm sure I don't remember much." She swallowed. "But I can try."

"Splendid. You and Lula can help me interpret these recipes. One book is English, but the other is written in French. I speak French, but I can't read a word of it. We have to learn. There are so many wonderful dishes. Our guests will be so surprised."

Catherine left the kitchen, and Grace turned to Lula. "I don't know how we're going to convert recipes from a French cookbook," Grace said. "I don't speak a word of French. And the measurements aren't even the same."

"Don't worry about it," Lula said. "There's pictures in there. We can figure it out. I have hundreds of recipes right here in my head. Besides, no recipe tastes the same all the time. We'll cook by sight and smell and feel. That's the way I do it."

Grace knew nothing about French cuisine, but she stayed awake late into the night and struggled with the French translations. She read her notes to Lula, and they compromised here and there and incorporated local ingredients until finally, they created the Horseshoe Hill version of French cuisine. They had a southern-style beef bourguignon, a braised cottontail rabbit, and meat pies stuffed with local game. They prepared duck confit from ringnecks and wood ducks. And chocolate soufflé for dessert. Catherine was thrilled. She adapted a new daily greeting for her entry into the kitchen, "How is everyone in the bistro today?"

Day by day, Grace embraced the comforts of Horseshoe Hill and her new life. She transformed the tiny cottage into a heart-warming home. She covered the bare windows with curtains sewn from remnants of cloth she found in the sewing room. She swept the cottage floor twice a day. She kept fresh flowers in a vase on the kitchen table, and she found a wooden mirror that she hung over the fireplace. For the first time in years, she looked in a mirror and touched her face. She took one of Catherine's handed-down dresses from her closet and held it to her body. She smoothed her hair and managed to smile.

While Grace worked, Luke sat alone on the porch for most of the day. He watched wagons, horses, and men with dogs pass by the cottage. He watched gardeners and cooks go to work early in the morning and return home in the afternoon. He was an outside observer, a bird perched on a limb above a river of fish. He kept to himself. He didn't run and play like a six-year-old boy. The porch was a self-imposed prison that barred him from doing wrong. Lula sent lemonade and cookies from the kitchen. Horse grooms nodded when they passed, and dog trainers tipped their hats. Weeks went by, but Luke never left the porch. Then he met Eugene.

There were white families and black families living on Horseshoe Hill. Eugene was black. He was Roosevelt's son. He was a year younger than Luke, and Eugene was not shy. Eugene played in the gravel drive beside Luke's house. Day by day, he inched closer and closer to the house and occasionally looked to see if Luke was watching. Finally, Eugene played his way right up to Luke's porch and stood on the steps. Luke said nothing.

Eugene hopped onto the porch and swung around the porch column. Then he stopped.

"You must have done something real bad," Eugene said.

"Why do you say that?" Luke asked.

"'Cause your momma doesn't ever let you leave the house."

"I can leave if I want to," Luke said.

"Then why don't you?" Eugene swung around the porch post.

"Don't want to."

Eugene switched hands and swung around the post in the other direction.

"Why don't you want to?" Eugene asked.

Luke didn't answer. "Do you live around here?" he asked.

"Yep, my daddy's the mule skinner here on this plantation," Eugene said. "Can't everybody drive a mule wagon, but my daddy can. He's the best. Everybody says so. Where's your daddy?"

"My daddy don't live here. Momma says he's looking for work out of town. He does that a lot. We've got a house of our own out in the country. We're just living here till my daddy finds work."

"You want to go to the creek and go fishing?" Eugene asked.

"Ain't got a fishing pole," Luke said.

"We have plenty of poles. And I know where to dig worms, too."

That afternoon, Luke and Eugene fished the big hole at the creek. They fished the following day, too. And they fished every day after that for a week. When Luke and Eugene weren't at the creek, they walked barefoot in the woods and explored the barns and kennels. They caught frogs and shot at quail and squirrels with homemade slingshots. When they got hungry, they went to the kitchen door and Grace brought them ham and cheese sandwiches on white bread. They ate the sandwiches with tall glasses of milk fresh from the dairy cows. In the afternoon, there was always a pitcher filled with ice and lemonade.

The hot summer days stretched into weeks and the weeks stretched into months. Grace and Luke blended into the Horseshoe Hill family like they had lived there all their lives. No one remembered a time when they were not there. They were home. And that suited Grace and Luke just fine.

CHAPTER 2

Horseshoe Hill was home to white people, home to black people, and Horseshoe Hill was home to one brown man. His name was Joe Green, and he was a full-blooded Native American. Joe Green was small in stature. He had dark skin and dark eyes that always seemed to be focused, even when he was looking at nothing. He had black hair that was closely cropped, and he wore a sweat-stained cowboy hat that rarely came off his head. If Joe Green stepped on a rattlesnake, he picked it up like it was nothing. But Joe Green never stepped on rattlesnakes. Nobody knew where he came from or how he got his name. It was not the sort of name you expect a Native American to have, but that was his name, Joe Green.

One afternoon, Roosevelt told Luke and Eugene about a litter of bird dog puppies. The news sent the two boys running for the kennels. When they arrived, they stood on the fence and peered through the boards where six brown-and-white puppies squirmed and searched for milk on their mother's belly.

"Look at that, Luke," Eugene said. "They ain't even opened their eyes yet. I bet they were just born last night."

"When you reckon they'll open their eyes?"

"Maybe a week, maybe two," Eugene said.

"Can we hold one?" Luke asked.

"You ain't supposed to pick them up until they open their eyes. We'll come back tomorrow and check on them."

The boys woke early the next morning and ran to the kennel where the momma dog cared for her pups.

Luke pointed to one of the pups in the corner of the kennel. "I like that little one there with the patch over his eye," he said. "He keeps to himself, but he crawls around real good."

"He looks like he's lost," Eugene said. "While all those others are getting their milk, he's just crawling around in circles."

"He can't find a teat with his eyes closed like they are. Look at him. He doesn't know where his momma is." Luke slid off the fence and landed in the kennel. "I'm going to help him." He picked up the puppy carefully and held him to his cheek. Then he laid the whimpering puppy on his mother's belly. The pup rolled off and crawled away. Luke retrieved the pup and once more placed him on a teat. Over and over again, Luke guided him to his mother, but the pup crawled away. "That puppy's going to die if he doesn't get milk," Luke said.

"Leave him alone," Eugene said. "He'll find her on his own. When you pick him up, he gets your smell on him. And his momma doesn't like that."

Luke put the pup back. The two boys visited the puppies every day for the next two weeks until finally, they opened their eyes. The boys watched them squirm around the kennel and roll on and off each other making the soft sounds that puppies make. Luke's favorite was the loner, and he named the pup "Patch" because of the black spot that covered his eye like a pirate patch.

When the pups were two months old, Luke and Eugene took them from the kennel and placed them on the grass where they sniffed the dirt and poked their noses at insects. Patch sat in the same place and watched the others but did not move. Luke returned him to the kennel, and Patch came to the wood fence and whimpered. He stuck his nose through the boards and licked Luke's wiggling fingers.

"I'm going to take Patch home with me," Luke said.

"You can't do that." Eugene reached out and grabbed Luke by the shirt. "If you do that, you're going to get a real whupping. I might get a whupping, too."

"They ain't going to miss a little one like Patch," Luke replied. "They already got fifty dogs around here, and they can't train all these puppies. Besides, if he doesn't get milk from his momma, he's going to die. I can get milk from our refrigerator and feed it to him on a plate."

Despite Eugene's objection, Luke climbed the fence and took Patch in his arms. He wrapped Patch in his shirt and the boys ran as fast as they could to Luke's house. They found a cardboard box and lined it with an old towel, then placed the box in the corner of Luke's room.

That evening, when Grace came home from work, she looked at Luke's sheepish face. "What have you done, Luke?"

"I ain't done nothing wrong, Momma."

Muffled whimpering and scratching came from Luke's room. Grace opened the door. Behind the door was a tiny pup with a dirty sock hanging from his mouth.

"Luke." She pointed her index finger in his direction. "Where did this dog come from?"

"The kennel."

"Did someone give you this dog?"

"No, ma'am."

"Does Mr. Parker know about this?"

"No, ma'am."

"What made you think you can take one of the puppies and bring him home like you did?"

"I don't know." Luke hung his head.

"Well, you've got to tell him. It's not right to take one of his puppies like that. You'll get us thrown off this place for sure, and we don't have anywhere else to go. Does Roosevelt know?"

"No, ma'am."

"Well, I expect you better tell him, too."

Angus Parker did not care that Luke had taken a puppy. But he pretended that he did. He recited the rules to Luke with a stern face and then softened a bit when tears fell from Luke's eyes.

"The good part of all this is that I see you have an interest in dogs," Angus said. "I figure that dog won't amount to much unless he gets special attention. So, for your punishment, I'm going to put you in charge of working that dog. I want you to feed him, bathe him, and train him. And I'll be keeping my eye on you to be sure you do a good job."

Luke wiped his tears. "Yes, sir, Mr. Angus. I'll do that for sure."

That was the day young Luke became a dog trainer. He named Eugene as his assistant dog trainer, and from that day on, wherever Luke and Eugene went, Patch went with them.

One summer afternoon, Luke, Eugene, and Patch went to the fishing hole. The boys led the way and Patch followed closely behind. "My daddy says you can't make a house dog out of a pointer," Eugene said.

"Everybody says that, but Patch is different. And besides, I'm going to train him to point birds, too, because that's what Mr. Angus told me to do. I'm going to train him to run in the field trials. If he gets good enough, they'll paint his picture and hang it in the living room like all those others with the silver bowls and blue ribbons."

"You don't know anything about training bird dogs," Eugene said.

"Don't have to train him," Luke said. "Bird dogs already know how to hunt. You see the way he's always watching and chasing after birds around the yard? He already knows how to do it. Besides, your daddy can show me how. He knows all about working the dogs. I've seen him do it."

One morning, Luke woke to find Joe Green and his horse, Dancer, in the front yard. "Bring the puppy outside," Joe Green said.

Luke went inside and came back with Patch. Joe Green slid from his horse. "Don't train that dog hard," Joe Green said. "He has the spirit of a hunter, but he hides it. Listen to his spirit and teach him to trust you." Joe Green raised Patch from the ground and looked him over good. "Come to the kennel in the morning and I will show you. He will be a better dog if you are the only one who trains him."

Joe Green and Luke established a routine. In the mornings, Joe Green trained kennel dogs, and in the afternoons, he helped

Luke. They started Patch in a small field behind Luke's cottage. Joe Green pulled a quail from the field bag and tied Patch to the porch while Luke dragged the quail around the backyard. Then, Luke hid the bird in Grace's flower bed. Patch hit the scent trail. He twitched his tail and sniffed the ground. He followed the trail to the flower bed, pounced on the quail, then paraded around the yard with the prize in his mouth. Luke praised him with words and gentle strokes. When they finished training for the day, Luke and Patch wandered around the barns and paddocks and walked to a nearby field and stayed outside until Grace called Luke to supper.

After Patch honed his skills finding dead birds, Luke tied a wing on the end of a fishing pole and dangled it in front of Patch, who pointed the moving wing like it was a live bird. Luke moved the bird closer and closer to Patch's nose until he jumped at the wing, then Luke snatched it away. That was the way veteran dog handlers taught dogs to hold point. Patch learned quickly. If he jumped, the bird left. But if he did not move, the bird did not leave. And when Patch did not move, Luke praised him. "That a boy, Patch. Hold him tight, Patch. Good boy. Good boy."

One morning, when Patch was eight months old, Joe Green knocked on Luke's door. "I'm done helping you. The dog is ready to learn on wild birds. And he needs to learn from you."

Luke took Patch into the woods on a short leash and let him hunt for live quail. He did that day after day. Once Patch was accustomed to the short leash, Luke used a longer leash, then a longer leash each time they went out until, eventually, he had no leash at all.

Despite everyone's doubts, Patch made a good pet and companion for Luke. At night, Patch slept at the foot of his bed. In the early mornings, he jumped on the bed and woke Luke by licking his ears and face. In the afternoons, Luke and Eugene and Patch fished the creek for tiny bream. On their way home, they pulled fresh grass and fed it to the horses in paddocks. They stopped by the kennels and looked over the pointers, and they ventured into the pines and searched for quail. And at night, Luke lay in bed and imagined Patch next to a silver bowl with his tail held tight and his head high as he posed for the painted picture that Luke would hang over the fireplace in their tiny cottage.

CHAPTER 3

It was late summer in 1984. Luke and Grace had lived on Horseshoe Hill for a year. They sat in rocking chairs on the front porch and waited for the sun to go down. Patch sat on the floor at Luke's feet.

"Momma, look at the way Patch is wagging his tail," Luke said. "He wags it all the time. Except when he's locked down on a bird scent."

"He wags his tail because he's happy," Grace said.

"If I had a tail, I'd wag mine," Luke said.

"Me, too, Luke. Me, too."

Just then, they looked past the big house and saw a rusted blue Pontiac sedan rattling up the drive. The car passed the big house and drove toward Grace's cottage. Grace stiffened in her rocker, and lines of worry formed on her face.

"It's your pa, Luke," she said. "Go inside." She shoved Luke inside and slammed the screen door behind him.

Luke went to his room with Patch and buried his head in his pillow. He stayed quiet and listened to the sound of a man's voice that was sweet and kind. He clenched the sheets in his hands as the man's voice changed from sweet and kind to desperate begging and pleading. The talking went on and on and sometime during the night, Luke fell asleep.

Luke woke up the next morning and cracked his bedroom door. He peeked into the living room and saw Grace dressed in a fresh floral dress gifted to her by Catherine. Her hair was brushed and tied with a blue ribbon. The old, tattered suitcase was open on the sofa and their clothes were packed neatly.

Luke heard a car engine crank and looked out the window. The rusted blue Pontiac sat idling with the trunk open.

"We're going home, Luke," Grace said.

Luke gathered Patch in his arms and stood in the doorway while Grace checked the dresser for clothes. She took a final look under the bed, then carefully closed the door to the small cottage that had been their home for nearly a year. As they drove away, Luke and Patch looked out the back window and waved goodbye to Eugene, who stood in the yard with two fishing poles perched on his shoulder.

The folks on Horseshoe Hill did not hear from Grace for a long time. At least it seemed like a long time. Then, three weeks after they had gone, Roosevelt found Grace and Luke on the oak-lined driveway walking toward the big house. Grace had the old suitcase in one hand, and she held Luke's hand with the other. Her hair was matted, and beads of sweat wet her brow.

Roosevelt slowed the truck. "Miss Grace, y'all need a ride?"

"Please, Roosevelt. I'm here to see Mr. Parker." Grace spoke as if she was speaking to a stranger. She and Luke climbed into the truck and sat next to Roosevelt.

"You should have called somebody to pick you up," Roosevelt said. "No use you walking in this heat like it is today."

"I needed the long walk so I could think about things," Grace said.

They rode in silence to the big white house with tall columns. Angus saw them from the window and met them at the door. He greeted them with a smile. "It's wonderful to see the two of you," Angus said. He looked at the suitcase. "Why don't you come inside? I'll get you something to drink."

Grace turned to Luke. "Luke, please wait on the porch. I need to speak with Mr. Parker."

"I'll send Lula with some water," Angus said. He offered a chair in the foyer, but Grace did not sit. Her lips trembled, and tears welled in her eyes. "I know I left you, and Miss Catherine in a bind, Mr. Parker. But I've come to ask a favor. I'd like my old job back. If there's any way you can consider it."

"Of course," Angus said. "We've missed you. Both of you. We hoped you would come back. Take your things to the cottage. Everything is just as you left it. Catherine will be thrilled. And Lula, too." Angus reached out to hug her, but Grace flinched when he touched her shoulder.

Grace was back, her cottage was back, and everything should have been the way it was before. But it was not. Grace and Luke were not the same. Grace looked older. The lines on her pretty face were deeper. The shine was gone from her hair. She spoke in whispers and flinched when pans fell to the floor or when someone in the kitchen brushed her as they passed. When Grace finished her work, she opened the cabinets and laid every piece of silver on the dining room table. She polished it until her fingers bled.

Luke was different, too. He stayed in his house all day long. It took two weeks for the purple bruise on his face to fade into yellow. It took another week for the yellow bruise to fade into his freckled face completely. Eugene walked by the cottage every day, but Luke would not go outside. After three weeks, Eugene gave up.

One day, Grace stood in the kitchen and watched Luke as he sat alone on the porch. She wiped the sweat from her forehead and untied her apron. "Lula, excuse me for a moment. I have something I have to take care of."

"It's time," Lula said.

Grace walked to the cottage and took Luke by the arm. She led Luke to the doorstep of Roosevelt's cottage and called Eugene outside while she stood at the door with a firm grip on Luke's arm.

"Eugene," Grace said, "I think Luke wants to go down to the fishing hole today. Does that sound like fun to you?"

"Yes, ma'am. It sure does."

"I can help dig the worms if you don't have any," Grace said.

"No, ma'am. We can dig our own. I know just where to find them." Eugene ran to the back of the house and came back with two cane poles and a rusted coffee can.

Eugene and Luke dug worms, then walked slowly and quietly to the creek. When they got there, Eugene threaded a wiggler on his hook and threw his line in the water. Luke's pole lay untouched on the bank. He tossed tiny sticks in the water and watched them drift away. He had not said a word since they left the house.

"Where's Patch?" Eugene asked finally.

"My pa shot him."

"Huh?"

Tears rolled down Luke's cheeks. He dropped a stick from his hand and covered his eyes and then a flood of tears seeped between his fingers. His chest heaved in and out as he sobbed. "He said he didn't like the way Patch barked. He never barked bad, but Pa took out his pistol and shot him dead. Just like he was nobody."

CHAPTER 4

The Red Hills are important to two kinds of people: those who hunt quail, and those who breathe air. It's a good place for healing.

A year passed by, and with the help of Eugene's companionship, Luke returned to his old self. When he was not with Eugene, he wandered about the plantation. One day Joe Green rode Dancer to Luke's cottage and stopped at the front porch. Joe Green had a black-and-white puppy tucked under his arm. He slid off his horse and extended the puppy to Luke.

Luke looked down and did not speak.

"I brought a dog," Joe Green said.

"I don't want another dog," Luke replied.

"The dog is not yours. I only came to show him to you." Joe Green placed the puppy on a patch of green grass. "Look how his nose goes straight to the ground and works back and forth."

"He is just a dog," Luke said.

"No. This one has the soul of a hunter. He'll make a good dog. Maybe a field trial winner. Maybe a picture dog. I want you to train him for me. The way you trained Patch."

Luke dropped his head and tears welled in his eyes.

Joe Green put his hand on Luke's head. "Your dog Patch is not gone." Joe Green pointed to the sky. "He is with the wind now. Everything that is good on the earth goes to the spirits when they leave the Earth. And everything that was yours on Earth is yours again in the sky. Patch is there for you because you were good to him. He is your spirit now. And the more spirits you have in the heavens, the stronger you will be."

Luke sniffled, and Joe Green continued. "Train this dog and he too will be your spirit."

The next day, Luke found Joe Green at the stables, sitting on a feed bucket, and chanting to his horse. Without saying a word, Joe Green stood and walked to the kennel with Luke in tow. He reached into a wooden box where six English pointer puppies tumbled like otters. Joe Green pulled a lemon-and-white puppy from the chaos. A female. He placed the puppy on the grass at Luke's feet then reached in and plucked a liver-and-white male.

"Start with these two. Work them as a pair, then put them back and take two more. Work all the puppies every day."

"Work them how?" Luke asked.

"Like before. Play with them. Play hunting games. Pretend they are running in the field trial. Be gentle in the beginning."

Every morning Luke walked to the kennel and played with the puppies. When they were three months old, Luke worked them with a cane pole and wing, and he dragged feathers through the grass in a game of hide-and-seek.

Every few days Joe Green stopped by to watch. One day he placed a pup on a wooden table. "Do this," Joe Green said. He stroked the pup's tail from the bottom up, so it stood tall and stiff. "That's the way a judge likes a tail on point. Tall and straight. Like twelve o'clock on a wall clock. Try it."

Luke stroked the tail just as Joe Green had. The tail stood tall and straight. A smile came over Luke's face. The first smile since he had returned to Horseshoe Hill. Joe Green took the dog down and placed him in the kennel.

"Remember," Joe Green said, "these are the working dogs. Be gentle but be firm. We want them to be warriors. They're not for the house."

Luke trained puppies that summer and would have trained during the fall if not for school. He was plenty smart, but school interfered with hunting season when everyone on Horseshoe Hill was in the field. Every day, when the final bell rang at the end of school, Luke jumped from his desk and ran to the bus that he and Eugene rode home. Eugene went straight to his cottage to do his homework, but Luke ran to the barn as fast as he could and looked for anyone to tell him the details of that day's hunting.

Fall turned to winter and on a cold Saturday morning in February, Joe Green rode to Luke's cottage and called him outside. "Come with me," Joe Green said. "It's time for you to go with the hunters." He held his arm low and swung Luke onto the back of his horse. They rode to the horse barn where the hunting group had gathered. Angus slid shotguns into scabbards. One of the scouts checked the tack on the horses. And Roosevelt hitched a matched pair of grey mules to the wagon.

Angus helped Luke onto the wagon, and he sat between Roosevelt and a young girl dressed in a perfectly white field jacket and a red headband that matched the red caps worn by the hunters and scouts. "This young lady is my daughter, Annabelle,"

Angus said. "She has recently returned from visiting family up north." Luke and the girl exchanged looks, but neither spoke.

Angus and Joe Green rode horses along with two scouts wearing white jackets and red caps. The scouts had brass whistles that hung from their necks and each one had a place in the formation that came together quickly.

The choreographed parade of wagon, horses, men, and dogs lurched forward and settled into a rhythm. They rode over gentle hills and skirted the edges of thickets and small fields in search of birds. Each player had his part and the parade rose and fell as they covered the land. It jingled and clicked as wagon parts, horse bits, and the iron latches on dog kennels shifted with the terrain. Dogs ran, scouts sang, and Roosevelt clucked at his mules.

Annabelle reached into the cooler on the back of the wagon and brought out two bottles. "Do you want a Coca-Cola?" she asked.

Luke accepted the Coke and Roosevelt popped the tops with a bottle opener. Luke leaned forward and watched with eyes opened wide like he was seeing his first circus show. Two pointers ran a crossing pattern through the woods, then suddenly both dogs stopped and stood rigid with tails held tight. Angus dismounted and put two shells in his over and under. He walked briskly to the dogs and the scout thrashed the cover with a flushing whip. The covey burst skyward, and Angus dropped two birds with two shots. Luke stood on top of the bench seat and watched with his mouth wide open.

The hunt ended as twilight began. The wagon returned to the barn, and Luke jumped off and ran home. He was out of breath when Grace met him at the door. "Momma, Roosevelt can drive that wagon like a truck on the highway. And those pointers can smell a bird a mile away. They've got a bird dog named Sam that's the best bird dog in the whole country."

"It sounds like you had fun," Grace said.

"I sure did. They even had cookies on the wagon. And there was a girl named Annabelle. She gave me a Coca-Cola. We brought back fourteen quail and Miss Lula's going to cook them for lunch tomorrow. You should have seen it, Momma. I can't wait 'til I'm bigger. I've got to learn to ride a horse so I can go out on the hunt every day just like the scouts."

Horseshoe Hill was like a winter carnival that fall. Guests came and went. Hunters hunted, and the crisp air held the smell of horses, leather saddles, gun oil and hickory logs burning in fireplaces. Catherine planned parties and hosted lunches and afternoon teas for charitable organizations. At nighttime there was a revolving circuit of dinners and events at the plantations and a carefully planned calendar of exhibits and festivals in town.

Guests took to the field every day, and at day's end they gathered for cocktails and conversation while dressed in field jackets and canvas trousers tucked into tall boots. They stood by the fireplace, on the porch, and sometimes they gathered with cocktails around a wagon parked on the lawn and plucked salted pecans and cheese straws from silver platters.

Dinner called for black tie and dinner gowns at Horseshoe Hill. Guests sat at the long table that seated twenty-four while servers in crisp white jackets and cotton gloves served each course. Conversation revolved around hunting and no business talk was allowed at the table. They politely argued best shots, best guns, and best dogs. They talked about cold weather and hot weather and bird populations and forest management ideas, old and new. And, without fail, they sadly toasted old companions who had passed away as if they knew that this life in the Red Hills would be gone one day. Maybe it was gone already, and they just didn't know it.

CHAPTER 5

HUNTING SEASON ENDED. WINTER DIED out. The ducks and the geese flew north. And a green spring spread over the Red Hills. Turkey gobblers gobbled and bobwhite quail whistled all day long. On Horseshoe Hill, Angus and Catherine Parker stood outside the house and made plans for a flower garden while Annabelle chased butterflies across the lawn. A blue Pontiac appeared in the driveway coming slowly toward the house. The sedan came to a stop in front of the house and a tall man in a denim jacket stepped out. He flipped a cigarette butt on the ground.

Angus walked to the man. "Can I help you?" he asked.

The man's eyes were red, and he swayed a bit as he greeted Angus. "I came to see my wife and boy," he said.

"Who is your wife?" Angus asked.

"You know who she is," the man said. "She's the white woman you have working in the kitchen."

"Then you must be Mr. Walker."

"That's right, Jason Walker."

Grace and Luke recognized the voice and ran to the kitchen window. Grace grabbed Luke by the hand and burst onto the porch dragging Luke behind her. Her face was flushed, and veins stood out on her temples. Angus stepped between Grace and the man with red eyes as he walked toward the porch.

Angus held out his hand and attempted a smile. "It's warm out here for March, and you look a bit parched," he said. "Why don't you come inside, and we'll have a drink. My name's Angus Parker."

"Yeah, I could use a drink," Walker said.

Catherine walked to the door and reached for the handle, but Angus grabbed her hand. "Catherine, you and Grace wait here with Luke," Angus said. "We'll be back out in a minute." Angus shouted toward the kitchen. "Lula, please bring us a couple of glasses of iced tea."

"Iced tea?" Walker huffed. "I thought we were having a man's drink."

"You'll like Lula's iced tea. It's the best in the Red Hills."

"You got something else?"

Angus ignored the question and the two men walked into the study and stayed there for half an hour. Roosevelt and Joe Green were in the front yard on horseback when Walker and Angus walked out.

Walker looked at the men on horseback and turned to Angus. "Now, I'll have a word with my wife," Walker said. He walked to the corner of the porch where Grace held Luke in her arms.

"Why don't you come back tomorrow?" Angus asked. "Grace is helping prepare dinner for guests coming tonight, but she has the day off tomorrow and you can talk with her then."

Walker stared at Angus and smirked. "Alright, I'll come back tomorrow." He looked around. "Nice place you have here," he said.

Angus walked down the stairs and approached Roosevelt. He spoke quietly so only Roosevelt could hear. "Looks like he's got a pistol tucked in the back of his pants. When he leaves, make sure he knows he's not welcome to come back. I'll have the sheriff meet him at the gate."

Roosevelt nodded his head. Walker leaned in and attempted to hug Grace, but she pushed him away. He tried to tousle Luke's hair, but Luke hid behind Grace. "I'll come back tomorrow," he said.

"It's late and we have locked the front gate now," Angus said. "Roosevelt, you and Joe Green show this gentleman out the back gate. Maybe he would like to go by the hill and rub the horseshoe for good luck."

Roosevelt tipped his hat. He and Joe Green wheeled their horses and trotted off, followed by the blue Pontiac.

That was the last time Jason Walker visited Horseshoe Hill, or anywhere else for that matter. The story was never clear, but Sheriff Barnes never had the chance to confront Jason Walker. When he saw the sheriff waiting at the gate, he drove through a wire fence and sped off. The sheriff flipped on blue lights and pursued the speeding Pontiac but lost him during the chase. The next morning, the blue Pontiac was upside down at the bottom of a broken bridge. Jason Walker's lifeless body was still behind the wheel.

CHAPTER 6

Three years after the day Grace and Luke arrived at Horseshoe Hill, no one could have imagined the struggles they had known. Grace never had to look far to find a friend. She had more friends than she had ever had right there on Horseshoe Hill. And Luke, well, Luke just smiled. He smiled all the time and never stopped smiling. He woke up with a smile, carried the smile throughout the day, and went to sleep at night with the same smile.

The school year ended, and the long-awaited summer began. It was barefoot weather for Luke and Eugene. The days passed slowly. Each day Luke fed, washed, and exercised a dozen bird dogs while Eugene watched. When Luke finished with the dogs, he and Eugene walked the trails picking honeysuckle and blackberries on their way to the fishing hole.

One afternoon, they passed the big house kitchen and the smell of fresh-baked cookies drifting through the screen door stopped them in their tracks. They peered into the window and saw three cooling racks on the counter. Each rack was covered with chocolate chip cookies.

"Let's get some of those cookies," Eugene said. "We can take them down to the fishing hole with us."

Eugene eased the kitchen door open and let it close slowly so as not to make a sound. Both boys put a cookie in their mouths and quickly filled their hands with as many cookies as they could hold. They slipped out the same way they came in and just as they were about to break into a run, a girl shouted from an open window, "I see you taking those cookies!"

Eugene and Luke stopped and looked back. It was Annabelle. She ran through the kitchen and caught up with the boys outside.

"We ain't stealing these cookies," Eugene said. "Lula gives us some all the time."

"She only lets me have one at a time and look how many you have. You have more than ten cookies." Annabelle crossed her arms. "If you eat all those, you'll get a stomachache."

"We're taking them to the fishing hole 'cause we always get hungry while we're fishing," Luke said.

"I want to go with you to the fishing hole." Annabelle said. "I'm bored around here in the summer."

Luke and Eugene looked at each other. "You'll get muddy and everything," Luke said. "Girls can't go to the fishing hole."

"Can too," Annabelle said.

"Can't neither," Eugene said.

"I'll tell on you for taking all those cookies if you don't take me with you."

The boys looked at each other and shrugged. "Well, come on if you have to," Luke said.

Luke, Eugene, and Annabelle walked toward the fishing hole and ate cookies along the way.

"What school do you go to?" Eugene asked.

"The private school," Annabelle replied.

"Oh," Eugene said. "We've seen you riding that black-and-white pony in the horse ring."

"Her name is Daisy," Annabelle said. "I'd much rather ride a horse than take piano lessons and ballet lessons like Catherine makes me do."

"You call your momma Catherine?" Luke asked.

"She doesn't care. I think she likes it. It sounds so much better than 'momma.' What do you call yours?"

"I call mine Momma," Luke said.

"I don't call mine anything," Eugene said. "She died when I was just a baby."

"We saw you jumping cane poles with that pony," Luke said.

"And we saw you fall off," Eugene said. "Remember that, Luke?"

"I sure do remember that," Luke said. "We about busted our sides laughing because she came off the ground with a mouthful of dirt."

"At least I didn't cry," Annabelle said. "I never cry. I'd like to see either one of you jump a pony like I can."

"I bet I could," Luke replied.

"Me, too," said Eugene. "But we ain't riding ponies today. We're fishing. And we're going to see who can catch fish the best."

They arrived at the creek with two cane poles and a coffee can full of worms. Luke and Eugene laughed at the way Annabelle took a worm from the coffee can and held it by the very tips of her fingers. She fumbled with the hook until Eugene finally took the worm from her, threaded it on the hook, and handed the pole back to Annabelle. Within seconds, the red-and-white bobber quivered, moved to the left, and then shot under water. Annabelle squealed and pulled back hard. The pole bent double, then snapped back and sent a palm-sized river bream flying onto the bank.

Luke ran to the fish. "Look at the size of that bream."

"He's mighty big to come out of this creek," Eugene said. "Biggest fish I've ever seen caught around here."

"It's the biggest fish I've ever seen anywhere," Luke said.

"Let's put him back," Annabelle said.

The boys looked at each other and gave in to her wishes. The big bream went back in the creek, and they fished that day until it was time for supper. On their way home, the boys whispered to each other that Annabelle was alright for a girl. From that day on, Luke and Eugene had a new fishing pal at Horseshoe Hill. And with Annabelle as their friend, Luke and Eugene gained privileges. She had permission to take anything they wanted from the kitchen and that included chicken drumsticks, pickled peaches, and cookies. Always cookies.

One day, the boys woke early and ran to the kitchen to meet Annabelle. She had a wooden picnic basket with a red bow tied to the handle. She placed a red-checked tablecloth and sterling silverware in the basket along with apples, grapes, and pimento cheese sandwiches.

"We're going to have a real picnic at the fishing hole today," Annabelle said. "And Daisy is going with us."

Daisy was small enough that the trio could slide on and off with ease which made it easy to take turns riding, but mostly, Annabelle rode while the boys walked with their cane poles and coffee can of worms. They never carried three poles, just two, because there was only room for two lines in the fishing hole. That didn't matter, and it didn't matter if the fish didn't bite. On those days, they followed the creek barefoot and looked for crawfish, frogs, and salamanders. That's the way it was, day after day, and all summer long.

CHAPTER 7

At its best, Horseshoe Hill was a universe unto itself. It was colorful. The big white house and the green lawn and white people and black people coming and going. Field workers and dog handlers walked the same path as black-tie guests who came for dinner. There were black Labs and white pointers. Hunters wore white jackets and red hats. They rode brown and white and buckskin horses. Some rode in black wagons with red-spoked wheels behind handsome gray mules. The colors blended beneath tall pines spread over hills and valleys of grasslands that turned green in the spring and faded to brown in winter. It was home to many living things.

It seemed that they grew up overnight. After two years of picnics, creek fishing and horseback riding, Annabelle, Luke, and Eugene started middle school and that is where their interests began to change. Eugene liked school, Luke liked dogs and horses, and Annabelle liked Luke.

One afternoon, Luke was training a puppy in the pasture next to the kennels. Annabelle rode by on Daisy and stopped at the pasture. She began riding in circles and jumping limbs and sticks and anything else that looked like a real jump. She kept her eyes on Luke, and Luke kept his eyes on the dog.

Finally, she stopped. "What are you doing?" she asked.

"Training dogs. I'm getting to know this pointer puppy. He's going to be a good one. He's not two months old yet and he's already pointing a wing. Pointing pretty, too."

"Can I watch?" Annabelle asked.

"Nobody's stopping you."

Annabelle slid from her horse, hitched the reins to a fence post and sat on the rail. "My daddy says you're going to be the best dog man in the Wiregrass Field Trial Club when you get older," Annabelle said.

"I might be the best now if Joe Green would let me enter one of these pointers in the field trial."

"Wouldn't that be exciting if you could win one of those big silver bowls?" Annabelle asked. "I'd put it in the trophy case right in the middle of all those other ones. And I'd put your picture right beside it. You and your dog, and me."

"Whoa, whoa." Luke tugged on the check cord with the pup chewing on the other end.

"My daddy says you know what a dog is thinking," Annabelle said. "That's why you're good with dogs. Do you know what a dog is thinking? Can you really know that?"

Luke ignored her. He gently added tension to the rope and kept the dog in check.

Annabelle sighed and touched her hair. "Do you think I'm pretty?"

Luke coiled the rope and looked up at Annabelle. She wore blue jeans, cowboy boots, and a white blouse with the sleeves rolled up. Her braces were gone, and her teeth were straight.

Her wavy blonde hair hung midway down her back, and she wore a blue velvet riding cap strapped to her head.

Luke tugged at the pup. "I guess so."

Annabelle stayed a moment longer, then jumped from the fence, untied the reins, and sprung onto her horse. She wheeled the pony and galloped home. She arrived at the house, dropped the reins, and ran inside. She found Angus in his office with a stack of papers.

"Daddy, I'm going to marry Luke Walker."

"No, you're not," Angus replied.

"Why not?"

"Because you're too young to get married."

"I don't mean now, Daddy," Annabelle said. "I mean when I get older."

"Then we'll talk about it when you get older."

"Okay, Daddy. But I *am* going to marry him."

CHAPTER 8

THERE WERE TWO PARTS TO the year on Horseshoe Hill. November until March, known as "the season," was dedicated to hunting. April through October was the slow season when men worked the fields, mowed grass, and nailed boards that had fallen from fences during the winter. It was an established routine year after year. But the spring of 1991 came with an added dimension.

After a quiet dinner, Angus and Catherine took their coffee into the library. Angus read a newspaper while Catherine browsed the pages of magazines. Thirty minutes later, Lula came in and freshened their coffee. On her way back to the kitchen, Lula looked out the window and gasped. "Lord have mercy. Look out there in the yard."

Catherine looked up from her magazine. "What is it, Lula? Another fox on the lawn?"

"You have to come and see for yourself."

"Is it deer?" Angus asked. He set his newspaper down and joined the two women at the window.

In the middle of the lawn, silhouetted by the glow of a full moon and a blanket of stars, Luke and Annabelle stood together. Luke had Annabelle's hand in his. From behind, they looked like a matched couple on top of a wedding cake, or a young prince and princess gazing into the starlight. Annabelle stood tall and lean. And Luke stood even taller with a taut frame and strong jaw. His unparted hair was thick and brushed back in lazy waves.

"I hadn't even noticed, but they're all grown up now," Lula said. "That's not children out there anymore. That Luke has turned into a handsome young man. And Annabelle, well there's no prettier girl in Georgia."

Catherine sighed. "I thought Annabelle was in her room. Angus, go out and tell her to come inside."

"They're just enjoying the stars and the fireflies. Let them be."

"Yes, but..."

"They're sixteen now, and he's a fine boy, Catherine. If you tell Annabelle she can't spend time with Luke, they'll be together for sure. Just let it be. It won't last."

On the lawn, Annabelle leaned on Luke, and squeezed his hand.

"She's your daughter through and through," Catherine said. "She'll stay out there all night long if we let her. Now please, call her inside."

Angus ignored her.

It was the first Saturday in April. Luke was alone in the cottage while Grace worked in the big house. Outside the cottage, a tractor stopped, and someone revved the engine again and again.

Luke went to the window and saw Annabelle on a rusted John Deere. Her hair was tied in a ponytail, her sleeves rolled to the elbows, and she wore a sweet grin on her face.

Luke ran outside. "What are you doing?" he asked. "Who gave you permission to drive the tractor?"

"No one gave me permission. I took it on my own."

"Who taught you how to drive a tractor?"

"Nobody. I want you to teach me." She patted the fender and invited Luke to join her. "I had a little accident coming over here, and the tractor knocked a few boards off the fence. But we can fix those later. Hop on and show me how to plow firebreaks."

Luke shook his head and walked toward the tractor. "You'll get me in all kinds of trouble." He climbed on. "You better let me drive around the house in case someone sees us."

Luke took the wheel and drove the tractor to the barn. He hitched a harrow and they drove off to a secluded area called the Outpost. When they got there, Luke slid over, and Annabelle took control. She plowed breaks and turned overgrown weed fields into fresh dirt. They stayed on the tractor for most of the day, and on their way home, they rode the backroads so no one would see them.

They had nearly reached the barn when they rounded a curve and there stood Angus, Catherine and Roosevelt looking at the damaged fence. They turned around when they heard the tractor. Annabelle was sitting in the driver's seat, and Luke stood behind her with his hands on her shoulders. They didn't stop and they didn't slow down. Annabelle gave a timid wave as they drove out of sight.

Catherine shot a look at Angus after the tractor passed. "Do something, Angus."

That look on Catherine's face was enough to make them slow down, but it didn't stop the thing that couldn't be stopped.

On Luke's seventeenth birthday, Angus asked him to meet at the horse barn. When Luke arrived, Angus handed him the reins to a chestnut gelding with a white blaze. The horse's name was Renegade, and he stood fifteen hands high.

Angus handed the reins to Luke. "Happy Birthday, Luke. Treat him well."

Luke's eyes grew wide. He took the reins from Angus and led the horse in a slow circle. "Renegade," Luke said. "He's my favorite of all the horses here."

"I know."

"Can I ride him?"

"He's all yours. You can ride him whenever you want."

Luke had tears in his eyes. He put a foot in the stirrup and eased into the saddle. He sat tall and straight and looked about as if he was seeing the world for the first time in his life.

"Thank you, Mr. Angus. Thank you." He wiped a tear from his eye, tightened the reins, and galloped down the road.

The next day, Luke found Joe Green outside the barn. Luke wore a large grin on his face as he tied his new horse to the rail.

"So, you have a horse now?" Joe Green asked.

"Yes, I do. And I came to ask you a favor. Can you teach me to ride like you? I've never seen anybody ride a horse like you can."

"I'll teach you. But not here. We'll go far from the barn where people don't go. Your horse can learn like a horse in the wild and you can learn the same way."

Joe Green was the best there was on a horse. He mounted and dismounted as easy as a bird folding his wing. He could go forward, he could go backwards, and he could go sideways. Joe Green rode with the reins in one hand, but he did not need them. Dancer knew what to do when Joe Green was in the saddle, with or without the reins.

Joe Green and Luke rode far from the barn. They stopped at a fork in the road and Joe Green removed the bridle from Renegade. He tied a red bandana so that it covered Luke's eyes like a blindfold.

"Now ride your horse," Joe Green said.

"I can't see a thing."

"Trust the horse."

Luke took a handful of mane in his right hand and nudged Renegade forward while Joe Green rode alongside.

"Listen to the horse and feel the earth through his feet," Joe Green said. "Feel the wind and taste the air and you will know where you are going."

Renegade walked slowly at first, then picked up the pace.

"Listen to the birds and the other animals when you ride," Joe Green said. "Be a part of it. That will make you a better hunter. And a better man."

After two weeks of riding blindfolded, Luke took the stairs to Annabelle's room and knocked quietly at her door.

"Who is it?" Annabelle asked.

"Luke," he whispered.

She smiled and closed her book. "Come in."

Luke poked his head inside the door. "What are you doing right now?" he asked.

"Summer reading. It's such a bore. I wish we never had school."

"Come with me," Luke said. "I want to show you something."

Annabelle jumped from her bed. "What? A surprise? You have a surprise to show me?"

"Not actually a surprise, just some things."

"What things?"

"Things around Horseshoe Hill. Interesting things I think you'll like. I have our horses saddled outside. Come on, we'll be back before dinner."

Annabelle unhitched her horse, placed her boot in the stirrup, and swung effortlessly into the saddle. Luke draped the reins over his horse's neck. He walked back, took four fast steps, placed his hands on the horse's rump, and vaulted into the saddle. Annabelle grinned in delight and Luke stood in the stirrups and took a bow as though it were nothing.

They set out with Luke in the lead. They rode single file for the first few minutes, then Annabelle nudged her horse closer to Luke. She rode closer and closer. Sometimes so close that the saddles rubbed against each other. The horses did not mind and neither did Luke.

"You see that hole in that pine tree up there with the sap all around it?" Luke pointed to a large longleaf pine in the distance. "That's a red-cockaded woodpecker nest. And there's another one over there." Luke pointed to a distant tree. "They're just about extinct, but I've found three colonies already," Luke said. "The research station is making a study on them, and they want me to help find the colonies. They're not hard to find really, if you know where to look."

Annabelle exhaled and melted into her saddle. "I love it when you say things like that. I can just imagine you and Renegade riding these woods and studying the animals. You should study biology in college. You'll be famous like Audubon, or Darwin."

"I don't care about being famous. I just like to do it. The research team is coming back tomorrow, and they'll try to catch some of these right here and tag them. You should come out."

"Are you going to be here?" Annabelle asked.

"I can't," replied Luke. "I have to work dogs tomorrow, but you should come and watch."

"Maybe I will," she said. "But I wish you could be with us." Annabelle reached out and took Luke's hand in hers. They rode for a long time with neither one speaking. They stopped at the fishing hole. Tea-colored water flowed over the sandy bottom and into the deep pool where it swirled in the bend then crept downstream, carrying tiny brown leaves in the current. Luke nudged Renegade and leaned in toward Annabelle. She met him halfway and their lips came together. Annabelle took a breath, wheeled her horse, and rode away at a gallop. She stopped, turned around, and galloped back for a longer, sweeter kiss. Then she was gone again.

The next day, Luke trained dogs in the field. He finished training for the day and fed the dogs. As he started for the cottage, he saw Annabelle riding toward him at a gallop. She came to a sliding stop, dropped the reins, and jumped from her horse. Her face was flushed, and she could barely speak.

"What in the world happened to you?" Luke asked.

Annabelle gave him a strong hug and then backed away. "I held one, Luke. I held a red-cockaded woodpecker in my hands.

He was so tiny. And he was so light and so fragile, and Luke… he felt just like a feather. Like one single feather. It was like I was holding nothing, but I opened my hands, and he cocked his head to the side to look at me and it was like he knew I would watch over him."

"Slow down and tell me," Luke said.

Annabelle exhaled. "It was like he was completely calm when he looked at me. Like he knew I was not going to hurt him. And then he flew away and went right back to his nest high in the tree. Luke…"

"What?"

"We must protect them. You and me. You must protect them. Will you, Luke? Promise me you will. Promise me right now." Annabelle was out of breath.

Luke flashed a devilish grin. "Give me a kiss and I'll promise," he said.

Annabelle grabbed him by the neck and drew his lips to hers. She pressed her chest into his chest and kissed him hard. Luke was breathless when finally, she broke away. He staggered back and caught his breath, "Those woodpeckers are going to have a long, happy life. I promise you that."

One day, in early fall, when the leaves turned red and yellow and the weather cooled, Luke and Annabelle saddled their horses. They rode side by side and held hands and kissed as soon as they were out of sight. They returned to the barn and bathed the tired and lathered horses, then climbed the hayloft ladder and tossed down fresh hay. At the far end of the loft, they made a room from hay bales and propped their boot heels on the bales.

They held hands and kissed until the light faded and darkness sent them home.

The next day, Annabelle was unusually quiet as they rode horses along a pine ridge. "Catherine wants me to go to finishing school," Annabelle said.

Luke stopped his horse and looked at her. "I don't even know what finishing school is."

"That's where girls go to learn how to be perfect ladies. They teach manners and fashion and everything that a girl needs to know about finding the right husband." Annabelle sighed. "Don't get me wrong, Luke. I want to be the perfect lady, but I want to be the perfect lady here. I don't want to leave Horseshoe Hill and live someplace else. I'm sure of it. As sure as I can be."

"I think your mother wants you to find a husband with lots of money and nice clothes," Luke said. "Maybe a doctor or lawyer."

"Don't be silly. I want to marry somebody like you." Annabelle nudged her horse next to Luke and kissed him hard on the lips. "I want you," she said.

"What if I was a lawyer in New York? Would you want me then?"

"Oh, Luke. Why are you asking me something like that? I could live in New York if you were there. Or maybe we could move to Madagascar and eat the fruit from the trees. But why should we when we're the same? We love the woods and horses and dogs and hunting, and I can't imagine any place better than this. I can't imagine being a housewife every day. I want to be out here and do the things that you do."

"If you go to a school like that, maybe you'll change your mind," Luke said.

"I won't."

"If you go, you'll know for sure," Luke said. "And your mother will be happy."

"You won't miss me?"

"Of course, I'll miss you. I'll miss Eugene too when he goes to Georgia Tech, but I won't try to stop him."

"Are you telling me I should go?"

"I'm telling you that all of Horseshoe Hill, and me too, will be waiting for you when you get back."

Annabelle's face turned red. She tightened the reins and wheeled her horse toward the barn. "I hate you, Luke!"

Annabelle did not hate Luke. She wrote to him every day. She came home for Christmas and ran straight into the library where her father sat behind his desk.

"Daddy, can I borrow a tuxedo from your closet?" she asked.

Angus looked over his reading glasses. "Where's my hug?" he asked.

Annabelle ran to the desk and gave him a strong hug. Then she backed away and asked again. "What about the tuxedo?"

"What does a pretty young woman like yourself need with a tuxedo?"

"It's for Luke," she said. "I invited him to our Christmas party. He doesn't have a tuxedo. You know that."

Angus Parker crossed his arms. "Have you asked your mother about this?"

"Of course not," Annabelle said. "There is no telling what she might say."

"She might think it's not a good idea," Angus said.

"That's why I want you to tell her. She listens to you. If I ask her, she will say no for sure."

"I need to think about this. You know we love Luke, and he is part of the family, but I imagine your mother made the guest list a long time ago."

Annabelle clasped her hands together under her chin. "Please, Daddy?" she asked. "I'm going to that school like she asked me to, and I do all the things you think are good for me. But please, I only want this one thing. When the Christmas break is over, I'll go right back to finishing school. Did you know it's cold in Virginia? I'm freezing up there. It's so cold. But I'll go back because I know that's what she wants me to do."

"Alright," Angus said. "I'll speak with your mother."

On the morning of the Christmas party, Annabelle pulled Luke into the dining room. She sat him in a chair and in front of the chair was one complete place setting with what Luke stated was an overabundance of forks, spoons, knives, and glasses. Annabelle leaned on Luke's back, placed her hand on his shoulder and carefully explained the purpose and order for each utensil. She was nearly finished when Grace walked in the door. Luke's face turned red.

"I'm showing Luke everything I've learned in finishing school," Annabelle said. "We are going to have so much fun tonight."

"Luke is pretty good with his table manners." Grace reached in and straightened his salad fork. "But I'm sure he pays better attention to you than he does to me. Do you mind if I have a word with Luke?" Grace asked.

"I think we're all done," Annabelle said. "I'm so glad to know that Mr. Randolph is here to join us tonight. Aren't you, Grace?" Annabelle winked at her.

Grace blushed. "Yes, I am."

Luke stood from the table and walked with Grace to the cottage.

"Luke, have a seat on the sofa. I need to tell you something,"

"What is it, Momma?"

"I don't know how to say this other than just saying it." She sat on the sofa next to Luke. "I'm thinking of leaving Horseshoe Hill," she said. "Actually, I have already quit work. Just recently."

"Quit work? What do you mean? I thought you loved it here."

"Oh, I do, Luke. So much. It has been wonderful here with you." She placed her hand on Luke's knee. "But sometimes I feel lonely. I never felt that way when you were young, but now you are always working the dogs and hunting and staying in the woods all day. You don't need me anymore. And I need to tell you, I've met somebody." Grace took Luke by the hand.

"You met somebody?"

Grace nodded.

"Who?"

"I think you've met Randolph Richardson."

"Mr. Richardson? Of course. We've hunted together, and he's always nice on a hunt." Luke stopped talking and Grace broke into a smile.

"That's it," Luke said. "I saw you sitting with him today. I knew the two of you looked mighty friendly."

"He is a nice man. A real gentleman. We've kept it a secret, and even Angus didn't know until recently. I didn't think it would be proper, but we've been seeing each other for a couple of years now. And I need to tell you something else." Grace squeezed

Luke's hand. "I've been lying to you. All those nights when I told you I was going into town to take classes...well, I was seeing Randolph. Going to dinner, taking in a movie, and sometimes just walking together."

Luke patted her hand. "I think that's wonderful, Momma. You deserve to be happy. But I don't know what I'll do if you leave Horseshoe Hill."

"You're eighteen now, and you're a grown man. You have your own kind of family here. I know it must seem selfish of me, and I have so much to be grateful for…but I want a partner in life. I want to have something of my own. I believe…no, I'm sure, Randolph is that man. And I love him so much. He is kind and patient and humorous. In a dry sort of way. I know it seems sudden, but we both know what we have with each other. He is a wonderful man."

"But can't you stay here?"

"No. We'll visit, but we can't live here."

"Where will you live?"

"New Jersey. He has a beautiful home there and a big extended family of his own. He wants us to be married and live together in New Jersey." Grace hugged Luke. "You are the most important person in my life, and always will be," she said.

"I am happy for you," Luke said.

"I'm so happy, but I feel scared. I'm scared that something bad is going to happen because in the pit of my stomach I feel like we don't deserve to have this much good fortune."

"You deserve all the goodness that God can give you, Momma. It was meant to be. For both of us."

As the day progressed, so did the preparations in the kitchen. Cooks and servers washed holiday dishes, polished silver and separated groceries into bins and baskets precisely organized on marble countertops. Catherine walked in with a pretty dress on a hanger, and everything stopped.

"Grace, I found this dress I thought you might like to wear to the party tonight," Catherine said. "I think it will fit you perfectly."

Grace looked at the dress and felt the silkiness of the fabric. "I can't, Miss Catherine. I'm not going to the party. I'll help Lula in the kitchen if that's alright with you."

"No, no. We want you to join us at the table. It would be awkward for Randolph if you're serving."

Lula chimed in. "You go on to that party, Grace. We'll be just fine here in the kitchen."

"I've already spoken with Randolph, and he understands. I'll be fine with Lula. We've been planning and working for weeks now. I can't abandon her at the last minute."

Catherine looked about the kitchen and then looked at Grace who had not changed her expression. "Alright…but think about it. It seems very awkward to me."

"I'll think about it. And thank you, but the answer is still no."

The holiday party was a festive whirlwind of black jackets, sequined gowns, black ties, silver bowls, music, and cocktails. Twenty-six people attended the candlelit dinner including the Parker family, house guests, town guests, Randolph Richardson, and Luke.

Luke looked handsome in his borrowed tuxedo. Thanks to Annabelle, it was the newest and best from Angus's closet. No one could have imagined it was Luke's first black-tie social event. He circulated the living room during cocktail hour and chatted easily with every guest. He held the chair for Annabelle at dinner and used the right fork at the right time and drank from the right glass. He joined the conversation at the table, and shared his thoughts on land management, quail habitat, food plots and their prescribed fire practices. Every time Luke spoke, Annabelle reached beneath the table and took his hand.

Grace entered the dining room with a tray of desserts and Luke stood and clinked a champagne glass with his knife. When he had everyone's attention, he took a deep breath. "I saw this in a movie once, so I guess this is the way to make a toast." He looked down at Annabelle, and she nodded with a smile. "I want to toast my mother, Grace, and I want to wish her all the happiness in the world. As most of you know, she is leaving Horseshoe Hill. And most of you know why." Luke hesitated. "And I also want to congratulate Mr. Randolph for finding the kindest and best woman I have ever known in my life." Luke extended his glass in her direction. "Here's to you, Momma."

Grace, with a flushed face and tears in her eyes, took a bow. Behind her, Lula stood at the door to the kitchen with her hand on her heart.

The dinner lasted for hours, and when they were done, the family and guests dispersed and then regrouped in front of the fire in the living room. Annabelle gathered Luke by the arm, pulled him into the library and kissed him firmly on the lips. "You are the consummate party guest and such a gentleman." She kissed him again. "I love you more than ever."

The wedding was simple. Grace and Randolph were married in front of a warm fire in the living room at Horseshoe Hill. The guests were Luke, the Parkers, Roosevelt, and Lula. The rest of the kitchen staff stood in the background. After the wedding, Grace packed three bags with all her personal belongings. She placed the bags on the porch steps and hugged Luke while Randolph brought the car. As they drove away, Grace gave Luke a final wave. He held his tears until they were out of sight.

Two days later, Annabelle went back to school, and Luke was alone. He spent his days working dogs, mowing, and turning food plots with the tractor. The work was hard, but he didn't mind. Every night, he opened the oven and found a plate of food that Lula had left for him. Some nights, Luke went to the hay barn and climbed the ladder to the loft where he kept a blanket, a cushion for his head, and a bare light bulb that he hung from the rafters for reading. He sometimes slept there all night, surrounded by the smell of hay and horses and the memory of secret rendezvous with Annabelle.

One night, Angus strolled over to Luke's cottage and found him reading at the kitchen table. "What are you reading there?" Angus asked.

"It's called *One Hundred Years of Solitude,*" Luke said. "Annabelle recommended it to me."

"That title is somewhat appropriate, I guess," Angus said.

Luke chuckled. "I know."

"Say Luke, I've spoken to Catherine, and now that your mother is gone, why don't you move in the main house with us?" Angus asked.

Luke closed the book. "I appreciate that, Mr. Angus, but if it's alright with you, I'd like to stay in the cottage. I've gotten comfortable here and the bed fits me just right."

"That's alright with me, Luke. You can stay there as long as you like. Just know that you have a room in the house whenever you want."

"Thank you, Mr. Angus."

"I'll leave the offer on the table," Angus said. "And by the way, I appreciate the work and long hours you put in around here. Why don't you and I saddle horses tomorrow and ride the courses? I'm thinking about adding a new course on the old Brown place. You can help me lay it out," Angus said.

"I've been thinking the same thing. There're a lot of birds over there."

"Then let's plan on it." Angus said. "You saddle the horses and I'll meet you at the barn around nine tomorrow."

Angus and Luke rode the Brown place that next day and they rode together the following three days as well. They laid out the hunt course and when they finished, Angus asked Luke to join him for an informal timber survey on the entire property. The survey took three weeks. The next project for Angus was a kennel renovation. He showed Luke a hand-drawn sketch and put him in charge. It seemed that every time there was a new project or task, Luke was involved. And every time that Luke was involved, Angus was there.

One night at the dinner table, Catherine had a question for Angus. "You certainly are spending a lot of time with Luke," she said. "Do you think he will get the wrong idea?"

Angus set his wineglass on the table. "What do you mean by wrong idea?"

"You know what I mean. Are you teaching him about the management on Horseshoe Hill because you think he will make a good manager in the future, or are you treating him like a son-in-law?"

"He's smart and has skills," Angus said. "He loves the land as much as I do, and we need someone young who knows how the plantation operates. Luke is a natural." Angus hesitated. "Annabelle is a natural as well. This place will be hers one day. Would you rather Annabelle stay home from school and learn the things I am teaching Luke?"

"Oh, Angus."

"I'm serious. We must think of these things. Which one would you prefer?" Angus asked.

"Which one would you prefer?" Catherine asked.

"I think they could manage it together. As a team," Angus replied.

Catherine patted her mouth with her napkin. "That's enough of this talk, Angus. Annabelle is not going to spend her adult life on a farm."

"You had better ask Annabelle about that," Angus replied.

It was late at night when Luke heard a tap at his bedroom window. He sat up in bed and rubbed his eyes. Then another tap. Luke opened the curtains and saw Annabelle looking in. He rubbed his eyes again and opened the window.

"Annabelle, what in the name of Jesus are you doing here?"

"I came to see you. Let me in."

"It's one o'clock in the morning."

"Let me in."

"The door is unlocked."

The front door opened, and Annabelle bounded into Luke's bedroom. She straddled Luke, placed her hands on his cheeks and kissed him.

"You're supposed to be in school," Luke said. "How did you get here?" he asked.

"I borrowed a car from my roommate's sister. I drove all the way here, straight through. I only stopped for gas."

"You're crazy," Luke said. "You can't be here now."

"I'm crazier than you know." Annabelle straightened up and put her hands on her hips. "Let's have a baby, Luke."

Luke sat up fast and Annabelle fell off the bed.

"You have lost your mind," Luke said.

Annabelle frowned. "No, I haven't. I'm wasting my good years in school while you're here living the life I want to live. You are going to find somebody else."

"No, I won't."

"You have a purpose and I'm studying to learn things I don't even care about. If we have a baby, Catherine will have to let us get married."

"And they'll hate me for the rest of their lives."

"No, they won't. They'll get used to it. Besides, they love you. Don't you want to marry me?"

"Yes, but not now. You have to finish school. And I have to earn the right to marry you. Your dad is already working me to death. Maybe it's a test, or maybe he is trying to get rid of me. I don't know which one it is, but he's driving me hard."

"Oh, Luke. Can't you imagine us living together and having babies and riding horses every day and having parties at night? I hate it when I think of you here alone. I know one day you'll see a pretty girl who likes hunting and tractors and you'll fall in love with her while I'm stuck in that cold prison with girls who only care about boring things." Annabelle sighed. She lay next to Luke and placed her hand on his chest.

"You're crazy." Luke rubbed her cheek with his thumb. "Maybe you'll meet a handsome boy up north and he'll be good at hunting and riding, and you'll fall in love with him."

"There aren't any boys like that where I go to school," Annabelle said. "Besides, Daddy says you are the best in the Red Hills at training bird dogs."

Luke laughed. "Sometimes I think my dog training is the only reason you love me," Luke said.

Annabelle took him by the shoulders and kissed him. Luke took her hands into his and they closed their eyes and they kissed again. Annabelle exhaled. "You see, Luke, training bird dogs is not the only thing you're good at."

They fell asleep sometime during the night and woke well past sunrise when bright sunlight came through the curtains. Annabelle slipped out of bed and walked barefoot into the living room. There were maps with handwritten notes tacked to the walls. Torn pages from bird dog magazines and pictures of fine shotguns and ads for tractors filled empty spaces.

Luke rubbed his eyes and joined Annabelle in the kitchen. "You have to go back," he said. "Won't they call your parents when they find out you're gone?"

"They won't know. My roommate is covering for me... hopefully." Annabelle looked around the room. "I love your decorating."

Luke chuckled. "I did it myself."

"I was only joking. I love it. I would be disappointed if it was any different."

They washed their faces and brushed their teeth in the kitchen sink, then peeked out the window. No one was there. They eased out the back door and walked quickly to the car parked behind the barn.

Annabelle sat inside and started the ignition. "Think about what I said."

"I won't. That's the craziest idea you have ever had, and you know it," Luke replied. "Now you better get going. Be careful. And call me when you get back to school."

"Okay." Annabelle shifted the car into drive. "I love you."

"I love you, too."

The very day Annabelle finished the school year, she came home for summer. She spent the long summer days by Luke's side. During the weekdays, Annabelle followed Luke while he fed and worked dogs, and tended to the horses. On weekends, they swam at the pool during the day. At night, they sat on the steps of the big house and listened to frogs bellow and crickets chirp and watched the sky for shooting stars until Catherine called Annabelle to the house.

One night, Luke and Annabelle sat on the front steps waiting for Catherine to call her inside. "I can't bear the thought of going back, Luke," she said. "I hate it there."

"It's only one more year, Annabelle," Luke said. "I'll be waiting for you. All of Horseshoe Hill will be waiting for you. There's a lot more fun when you're around."

"A year is so long," Annabelle said. "I've been thinking about going to Florida State for college next year. Wouldn't that be something?"

"Florida State? That's only an hour away."

"Catherine doesn't like the idea. All her New York friends have daughters going to Ivy League schools and she is begging me to go." Annabelle puffed. "I'd rather die."

Annabelle did not go to an Ivy League school. She enrolled at Florida State University in Tallahassee. Her first two years there, she did well academically and proved to be a spirited member of the Kappa Delta sorority. But she spent every weekend at Horseshoe Hill.

During one of her return visits to Horseshoe Hill, she ran to Luke's cottage and pounded on the door after dinner with Angus and Catherine.

"What is it?" Luke asked.

Annabelle was breathing hard, and her eyes were livid. "Catherine has enrolled me in a study abroad program. A one-year study abroad program. In Italy. I don't even like pasta!"

"What did Angus say?"

"He's for it. Says it will broaden my horizons. I can't do it, Luke. I just can't."

"You should think about it," Luke said. "They only want what's best for you."

Annabelle's mouth fell open. "Don't you love me? Do you want us to be apart for an entire year? Overseas? Is that how you really feel?" Luke said nothing. Annabelle tossed her hair and stormed down the steps.

"I hate you, Luke."

As the day for Annabelle to leave for Italy grew near, tension seemed to build around Horseshoe Hill. Angus had few kind words for Catherine, and Catherine snapped at Angus over the least irritation. And there were endless irritations. Annabelle refused to pack. The empty suitcase sat open on the floor of her bedroom for two weeks. She barely spoke to anyone. Other than Luke.

Two days before Annabelle's departure, Luke walked into the library and stood in the doorway as Angus sat at his desk looking over a stack of financial reports. Luke knocked lightly on the open door and Angus peered over his reading glasses.

"Mr. Angus, can I speak with you for a moment?"

"Sure, Luke. What's on your mind?"

Luke stood in front of the desk. He was breathing hard and twisting a riding glove in his hands. "Mr. Angus, Annabelle wants me to...I mean, I want to ask you if it's alright. You know, Annabelle and I are in love." He took a deep breath and blurted it out. "We want to get married."

Angus removed his reading glasses and looked Luke in the eye. "Is this your idea, or Annabelle's?" he asked.

"It's both of ours."

Angus sat silent for a while. "You're both too young, Luke. God knows Annabelle is stubborn." Angus looked away then back at Luke. "But she is also very young. I know she thinks she is grown, but she is young. There's a whole world for her that she doesn't know. Maybe it doesn't matter. Maybe you are the right one for her." Angus pushed his chair back and crossed his arms. "I think the world of you, Luke, but I can't give you my blessing. And I'm sure Catherine feels the same."

Luke took those words like a punch to the gut.

And so it was. The shy boy who first arrived at Horseshoe Hill in bare feet and stained clothes was now a man. He knew what he had, and he knew what he wanted. He loved Horseshoe Hill, and he loved Annabelle. He could have one. But not the other. "Will of the wind" is what Joe Green, Roosevelt and other folks around Horseshoe Hill called it.

CHAPTER 9

ANNABELLE LEFT FOR ITALY, BUT she wrote to Luke every day. Then, the letters came every other day. Then it was only one letter a week. Then there were none. Luke tried to call her, but never could reach her by phone. Finally, the only news he got from Annabelle came from the postcards sent to Catherine and Angus that they left laying around the house.

Late one night, after a dinner party in the big house, Luke heard someone knocking on his door. He went to the door half-asleep and there stood Lula. "Can I come inside?" Lula asked. "I need to talk with you about something."

"Of course, Lula."

Lula walked inside and sat at the kitchen table. "I know it's late and you were probably asleep, so I'm going to tell you straight out."

Luke cocked his head to the side. "What is it?"

"Everybody 'round here is scared to tell you about Annabelle."

"Something is wrong?"

"No. Nothing is wrong. But she has gone over to Italy and she has found her a man."

"What?"

"She has a boyfriend. And they are already engaged to be married."

"An Italian man?"

"No. An American. A man from Boston."

"I didn't want to tell you, but you've got to know."

Luke started rocking back and forth in his kitchen chair. "She'll be back," Luke said.

"You can't think like that," said Lula. "You've got to forget about her and live your life."

"She'll come back," Luke said.

"Listen to me," Lula said. "You're a good looking man, and you work hard. There are lots of pretty girls out there. You need to be with one of them." Lula stood up. "I'm sorry I had to tell you."

On June 19, 1999, at twenty-fours years old, Annabelle married an investment banker from Boston. His name was Charles Henry McMillan, III. The wedding took place on Cape Cod.

After Annabelle's wedding, Luke worked harder than ever. For the next five years, with his help, Horseshoe Hill ran like a fine pocket watch. The forest grew healthy, and the quail thrived. The house was immaculate, the grounds were immaculate, and there was an endless string of guests from various places around the world.

Then, one cold February day near the end of hunting season, Annabelle came home. Alone. It was late in the evening when Annabelle arrived at Horseshoe Hill. She slipped through the back door, had tea with Angus and Catherine at the kitchen table then went upstairs to her room. The next morning Luke opened the kitchen door and froze in the doorway. She had the same seductive eyes, her pretty face was more defined than before, and her blond hair was cut in a bobbed style exposing her long, lean neck. She looked at Luke and spoke quietly. "Luke."

"Annabelle."

Luke twisted the riding gloves in his hands, and Angus broke the silence. "Luke, let's hunt the ball field course this morning," Angus said. "We should try to go out around nine." Angus glanced at Annabelle who had not taken her eyes off Luke. "Annabelle is going to join us, so can you get her Purdy twenty-eight from the gun closet and saddle a horse for her?"

"Yes, sir," Luke replied.

"I can saddle my own horse," Annabelle said.

"Of course, you can, but Luke will do it for you," Angus said.

They hitched the mules, loaded the dogs on the wagon, and set out on the course. Roosevelt drove the wagon and Luke rode with Andy, a young scout. Angus and Annabelle rode beside the wagon, while the pointers quartered the pines and wiregrass with twitching tails and heads held high.

Luke watched the dogs, and his face was intense. He called and whistled to the dogs while he kept them on the course. In a few short minutes, the dogs had the first point. Angus and Annabelle dismounted and removed shotguns from their scabbards. Luke gathered the reins and held the horses while Andy moved forward with the shooters and beat the brush with a whip. The covey exploded from the cover and swung hard to the right.

Angus watched as Annabelle fired two shots and dropped a double.

"I see you haven't lost it," Angus said.

A retriever fetched the quail back to the wagon while Luke led the horses to Angus and Annabelle. He handed the reins to Angus, then placed the reins across the neck of Annabelle's horse and held her saddle as she mounted from the other side. Their eyes met across the saddle, but neither spoke.

Ten minutes later the dogs had another covey. Angus took a bird with a single shot and Annabelle's shot brought down another. They mounted the horses, and Annabelle rode toward Luke and caught up with him. Annabelle seemed at ease, but Luke's face was tied in knots. They rode side by side and watched the pointers pattern the course without saying a word. Finally, Annabelle turned to Luke with a subtle smile. "You really love this, don't you, Luke?"

"I do," Luke said. "There's nothing better in the world than following a pair of pointers in the piney woods. But that's just my opinion."

Angus pulled his horse between Luke and Annabelle. "Luke, that Molly is going to make a fine bird dog," he said.

Luke gave way to Angus and created space between their horses. "She's pretty good for her age," Luke said. He called to the dogs, "Hup, hup." Then Luke broke away and left Angus riding beside Annabelle.

The hunt was over at lunchtime and the group returned to the barn. Angus slid off his horse and patted him on the rump. "Annabelle, let's see what Lula has for lunch," he said.

"I'm going to stay and help with the horses," she replied.

"I'm sure lunch is on the table already," Angus said.

"I'll be along shortly."

Luke and Annabelle stood close to each other while they watched Angus walk toward the house. They turned face to face and stood closer. Annabelle tucked her bobbed hair behind her ear and Luke put his hands in his pockets and shifted his weight from foot to foot.

"I guess I better go in," Annabelle said.

Luke pulled the saddle off her horse. "Enjoy your lunch."

The weather turned cold that night and Luke carried a load of firewood to the big house. It was dark, and he saw a light on in Annabelle's upstairs room. He watched her through the curtains pacing back and forth with a phone in her hand. He looked away and carried the firewood inside the house. Luke stacked the wood beside the fireplace and returned to his cottage. He found Roosevelt sitting on the porch.

"Going to be frost in the morning," Roosevelt said.

"That's what I heard. Do you have enough wood for your fireplace?"

"I have plenty."

Luke sat next to Roosevelt and looked toward the big house. In the window he saw Angus and Catherine seated on a sofa. Annabelle came down the stairs and stood by the fireplace. She crossed her arms and pointed her finger as she spoke. She put her hands on her hips and stood motionless while Catherine spoke and then she walked to the bookshelf, turned around and folded her arms again. Luke and Roosevelt didn't hear the words, but it was obvious that the conversation was intense.

"Something is going on," Luke said.

Roosevelt nodded his head. "I feel it, too."

"I wish I knew what it is," Luke said.

"I think it's best if we just mind our business. Especially you. If it has anything to do with us, we'll know in due time. The look on your face tells me everything I need to know about what's happening in your heart right now. It's best you sit tight and let the Lord work it out for you."

"That's hard to do."

"I know."

"How long will she be here?" Luke asked.

"I don't know."

Annabelle stayed until the end of February. There was no indication that she would return to Boston. Most days she hunted with Angus and his guests. If there was no hunt, she rode horses with Catherine or sat by the fireplace and read a book. At nighttime she had dinner with Angus and Catherine and their occasional guests. And after dinner she often paced back and forth in her bedroom, long into the night.

One morning, Annabelle surprised Luke at the barn. "Sorry if I startled you," she said. "I saw you from the window and thought you could use some company. What are you doing?"

"Reworking some tack," Luke said. He twisted a hole punch through a leather strap and attached the strap to a saddle.

Annabelle glanced around the barn. "Say, is that old tractor still around? The one with the dented fender."

Luke looked at her and smiled. "Oh, no," Luke said. "Don't even think about it."

"Seems like a long time ago," Annabelle said. She looked to the ground and gathered her thoughts. "I feel like there is something I need to say to you, but I don't know what that something is."

"No words necessary."

Luke stopped his work and Annabelle looked into his eyes. "I guess what I want to tell you is that…well, the time we spent together. I want you to know that was real." Luke breathed in and out and Annabelle went on. "I like to think about those times now and again. How you always took care of me and how I felt like the most important girl in the world when I was with you. And the talk about a future with you was what I was truly feeling."

"Are you happy you left?" Luke asked.

"I've learned a lot. Things were so simple and innocent back then. Now I know things that I wish I never knew."

"I know things, too," Luke said. He paused. "Do you know Lisa Donnelley?"

"Yes. Her family owns Tanglewood."

"I had a beer with her one night. In fact, I had several beers. It had been a hard day, and I was feeling sad. Sad about you. Sad about being a dog trainer surrounded by people with more money than I will ever have."

"I'm sorry."

"That's okay. It was a while back, and I don't really care anyway. But I asked Lisa if I should change my degree from forestry to law."

"Did you?"

"No. Lisa told me I shouldn't. She told me I would certainly earn more money as a lawyer, but then she told me that, no matter what, inherited wealth will always win out over earned wealth."

"And?" Annabelle asked.

"It's true, isn't it?"

"Did you sleep with her?"

"We're just friends."

"I know Lisa. She's pretty. Did you sleep with her?" Annabelle waited for an answer, then scoffed. "Of course, you did."

At that moment, Angus appeared at the barn door. "We have another hunt this afternoon. We'll go out at two."

CHAPTER 10

In the 1920s, the US Forest Service believed that any fire was a bad fire. But that was not nature's way. Like other plantation owners in the Red Hills, Angus Parker learned from Herbert Stoddard, a self-taught naturalist from Illinois, and the Red Hills Research Station that fire was an integral component of a healthy forest. Fire consumed straw leaves and dead branches. It took out invasive trees that shaded the forest floor. It exposed the soil to sunlight that fed native grasses and forbs. Fire opened the door for seeds and regeneration. In a natural way, it brought new life to the land. It was good for the land, and it was good for the animals that lived on the land. But the fire of the year 2004 consumed much more than dead brush and straw.

It was the end of March, and the end of quail season and Angus was anxious. "We're going to burn," he said.

Joe Green looked at the sky and shook his head. "Not a good day to burn."

"There won't be much wind in the morning," Angus replied. "We'll set a backfire and we'll be fine. I know it will burn hot, but we haven't had a hot fire in three years and the hardwoods need to be knocked back."

It was mid-morning and Angus met the burn crew at the equipment barn. Roosevelt, Joe Green, Luke, and two others stood by the tractors and trucks as Angus laid out the plan. After three consecutive years of wet weather hampering the burn, Angus was desperate for a good fire. Fuel was dry and thick in the understory and winter weather had been exceptionally dry. Grasses were brown and brittle, and leaves crackled underfoot. Pinestraw was dry to the dirt.

Luke joined the conversation. "We're not going to burn the west side of the winter pasture today, are we?" he asked. "There's a lot of fuel on the ground there."

"No, not today," Angus answered. "You ran a break around it, didn't you?"

"Yes, sir. I ran a double break. But I can keep an eye on it just in case anything jumps the break."

"No, Luke. I want you to take the tractor and run a fresh firebreak from the old dairy to the creek. We'll back burn a strip in there later today. Joe Green and I will watch the pasture."

"One other thing, Mr. Angus," Luke said. "I was supposed to saddle horses for Annabelle and Miss Catherine this morning. They're riding over to the Outpost."

"Andy can saddle the horses," Angus said. "I want you with us today. Let's get going now. We need to be done before the weather moves in."

Luke left for the dairy while Angus and Joe Green set fire on the east side of the winter pasture. Within seconds, a thin line of crackling orange grew and turned into the hot blaze that Angus wanted. Angus and Roosevelt extended the line of fire with drip torches while Joe Green watched the wind building in the treetops.

"No good," Joe Green said. His jaw was tight, and his eyes were like steel. He stared at the sky as if he were looking back a thousand years.

"What do you mean?" Roosevelt asked.

"The wind is restless. You can't stop the wind. And if the wind is angry, we won't stop the fire."

Joe Green was right. From nowhere, the wind came down and stirred the tops of the trees. It increased tenfold and changed direction from west to east, sweeping the fire with it. The fire burned hotter and hotter, and it seemed there would be no way for the breaks to hold, but the tall flames settled and died on bare dirt. There was a short relief, but far down the break the fire jumped, and it grew hotter and higher and tore into the driest and thickest part of the woods.

The angry fire blazed on. Flames grew fifty feet high and scorched green needles in the tops of the tallest pines. The fire inhaled the air from above and created its own wind, and the wind caught the fire and twisted it into cyclones that bent the trees back and forth. It grew tall and jumped from tree to tree and made loud popping and cracking sounds as it raced. The men slapped and dug at the fire with their shovels and rakes, but embers and hot smoke burned their faces.

Two miles away, Luke sat on the tractor and plowed fresh dirt from an old break. He glanced back to the west and dropped his jaw when he saw the tall column of thick blue smoke streaming into the sky. He nearly ran into a large oak before he raised the plow and turned the tractor to the west. He found the others and jumped from the tractor.

"Luke, plow another break on the north side!" Angus shouted. "Plow a break down the property line next to Peterson's land. We'll run one beside the Old Mill Road. We'll stop it there. Send more help."

Luke did as Angus said and plowed a wide break on the northern border. He was far from the fire, but he saw smoke and flames rising above the trees. He drove to the barns as fast as he could and gathered six men with shovels and axes and they joined the fight. They made a stand at Old Mill Road, where they plowed a double break and sawed a wide strip of trees. Smoke filled the forest and burned the eyes of the men. Sweat wet their clothes and smut stuck to the sweat. They fought the fire for three long hours until, finally, the destruction was done. The wind died and the fire burned out.

The men sat on tractors and truck tailgates and wiped sweat and ash from their faces. One by one, the men turned and stared down the road as a man emerged from the smoke. The man walked slowly with his head down. He held the reigns of two horses covered in sweat and ash. The horses' nostrils flared nervously, and the man walked with his head hung low. The two horses had saddles, but no riders. No one spoke while the man and the horses came closer. The man emerged from the smoke, and everyone saw it was Joe Green. His smutty jaw was clenched. Tears flowed down his cheeks and cut streams through the ash.

"That's Annabelle's horse," Luke said. "And Catherine's." The white of Luke's eyes shot through the dirt on his face. He looked like a crazy man as he ran down the road and grabbed Joe Green by the shoulders. "Where are they?"

Joe Green said nothing.

"Where are they?" Luke asked again.

Joe Green placed his hand on Luke's shoulder. "They're gone, Luke."

"Gone?"

"Gone." Joe Green looked straight into Luke's eyes and spoke with no emotion. "The fire came hot."

Luke stood shaking his head from side to side. "Where are they? Take me there."

"No."

"I want to see her."

"You can't see her. I wish I had not seen her."

Luke tried to run, but Joe Green reached out and grabbed Luke. They fell to the ground and Joe Green ripped the shirt off Luke trying to keep Luke from going. But Luke got away. He ran as fast as he could with his shirt torn and his crazy eyes and the smoke from the fire hanging in the road.

Two workers jumped in a truck and started to go after Luke.

"Let him be," Joe Green said.

"Where's Mr. Parker?" they asked.

"He's with his family," Joe Green said. "The sheriff will be there soon."

Friends and neighbors, and just about everyone in the Thomasville area was shocked by the news.

The fire cut a black swath through the pine forest, and the smoke choked the life from Angus Parker's heart. It would never heal. Angus could not look at Luke and Luke could not look at Angus. Roosevelt retreated to his cottage. And Joe Green found meaning in the tragedy. He never said what the meaning was, only that fire was a warning.

Catherine and Annabelle's remains were cremated a week after the fire. A month went by and it seemed that no one lived on Horseshoe Hill. When Angus finally emerged from the shadows, he searched for Luke. He found Luke at an empty horse paddock, sitting on the fence and staring into nothing.

"Luke, we need to talk," Angus said. Luke looked at him with swollen eyes. The man looked like Angus Parker, but he was not Angus Parker. The man who used to be Angus Parker continued. "I'm leaving Horseshoe Hill and going back north."

"How long will you be gone?"

"I'm leaving for good," Angus said. "I can't bear it here. If I see the woods burning, or a woman on a horse…" Angus choked back the tears. "I can't bear it. It was my fault and there's no way to bring them back."

"It was my fault, Mr. Angus. I should have stopped them from riding that day. I almost said something. But I didn't." Luke covered his face.

"This place is cursed," Angus said. "Cursed for me now." Angus caught his breath and shook his fist. "I want you to listen carefully," he said. "Annabelle wanted Horseshoe Hill for her and Charles. It would have been hers anyway, but she wanted it now." Angus gritted his teeth. "Charles was cheating on her."

"He what?"

"Charles has a mistress," Angus said. "He doesn't know that I know, but Annabelle told me everything. Now, he's asking about Annabelle's trust, and he is asking questions about Horseshoe Hill. I'll be damned if that son-of-a-bitch ever touches anything meant for Annabelle."

Luke's eyes steeled over, and he shook his head in disbelief.

"I need you to know something," Angus said. "Ownership of Horseshoe Hill is now listed as Joe Green Enterprises."

"You gave it to Joe Green?" Luke asked.

"I probably should, but Joe Green wouldn't want it anyway. I'm still the owner, but I don't want Charles, or anyone else, to know that. I've got to figure out the details, but for now, we're going to say Joe Green owns it. Nobody will mess with Joe Green." Angus put his hand on Luke's shoulder. "But I want you to run it."

Luke nodded his head.

"There is a trust that will provide the money you will need to keep things going," Angus said. "I've watched you since you were a young boy, and I have all the confidence in the world in you."

"I don't know if I can do it, Mr. Angus. I don't know if I can even eat again, much less run a plantation."

"You know about quail, and that's all you need to know. If you take care of the quail, everything else will fall in place." Angus said. "You will be alright, Luke. What you don't know, you will learn. Give it time. But me, I can't bear to be here another day."

"When are you going?"

"Today," Angus replied. "And Luke, there is something else I need to tell you." Angus ran his hand through his hair. "You've been like a son to me. You've grown up to be the man I hoped you would be. And I… I took something from you. Something that should have been yours, but I didn't know it at the time." Moments went by, then Angus looked Luke dead in the eye. "I'll make it up to you someday."

"You don't owe me anything, Mr. Angus. You've done more for me and Momma than we could ever ask for."

"Joe Green will explain everything."

They looked at each other like two fallen warriors lost in defeat. There was no hug, no handshake, not even a tip of the hat. Angus slowly turned and walked away. Luke sat on the wood fence and watched him go.

Angus Parker drove slowly toward the gate. There was spring growth on the leaves of the twisted oaks that lined each side of the drive and clusters of azaleas bloomed pink and red. He reached the end of the driveway, stopped the truck, and rested his forehead on the steering wheel. He stayed that way until a passing truck woke him from the daze. A bobwhite quail whistled in the distance. Angus turned his head, and there, as if nothing had happened, was the Cherokee Rose in bloom. It was white and beautiful and stood out against the dark green fence. The first blossom of spring.

CHAPTER 11

THERE'S NOT MUCH YOU CAN do when you lose the people you love. No amount of crying is going to bring them back. The only one you can bring back to life is yourself. And sometimes, you can't even do that.

The fire on Horseshoe Hill was the talk around Thomasville and the Red Hills. Friends called on Angus, but he was nowhere to be found. He would never recover, but no one imagined Angus Parker would walk away from the thirty thousand acres and the big white house with tall columns and the dogs and horses and quail. The details slowly emerged. The courthouse deed confirmed it in black and white. Angus Parker transferred ownership of Horseshoe Hill Plantation to Joe Green Enterprises. All thirty thousand acres.

Everyone moved out of the big white house on Horseshoe Hill. The furnishings were covered with white sheets. Only house staff that tended to the kitchen and laundry went inside. The land was neglected and soon looked much like one of the old cotton plantations left to ruin when the war ended. There were no guests. None. There was no hostess planning dinner parties and luncheons by the pool. There were no hunts, and no hunting parties like before that wandered the grounds admiring horses, dogs, and shotguns. The house staff shuttered the windows. Dog trainers, field workers, and groundskeepers stayed on, but the shine was gone from everything that once made Horseshoe Hill the star of the Red Hills.

Joe Green was the new face of Horseshoe Hill, but Joe Green was rarely seen at all. Luke seldom left the gates of Horseshoe Hill. He was still there, but the young man who had earned a respected role in the plantation community was not there. He rode the horses, trained the dogs, and spent hours every day on a tractor parked on a distant hillside. The unbroken smile was broken, and the passion in his voice was muted. He lost weight because he barely ate, and an unkempt beard covered his face. He was hollow-eyed and wild. As wild as any living creature on Horseshoe Hill.

For two and a half years, Horseshoe Hill was nothing more than an empty shell. The pristine plantation was nearly swallowed by weeds that choked the lawn and covered the roads. Vines climbed and covered fences and crept up the walls of seldom-used barns and wooden sheds. Non-native trees and shrubs crept in and invaded the tall pines. Shutters fell from windows, boards fell from the fence and the splendor faded like a lonely widow waiting for death.

In the fall of 2006, the day before quail season, the sun broke through the gray clouds. Cool weather swept in, and crisp air filled the pine forest. Luke lay in bed with the windows open and there was a soft knock at the door. He pulled on his pants and opened the door. There stood a woman with tender eyes and a warm smile.

"Momma," Luke said.

She stood tall and pretty with a layer of fullness that revealed a contented life. She reached out and placed her hand on the side of Luke's face. Tears welled in his eyes then rolled down his cheeks.

"It seems so long, Luke. I didn't know what to say to you at the funeral, and now, every time I call, you don't answer. If not for Roosevelt, I wouldn't know a thing about your well-being."

"I know." Luke rubbed his face with both hands. "It seems like talking to you would make things harder. And to be honest, there hasn't been much to say. I keep waiting for tomorrow, hoping to wake up and find out that things are better. But they never are better."

"Roosevelt is worried about you," Grace said.

"I'm doing fine," Luke replied.

"You don't look fine." Grace looked into his eyes. "Do you remember how we were when we first came here? We were in bad shape, Luke. Real bad shape." She wiped the tears from his face. "Our life changed here, and it changed for good. You know that."

"I know."

"Well," Grace said, "now you have to show your appreciation." She looked out the window toward the big white house lying empty in the morning sun. "Angus asked you to take care of this place."

"It's hard, Momma."

"I know it is. But life is hard. And now it's time for you to be the man that you were going to be before that fire. This place needs you." She brushed the tangled hair from his face. "Life is a gift from God. Not to be lived for yourself, but for everyone who needs you now."

"I know."

"Have you talked to Eugene?" Grace asked.

"Not in a long time."

Grace said nothing.

"When I think about him," Luke said, "I think about Annabelle."

"I think the two of you could help each other."

"I know."

Grace placed her hand on Luke's shoulder. "Randolph and I are going to an opening-day dinner party at Bentwood tomorrow night. All the plantations and their guests will be there. I want you to put on good clothes and go with us. I know it's hard, but you must."

"I don't want to be around those people from the past," he said. "They'll say things to be nice, but everything they say will remind me…I don't think I can do it."

"You must. Sooner or later, you have to hear those things. You must take small steps, Luke. Do you remember when we were in a bad way, and you took up dog training to ease all the hurt you were feeling?"

"I remember."

"Well, you are at your best when you are taking care of someone else. Just like you took care of me for all those years. You should find another dog. I've never seen anything that made you happier than that dog. A special dog that can take your mind off all the bad things that have happened. Small steps."

"That dog died," Luke said.

"We all die, Luke. That's why we must live while we are here."

Luke woke up the following morning and stood in front of the bathroom mirror. He turned his head from side to side. He took a razor from the cabinet and shaved his face. He took scissors from the drawer and cut his hair. He walked shirtless to the big house and found a white shirt and tweed jacket from Angus Parker's closet. He rummaged through the drawers and chose a silk tie to match. He took one last look in the mirror then met Randolph and Grace in the driveway.

"My goodness," Grace said. "That is quite the transformation. Now see if you can manage a smile."

"I'll be smiling like a Cheshire cat," Luke said. "Just for you."

They walked in the door at Bentwood Plantation and everyone turned and stared. No one had seen Luke since the fire and his entrance was met with awkward silence until Luke finally spoke. "It's been a while, but it's good to see you folks again," he said.

As the night wore on, Luke relaxed. He greeted and conversed with every plantation owner and guest alike. The talk of the evening was bird dogs and Luke knew a lot about bird dogs. Dog talk rekindled a passion and by the end of the night, he placed a wager with everyone willing to back their dog in the upcoming field trial. He concluded his bets and drifted to a table of ladies. He smiled despite the knot in his soul. He did alright.

The next morning, Luke washed his face and looked in the mirror. He smiled a real smile. A smile that said he was alive. A smile from the past. He walked out of his cottage with a clean face, clean clothes and a dog whistle hung from his neck. He walked toward the kennels with long strides and his head held high. He walked like a man with a purpose. Roosevelt, Joe Green, and the young scout named Andy watched from the barn.

"Look who's coming here," Andy said.

Luke passed the barn. Roosevelt, Joe Green, and Andy followed him to the kennel. Luke walked to a run with six young dogs that jumped on the fence with tails wagging and tongues hanging. Luke studied each one, then pointed to a pup lying in the shade of a pecan tree. The pup did not raise his head but looked at Luke from the corner of his eyes. His long tail moved slowly back and forth in the dirt. Luke called to him, but he did not come.

"You like that pup?" Andy asked. "That dog won't move out of the shade. He's healthy alright, but he's lazy. The laziest bird dog I ever seen. The fattest one, too."

"That's the one," Luke said.

Luke named the dog Whistling Willy because he was fat and happy and seemed as though he was just whistling his way down the road while other dogs tore through the woods and ran hard in search of quail. No one knew why Luke liked the dog and Luke did not seem to care if he was trained or not. Luke took Willy out every day, and day after day, Willy showed no interest in hunting quail, and every day Luke watched him amble down the road and lay in the shade of the wagon whenever it stopped.

When Willy was two and a half years old, he rose from the ground and left the shade of the wagon. He held his nose high, trotted to the edge of a cornfield and stopped with his tail parallel to the ground. It was not a pretty point, but it was a point. Luke slid his gun from the scabbard and ran to Willy. He stood with shotgun ready and watched Willy burrow his nose into the brush and root around while his tail wagged back and forth. Willy came out of the brush with a box turtle in his mouth. He paraded the box turtle to the wagon, laid in the shade, released the turtle, and barked.

Joe Green looked at the dog and then looked at Luke. "He has the heart of a lion," Joe Green said.

Roosevelt laughed so hard he shook the wagon. Andy turned away and hid the grin on his face.

"Yes, he does," Luke said. "Heart of a lion. Come on, let's get going. We're wasting daylight." Luke spun his horse and trotted down the road.

Whistling Willy was a joke around Horseshoe Hill plantation. He was a joke to everyone except Luke. When he was three years old, something happened to Whistling Willy. He trotted beside the wagon while two of their best pointers slashed the woods far ahead. Willy wandered along the edge of a food plot and winded something of interest. He stumbled to a stop and pointed a covey of quail with a drooping tail. Willy looked around and the two pointers backed him with heads high and tails tall and tight. The birds started running and Willy eased ahead a few yards and made another point. A better point. He turned and looked at the backing dogs still locked down. Willy turned back to the quail. Luke dismounted, eased behind Willy, and stroked his tail from the back to the front until it pointed skyward.

Luke spoke softly, "Whoa, Willy, easy now, boy, easy, you've got them. That's it." Then Luke stepped to the side and raised his gun to his shoulder. "Get them!"

Willy dove into a tangle of pine limbs and briars and twenty birds exploded from the thicket. Two blasts from the double-barrel twenty-eight folded two quail. Willy pounced on one of the fallen birds and pinned it to the ground while the backing dogs held steady, and a Lab was sent after the other.

Luke turned back to the wagon. "Did y'all see that point?"

"Sure did," Roosevelt replied.

"Andy, did you see him?"

"I saw him alright. But you're going to have to break that dog from pointing quail if you want him to be a champion box turtle dog."

Roosevelt, Andy and even Joe Green had a good laugh, but lightning had hit that no-care dog that day, and Luke knew it. From that day on, Willy outran every dog in the Horseshoe Hill kennel. He forgot about box turtles, butterflies, and garden snakes. He wanted quail. And as soon as a shot quail hit the ground, Willy was on it. It took time, but eventually, Luke trained Willy to hold steady and allow the Labradors to retrieve. And that was alright with Willy. While the Labs found the downed birds, he was already looking for the next covey.

Now enlightened, Willy worked harder than any dog in the field. He grew tall and the fat on his neck and ribcage dissolved into muscle. He was sleek with a smooth coat and paws the size of a grown man's fists. He ran like a tiger with long strides and paws that landed soft. His gate was effortless, and he jumped logs and crossed creeks with ease. And, little by little, Luke styled Willy, and perfected his form. At four years old, Willy was one of the best dogs in the kennel. At four and a half, he was the best dog in the kennel. At five years old, Whistling Willy was the best bird dog in the Red Hills.

One night, Joe Green and Roosevelt were sitting on Roosevelt's cottage porch when Luke walked by.

"Hey, Luke," Roosevelt said. "Come here for a minute. We need to talk about something."

Luke stepped onto the porch and took a seat.

"You want a drink?" Roosevelt asked.

"Sure."

"Bourbon?"

"That'll do."

Roosevelt walked inside and returned with the drink. He sat down and crossed his arms. "We have to burn."

Luke drank slowly from his glass and stared straight ahead.

"I know you don't want to think about it," Roosevelt said. "But if we don't burn this year, the hardwoods are going to take us over. I see hardwoods showing up in places where they've never been before. We've got to burn."

Luke took a deep breath and held it and Roosevelt rocked in his chair until Luke had exhaled and then he continued. "Did you know that Herbert L. Stoddard himself was the first one to set fire to the woods here on Horseshoe Hill?"

"Not so," said Joe Green.

"Not so?" Roosevelt asked.

"My people were the first ones to use fire in these woods."

"Maybe so, but the planters stopped burning, and Mr. Stoddard was the one who brought it back. Do y'all know the history?" Roosevelt asked.

"Yes, we do," Luke replied.

Roosevelt was undeterred by Luke's answer. "In the early 1920s, the quail population in the Red Hills went way down and nobody knew why. The plantation owners set about looking for a biologist who could figure out what happened to the quail. Well, they found a man from Illinois named Herbert L. Stoddard. And when they found Stoddard, they found gold." Roosevelt sipped his drink. "Herbert L. Stoddard teamed up with Henry Beadel and they started the Cooperative Quail Study Investigation. And do you know what they found?"

Luke did not have time to answer.

"Fire," Roosevelt said. "They found out a lack of fire was the reason quail were disappearing. In the old days, lightning strikes caught the woods on fire, and it just burned 'til it went out naturally. But paved roads and fields and fences stopped those fires. It wasn't natural. These longleaf trees need fire. It's good for quail. And if it's good for quail, it's good for all the wildlife."

Luke swirled the whiskey in his glass. "I guess you're right," he said. "We have to burn."

"I know I'm right," Roosevelt said. "Read Herbert L. Stoddard's book. It's called *The Bobwhite Quail*, and it's bigger than the Bible, but every word in it's important."

"I've seen it in the library," Luke said.

"Read it. You'll learn something," said Roosevelt. "This plantation can be the best in the country if we follow that book. And I know that's what Miss Annabelle would want." Roosevelt stopped talking and sat back in his chair while Luke stared straight ahead and said nothing.

Luke read Stoddard's book. Then he read it again. Then he mapped a plan that implemented Stoddard's recommendations for all thirty thousand acres of Horseshoe Hill. He hired foresters and loggers who thinned the timber in places where the canopy was tight. They removed the weaker trees and left the best for regeneration. Luke watched the foresters hand-mark each tree chosen for harvest with a slash of blue paint. They mowed and chopped hardwoods and non-native trees that had encroached into the savannas. And they plowed firebreaks deep and wide and thorough so there would never be another fire like before.

Luke brought regeneration back to Horseshoe Hill. He worked from sunup to sundown every day. The land improved and the string of bird dogs and stable of horses returned to their previous glory. It did not go unnoticed. Luke and the staff posed for the winner's photo at the Wiregrass Field Trial with regularity. Silver trophies, bowls and blue ribbons filled, then overflowed, the trophy case. And there, discreetly placed in the corner of the case, was a photograph of Luke and Annabelle riding bareback on Daisy.

Luke established himself as a smart land manager. Little by little, his reputation grew among his peers. He was a regular at cocktail parties, dinners, charity events and any other function where neighbors, sportsmen and land stewards gathered. He was popular with the plantation owners and well-heeled hunters. And he was popular with the ladies.

Wednesday night started as the informal staff meeting night on Horseshoe Hill. It turned into Wednesday night storytelling night for Roosevelt.

Roosevelt and Joe Green sat in rockers on Roosevelt's porch. They each had a drink and they packed tobacco in brown stemmed pipes while they waited for Luke. They waited for a half hour and then a silver Mercedes stopped in front of Roosevelt's cottage. Luke stepped out from the passenger's side, walked around to the driver side, and leaned in to kiss the attractive woman driving the car. The woman raised the window in his face, jerked the car into drive, spun the tires and left Horseshoe Hill in a cloud of gravel and dust. Luke stepped onto the porch with a crooked smile.

"I guess she doesn't see the importance of Wednesday night porch meetings," he said.

Roosevelt handed Luke a glass of whiskey. "You've been gone for two days, Luke. I don't reckon your momma would much approve of the way you get around with these women."

"Momma's not here," Luke said. He took a drink of whiskey and settled into a rocking chair. "Besides, they all know good and well I'm not shopping for a bride."

"I swear," Roosevelt said. "I'm glad Eugene's not around to learn any of your womanizing ways these days."

"Speaking of Eugene, how's he doing, anyway?" Luke asked.

"He's doing fine. I'm not sure he's fully adjusted to California, but his company is paying him a whole heap of money and he just moved into a new apartment. He won't tell me how high the rent is, but I imagine it's higher than a cat's back."

"I hope he does well out there," Luke said. "But I sure do miss him."

"He's made me proud," Roosevelt said. "I get tears in my eyes every time I think about him walking across that stage and receiving a diploma from Tech. But he says a college degree from Georgia Tech doesn't mean a thing where he works."

"I wouldn't worry about that. Eugene will make something of himself. He has common sense. Not all smart people have that."

"I'm just glad he got his mother's intelligence," Roosevelt said. "She was a smart woman. God rest her soul."

Luke poured a short glass of whiskey and sat back in his chair. Joe Green took a puff from his pipe, and Roosevelt crossed his arms. The storytelling began. "I can remember when I was just a boy," Roosevelt said. "I used to sit on these steps and listen to my granddaddy tell his stories. He was great storyteller."

"You're not too bad a storyteller yourself," Luke said.

"Maybe so, but he was some storyteller. I wish I could have recorded those stories. Times were hard back then but seems like he always had a story. He had a way that made everybody laugh. And he'd talk about those times like they were the good old days. Did I ever tell y'all about the time I met Miss Jackie Kennedy?" Roosevelt asked.

Luke rocked in his chair. "We've heard it, but I know it's one of your favorites. So, let's hear it again."

Roosevelt tapped his pipe on the arm of the chair. "I was just a small boy when I met Miss Jackie. It was 1963, a couple of weeks after President Kennedy had his brains shot all over the back seat of that Lincoln automobile in Dallas. Me and my daddy were working on Greenwood Plantation that day and I remember it like it was yesterday. We were outside the barn shoeing horses. I handed my daddy a rasp from the toolbox and when I looked up, I saw a woman walking toward the barn. She was tall and thin, and she wore a blue riding jacket and tan riding pants tucked into tall black leather boots. They were polished so that they shined in the sun. She walked like a show horse with her head held high and her shoulders back." Roosevelt sipped his whiskey. "It was Jackie Kennedy. She walked right past us like we weren't even there. But then she stopped. She turned back and smiled. She spoke slowly and carefully, and her voice was as kind as any voice I can ever remember. 'Good morning,' she said. 'You're doing a fine job on those shoes. An exceptionally fine job.' Then she walked away and my daddy and me never said anything about that. We just looked at each other without saying a word."

The three men drank whiskey and sat in silence.

"I guess Jackie Kennedy had a lot on her mind, wondering how she would go on with her life." Roosevelt paused. "But she handled it with class. We never said anything about Miss Kennedy when we went back to work. But that night, I prayed for her. And I pray for you too, Luke."

Luke drained the whiskey from his glass and stood from his chair. "I'm doing the best that I can."

CHAPTER 12

EVEN WEALTHY PEOPLE SWEAT IN a sinking economy. And when the United States economy hit rock bottom in 2008, everyone in the Red Hills felt it.

Early one morning the phone rang just as Luke was leaving his cottage. It was Angus.

"Luke, I caught wind of a plan at the Links Club last night. There was an overserved investment banker at the club, and he was talking about a group of technology billionaires backing an enormous development project. Do you know where?"

"I have no idea."

"The Red Hills. I think Charles is part of it."

"I haven't heard anything about a development here, Mr. Angus," Luke replied.

"It's Angus now, not Mr. Angus. Okay?"

"Yes, sir."

"Anyway, I didn't say anything. I just listened. They have done a demographics study, and the number one location is the Red

Hills. And ground zero for the Red Hills location is where you are standing right now."

There was a long moment of silence.

"How can they do that?" Luke asked finally. "There's no land for sale around here."

"Anything can be done with the right amount of money. And these people have it."

"You're not thinking about selling Horseshoe Hill, are you?"

"Hell, no. I will fight until my dying breath to see that Charles McMillan never makes a penny from anything I have ever owned."

"Then they will have to go somewhere else, right?"

"I'll never sell them Horseshoe Hill, but some of the owners around there are vulnerable. These oligarchs will choke it off and close in on it until they have it. Believe me, there are ways. These are dirty people. Dirty, greedy people. And I hear that one of our elected officials is already in their pockets."

"I can't imagine any of the large landowners selling out," Luke said.

"The good ones are getting older. The real land stewards are dying off. Some of their heirs can carry on, but most don't care about it. Those are the ones they'll go after. The heirs. They'll throw money at the heirs and make it seem like the right thing to do. They'll tout their *eco-friendly* line of lies."

Luke sunk into a chair and stared into nothing.

"I have a plan," Angus said. "Everyone thinks that Joe Green owns Horseshoe Hill because it's in his name. That's the way I set it up. Nobody will ever dig deep enough to uncover the truth. And nobody will question ownership if Joe Green says he wants to sell it. Most people see him as an eccentric old Indian."

"But Joe Green is smart. Real smart."

"We know that, but these people don't know it."

"Does Joe Green know about the developers?"

"Yes. He is getting old, and he is tired. But he is taking this personally and there is still some fight in him. He wants a taste of redemption before he's too old to care anymore."

"So, what are we going to do?" Luke asked. "Are we going to sell?"

Angus cleared his throat. "Let me explain..."

Miles Murphy, who owned Murphy's Guns and Sporting Goods along with his wife, Kitty, helped Luke load the last of twenty boxes of shotgun shells into his truck parked on Broad Street.

Oscar Thornton, owner of Dogwood Plantation, stopped his truck in front of the store. "Hey, Luke," Oscar said. "I'm glad I ran into you. I've got something I'd like to discuss if you have time."

Luke patted Miles on the shoulder, walked to Oscar's truck and leaned in the window. "I always have time for you, Oscar. When do you want to get together?"

"This afternoon at my place?" Oscar asked.

"You look worried, Oscar, what's on your mind?"

"I'd rather discuss it in private."

"Okay, how about five o'clock?"

"That's good. I'll see you at five."

Luke arrived at five, and Oscar met him at the door with a Scotch in his hand. It did not appear to be his first drink. His eyes were red, and his speech was slurred. Despite the drink, Oscar was neatly dressed in pressed trousers and shined loafers without socks. His tweed jacket fit perfectly with a hint of silver thread that matched his full head of hair swept back with a proper part.

"Come in, Luke. How are you all doing over there on Horseshoe Hill? Are you seeing many birds this year?"

"I think the hatch did alright," Luke replied. "But it looks like we might be down from last year. We had a lot of rain, and it was really wet over the summer. How about you?"

"We haven't scouted much as of late. I've been spending my time modifying our management plan. I can speak with you in confidence, right?" Thornton asked. He led Luke to the living room.

"Sure, you can, Oscar. What's going on?" Luke nodded to the glass in Oscar's hand. "Looks like you're starting a little early today."

"I'm sorry, how rude of me," Oscar said. "Can I make you a drink?"

"No, thanks."

"I've got problems, Luke. Real problems. It's this damn economy. My financial advisor called from New York yesterday. He says this recession is deeper than anyone knows and it's going to get worse. A lot worse. And quite frankly, Luke, I can't afford it to get any worse. I'm speaking in confidence, but I've got to tell you I've lost a third of the holdings that support this place. And I'm losing more every day." Oscar drained the Scotch from his glass and poured another. "Are you sure you don't want a drink?"

"No, thanks."

"The expenses are eating me up," Oscar said. "Are the expenses increasing on Horseshoe Hill?"

"They go up every year," Luke replied. "But we're managing."

Oscar took a gulp of Scotch. "It's always cost money to keep this place, but I had income from other sources. Stocks and a couple of trusts. But the recession has taken a bite out of our holdings. I've got to do something."

"What are you saying, Oscar? Do you have a plan?"

His voice trembled. "I have to sell it. That's the plan. I can't keep it any longer."

"Hold on, Oscar," Luke said. "Let's think this thing through."

"I've been thinking it through and I'm out of options," Oscar said. "Dirk Thompson called me the other day and he has a buyer looking for big tracts. I tell you, I'm out of options."

"Dirk Thompson means developers, Oscar. If you've got to do something, call Victor at Pine Ridge Realty. He's one of us and he's sold more plantations in the Red Hills region than anybody. He has the connections and every one of the tracts he sold has ended up in a conservation easement. Good land stewards. All of them."

"I've already talked to him," Oscar said. "He doesn't have anybody looking right now. His people are sitting on cash until this thing ends. If it ever does. Besides, nobody needs a tax deduction in this economy. I know Joe Green has Angus's trust that funds Horseshoe Hill. If it's big enough to keep it going, I'm happy for you. But we can't hold on much longer."

"Sure, we get money from the trust, Oscar. But we also run a tight ship. We've put off repairs and reduced the kennel to lower numbers than it's been in years. We've cut more timber and if it doesn't get any better, we'll have to lay people off. Hell, do you have bourbon?"

"I do."

"I'll have one on the rocks, please."

Luke took the bourbon from Oscar and continued. "We're hoping timber prices will bounce back soon, or we'll have to make even more changes. You've got to hold out if you can, Oscar. Your place is right in the heart of it all. If your place goes, there're going to be others and all this beautiful land is going to turn into strip malls and trailer parks. Can't you do a timber cut?"

"I can't cut any more trees without ruining the place. Besides, the market has gone to hell," Oscar said. "Has anyone talked to Angus?"

"Angus is aware of the situation," Luke answered. He sipped his bourbon. "Why don't you consider selling some hunts this year? You can get twelve, maybe fifteen thousand a day for a good wagon hunt and lodging on a legacy plantation like this."

"Are you selling hunts?" Oscar asked.

"We still have a long list of guests who we invite during the season. Guests who couldn't necessarily pay to hunt the way we do. So, we'll most likely honor that as long as we can."

Oscar took a deep breath. "I don't know, Luke. Look around at my place. It's in bad shape. The house hasn't been painted in twenty years. Both wagons need repairs, and I don't have the quality dogs in the kennel like I had a few years ago. They're old, too. Just like everything we've got." Oscar looked out the window. "We don't have a single dog that would make a respectable run in the field trials."

Luke placed his hand on Oscar's shoulder. "Think about selling some hunts," Luke said. "We've got a spare wagon, and Roosevelt can bring mules if you need them. He'll even drive for you if you want. That's no problem. And you can borrow our dogs if you promise not to steal any."

"Whistling Willy?"

"No, not Willy."

Oscar chuckled. "I didn't think so. And I wouldn't steal any of your other dogs. I might let a good one spend romantic kennel time with my bitches, but I won't steal any of them."

Luke and Oscar chatted for an hour about better days and hope for the future. Oscar poured another scotch, and Luke stood and walked toward the door. "I've got to go," Luke said. "Let me know if you'd like to borrow anything from our place and I'll send it over. If you are thinking about selling, please don't do anything with Dirk Thompson. We'll get together and figure something out."

Oscar held the door for Luke. "I'm the third generation to own this place, Luke. My grandfather, grandmother, and my mother and father are all buried here. They loved it like nothing else. I love it like nothing else. I can't bear the thought of being the one who loses it. Not all of it, anyway."

"I know. We'll figure out something."

Most days Luke worked long hours on Horseshoe Hill. But some days, he quit early, showered, dressed in clean clothes, and drove into town. He had a couple of favorite places. One of those places was Brinkley's Diner. The food was southern and good, and the servers were pretty. Brinkley hired family, and good looks ran in the Brinkley family. Another favorite place was Paul's Pool Hall. Sometimes Roosevelt went with Luke and sometimes Joe Green went with him. Joe Green liked chilidogs and cold beer at Paul's. Luke and Joe Green were at Paul's one night when they ran into Dirk Thompson.

Dirk was an arrogant real estate broker. He claimed to be the only real plantation broker in the South, and he never mentioned the fact that he had spent most of his life selling cars in Toledo.

Luke and Joe Green walked through the swinging door and George Strait greeted them with “Amarillo by Morning” on the juke box. Pool balls clicked on felt tables in the back. Luke and Joe Green sat at the far end of the bar and ordered two beers. A minute later, Dirk walked in and sat down. He spotted Luke and Joe Green, twisted his face into a big grin, then walked over and stood directly behind them.

“Hello gentlemen. Is Horseshoe Hill ready for opening day?” Dirk extended his hand, but Luke and Joe Green ignored it.

Several seconds later, Luke turned around and faced him. “Let me guess, Dirk, you’re about to get all friendly with us, and then you’re going to slip in some confidential information that you have developers looking for property just like Horseshoe Hill. They’ve got more money than God and they’re itchin’ to spend it. That right, Dirk?”

Dirk’s face soured. “Hey, you know developers are going to end up with it sooner or later,” he said. “I love this quail country more than anybody. I’d hate to see it developed by people who have no respect for the environment. I’d be out of business if that happened.”

“How about the Lovett Plantation you sold outside Tallahassee?” Luke asked. “How’s the bird count on those strip mall parking lots and condo balconies?”

Joe Green took a swallow of beer and looked straight ahead. Hank Williams Jr.’s “Family Tradition” came on the jukebox and Luke kept talking. “That was one of the prettiest stands of virgin longleaf in the Red Hills and look what they did to it. They ripped hundreds of acres of two-hundred-year-old trees out of the ground in one day. Now half those stores that moved in have gone out of business."

"I can't believe it either," Dirk said. "The people I sold it to are good people, but they're the ones who sold it to developers. It was big money, but I had nothing to do with it. I just handled the transaction for them. It would have been somebody else if it wasn't me."

"You forget, Dirk. You tried to get Joe Green here to sell Horseshoe Hill to them before you sold the Lovett place. Those guys had no idea what a bobwhite quail looks like. And you told Joe Green that they wanted a working quail plantation. Sometimes I lie awake at night thinking about what that would look like if those people had Horseshoe Hill." Luke took two large gulps of his beer and glared at Dirk who was red in the face.

"Hitting that beer pretty good today, Luke," Dirk said. "Too bad your daddy never hung around and taught you how to drink red liquor. I hear he was pretty good at it."

Luke placed his beer on the counter and stood face to face with Dirk. "You know something, Dirk? I was thinking of you just the other day. I was running a pointer in the north pasture by highway 91." Luke waved his hand as he set the scene. "It was cold, and frost covered the ground. She ran happy, like she knew she was making the first tracks in the frost. She circled the pasture twice then stopped on the hill. She hunched over and squatted right there with her nose held high in the air. And Dirk, when she finished, she left a smelly brown pile steaming on the ground." Luke picked up his beer and took a drink. "That's when I thought of you."

Dirk smirked and flattened the tone of his voice. “I know this economy’s hurting you guys. Running a quail operation’s not as cheap as it used to be.” He turned to Joe Green. “You let me know when your friends are ready to sell. I’ve got people looking. Just let me know.”

After Dirk left, Luke and Joe Green sat in silence before Luke spoke. “He’s an asshole,” Luke said. “They’re all assholes.” He cocked his head. “But maybe we are no better than they are.”

“Maybe not,” Joe Green said.

Luke took a drink from his beer. “But there is no turning back for us,” he said. “There is too much at risk now.”

“Maybe they will take the land,” Joe Green replied. “And when all the land is gone, they’ll have nothing to eat but their money.”

CHAPTER 13

It was a cold Wednesday night. Porch drinking night on Horseshoe Hill. Luke, Roosevelt, and Joe Green sat buttoned-up in barn coats.

"I remember when I was a boy," Roosevelt said, "and my granddaddy sat right here, on this porch, and told us stories. He was some storyteller. Of course, seems like there was a lot more to tell stories about back in his time. Or maybe it only seemed that way because he was a good storyteller. I remember his stories about the circus. Do you all know P.T. Barnum used to bring his circus to Thomasville?"

"Yes, we know," said Luke. "But I've got the feeling we're about to hear…" Luke never finished because Roosevelt cut him off.

"P.T. Barnum marched a dozen elephants down the middle of Broad Street. Right here in Thomasville. A dozen elephants. Can you imagine that? Do you know what they used to call P.T. Barnum's show?"

"Tell us," Luke said.

"'The Greatest Show on Earth.' Not the greatest show in Georgia. Not in the United States of America. The greatest show on *Earth*. And the greatest show on Earth came right here to

Thomasville." Roosevelt held a match to his pipe, took a couple of puffs, and leaned back in his chair.

Luke looked out at the distant tree line. The night was clear, and the stars shone brilliantly in the Red Hills sky. "I heard that Nathan Trammel's grandson was in town asking questions at the county building department about permits for developments," he said. "And someone saw him sharing a beer with Dirk Thompson in the pool hall."

Joe Green nodded, and Roosevelt puffed on his pipe. "Nathan is getting old," Roosevelt said. "He doesn't get around like he used to. I don't know what his plan is for Hickory Lane, but I imagine his children and grandchildren will sell it when it comes time. I don't think any of the children care for quail hunting."

Luke pointed to the west. "Their property line is about five miles that way. Think of the night glow from the streetlights and house lights and car lights. These stars would disappear."

Roosevelt pondered a thought. "That's called light pollution. It's a scientific fact. That sure would be a shame," he said. "I read a paper about it. Light pollution destroys the life cycle of animals. They might survive, but they'll never be the same."

"Maybe Nathan's family will sell it and the curse will move over there," Luke said.

Roosevelt sat up in his chair. "There is no curse."

Joe Green tapped the ashes from his pipe as he scanned the horizon. "People have died here. People we know and people we have never known. We'll all die someday, but the land will outlive us all. Men will try to break it and rule it in good ways and bad ways, but the land will have the last say. You have to love the land if you want to live here in peace."

It was late afternoon and tall pines cast shadows across the Plantation Parkway. An eight-point buck walked carefully toward the edge of the highway. The buck stopped, held his head high, twisted his ears and listened. In the distance, a humming sound grew louder and louder. A shiny black vehicle appeared on the crest of a hill with two identical vehicles close behind. The buck stood motionless while the three sedans with dark windows streaked by and disappeared into the distance. Turbulence spilled from the highway and rattled dried leaves on the roadside trees. The buck worked his nostrils. Change was in the wind.

Two miles down the road, the black sedans pulled to the side of the road and stopped on an empty stretch of highway. Eight men and two women stood around the lead car and one of the men opened a laptop computer on the hood. A man unfurled a map and placed it beside the computer. One of the men leaned over and pointed to the map and then to the computer and then to a stand of tall pines in the distance. The others nodded. The man pointed to the south then west and finally he pointed to the north and finished by sweeping his arm in a long arc while the others looked on.

On a wooded hill, hidden from sight, two men sat on horseback and watched. Joe Green looked like a warrior with his lips stretched tight and his leathered face and piercing brown eyes. "The wolves are here." He patted his horse on the neck. "If we act like deer, the wolves will eat us."

They stayed on their horses and watched in silence until the passengers returned to their cars.

"Did you go to Sam Horne's office?" Luke asked.

"Yes. He's a good man. And a good lawyer. These wolves call him every day."

"Remember, don't speak with them directly. They want to keep everything a secret for now so it shouldn't be a problem. Give them just enough to let them know they have a deal. We'll leak the story when it's time."

The cars sped off down the highway. They rounded the bend and surprised a gopher tortoise trapped in the highway. The first sedan clipped the tortoise's shell and spun him around. The tortoise crawled faster toward the safety of the ditch. The second sedan clipped him and spun him in the other direction. When the tortoise stopped spinning, he crawled even faster. The third sedan crushed him into a greasy mound of shell and guts.

Joe Green's horse shuffled his feet. "They are riding the horse of greed," Joe Green said. "It will take them to a place they don't want to go."

Three months after the black sedans left town, the *Thomasville Tribune* ran the story. A story that divided the citizens of Thomasville. A story that told of a tremendous change for Thomasville and the Red Hills region. A story that told of the sale of a huge block of land and a deal between an anonymous group of technology billionaires and a prominent landowner. To everyone's surprise, the huge block of land they referenced was Horseshoe Hill.

The resort project was slated to become the largest eco-resort in the world. Larger than Disney, and with more ancillary developments in the wake. The developer was the Rex Corporation, and they used the code name *Amadora* for the project. The detailed plan included a five-thousand-acre lake surrounded by nature parks, home sites, golf courses and sports fields. The large-scale plan included tentacles that would reach far into the countryside, adding RV parks, solar farms, and shopping centers. There was a Hollywood connection and plans for a film studio. But the most ambitious item of all was the plan to move the Tallahassee airport from the south of Tallahassee to a north of Tallahassee location. Right smack in the middle of the Red Hills.

Amadora sounded like heaven to some people in the area and sounded like hell to others. Closed-door meetings replaced social gatherings everywhere in Thomasville. Downtown merchants argued over parking and where to put it. City council members received requests from restaurants for Sunday liquor sales, and church congregations protested. There were rumors of historic buildings slated for demolition. Traffic jams and property tax increases were the talk of the town. Townspeople walked the streets and, for the first time ever, saw faces they did not know.

"I think those are film people at that table over there," someone said.

"I hear Warren Buffet is shopping for land here," said another.

"I've never seen so many BMWs in town."

"I'm thinking of putting my house on the market."

"My bank is too busy to call me back."

"It doesn't feel like Thomasville anymore."

Two weeks after the story broke, Luke saddled Renegade and rode out to check food plots. He had barely left the barn when he heard a car horn blaring at the front gate. The horn blared again and again and Luke wheeled Renegade and galloped to the gate. When he got there, Luke saw a red Toyota with the engine running. Inside sat an attractive woman dressed in business attire emptying papers from a briefcase into the passenger seat.

"Can I help you?" Luke asked.

"I'm here to see Joe Green," the woman said.

"And who are you?"

"I'm Heather Harrison. I'm vice president of the Rex Corporation. Mr. Green is expecting me."

Luke removed his hat, wiped sweat from his brow and took a closer look. "Joe Green's not around," he said.

Heather Harrison huffed. "Can you tell me when he will be around? I sent word a week ago that I would be here."

"Joe Green doesn't tell people where he goes, or when he'll be back."

"I'm here to discuss our contract. I sent notice to his attorney, but if he's not here, I can wait for him."

"Well, Miss Harrison, you can wait here, or you can wait at the house if you like, but there's no telling when he'll be here."

She looked around. "I'll wait at the house."

"Alright." Luke flashed a grin. "Follow me."

Heather brushed a strand of hair from her face and closed her briefcase while Luke opened the gate and motioned her to follow. He led her down the two-mile drive as slow as a horse could walk. They passed live oak trees with hanging moss. They passed dozens of green clumps of azaleas that lined the drive. Luke glanced back at the car riding on his heels. Heather had one hand on the wheel and a cell phone in the other. It took twenty minutes to reach the big house at the end of the drive. Luke dropped the reins and slid off his horse and directed Heather to the front porch. She took her briefcase and followed him to a row of rocking chairs.

Luke took a good look at his guest. She was tall with brunette hair that was smooth and neatly trimmed at her shoulders. Her eyebrows were full and natural, and she had blue-green eyes with gold flecks that gave her a captivating gaze.

"Are you staring at me?" she asked.

"I guess I was," Luke answered.

There was a moment of awkward silence.

"For what?"

"I was imagining you at a conference table with men and women in suits making decisions about what's best for the land here."

"We are enthusiastic about our plans. I will be happy to share them in more detail with Mr. Green."

Luke shook his head. "It's a nice afternoon," he said. "You can wait here on the porch. I'll get Lula to fix something to drink for you. Any preferences?"

"Do you have vodka?" Heather asked.

Luke arched his eyebrows. "Yes, we do," he said. "We have vodka. Plenty of vodka." He nodded his head and flashed a smile.

"On the rocks, please."

"Coming right up."

Luke returned with a bourbon in one hand and a vodka in the other. "To be honest, I don't think Joe Green is stopping by today," he said.

"Doesn't he live in the house?" Heather asked.

Luke chuckled. "No, Joe Green lives out there." Luke threw his eyes towards the woods.

"Out where?"

"Out there," Luke said. He pointed to the pines and wire-grass. "In the woods."

"Who lives in the house?"

"Nobody lives in the house."

"So, how do I find Mr. Green?"

"You can't find him, but don't worry, he'll be around," Luke said. "Just can't say exactly when."

"It's important. If you let him know I'm here, I can meet him tomorrow. Do you work for him?"

"I'm the manager here. You can wait, or you can come back tomorrow. That's up to you. But you have to be patient with Joe Green."

"Do you know a land broker named Dirk Thompson?" Heather asked.

"Yes, I know him."

"My company wants me to collaborate with him on land acquisitions. I'm supposed to meet him tonight."

"I heard Dirk helped y'all with the Horseshoe Hill deal. Rumor has it that he put your people in touch with our lawyer. For a fee."

Heather didn't comment.

"You and Dirk should get along just fine," Luke said.

Heather left, and the following day she came back. She waited for Joe Green on the porch while she read documents and made phone calls. Joe Green never came. Heather went to Horseshoe Hill the next day, and the day after that. Each day she was more restless. She paced the porch, talked on her phone, and scanned the grounds for any sign of Joe Green. In the afternoon of the fourth day, Luke joined her on the porch.

Heather stopped pacing, put her phone away, and sat in a rocker. "I've always heard that the people in Thomasville are friendly to strangers."

"That so?"

"That's what I heard. Of course, I'm not feeling the southern hospitality at this moment."

"Excuse me for a moment." Luke walked into the house and returned a minute later. "Now, what were you saying?" Luke asked.

Heather continued. "I know some people have objections to our development project. I sense that you are one of them," she said. "You don't even know the impact it will have on the community. The entirety of the plan is enormous. But trust me, it will be good. Good for everyone."

Lula came to the door and handed Luke a silver platter with pimento cheese, pickled okra, and roasted pecans with salt.

Heather waited until she had gone back to the kitchen. "And don't worry," she said. "We'll take care of anyone who becomes displaced."

"What do you mean?"

"I mean we'll see to it that they have opportunities."

"Who are you talking about?" Luke asked.

"The people who work around here. People like yourself."

Luke cocked his head to the side. "What kind of opportunities?"

"I've done my research, and I know about you," Heather said. "Maybe we can help each other. People say you know everything about plantation life in the Red Hills, and they say you can get things done. This may be your opportunity to parlay that into a future."

Luke's throat tightened. "You mean I could finally *be* somebody?"

"Yes, exactly."

Luke stood from his chair. "Listen, Miss Corporate High Achiever, maybe I don't *want* to be somebody. As a matter of fact, I always wanted to be nobody. But, despite all my efforts, I am somebody. People call me about dogs and quail, and they call me about anything to do with hunting. I settle feuds and dance with the ladies who need a dance partner. I drink bourbon with the boys, and I help ladies on and off wagons. It's a good life. The best life I can imagine. But you know what?"

"What?"

"If it all goes to hell tomorrow...I'll be just fine being nobody." He settled in his chair and took a swallow of bourbon. "And what kind of opportunities do you envision for the other folks working here on Horseshoe Hill?"

"The kind of opportunities they don't have now," Heather said. "I'm talking about jobs with benefits. What happens if Lula gets sick? Who would pay her hospital bills?"

"Her insurance."

"Who pays for her insurance?"

"Horseshoe Hill."

"Okay. But what about the cycle of poverty?" Heather asked.

"Cycle of poverty?" Luke's throat tightened once again. "Has it crossed your mind that people around here work their jobs because they like what they do? And they're good at their jobs. And that makes them happy being a part of a community that supports each other."

"Have you asked them?"

"No, I don't need to. I'm one of them. We're happy here and we're all part of a big family. You need to be a little mindful until you know more about how things work around here. You don't need to fix things that aren't broke," Luke said. He placed his hat on his head. "Now I'm going to my humble home. Tomorrow I'll be smiling all day long because I like my little one-bedroom cottage just fine. I like everything around here just fine. So does everyone else. With or without your opportunities."

Joe Green never came around that day, and when Heather came back the fifth day, Luke stopped her at the gate. He spoke politely with a genuine smile on his face. "Look, we're running out of vodka. If you're going to be hanging around, you might as well be doing something. We're going quail hunting this afternoon. Why don't you go with us?"

"Will Mr. Green be there?"

"There's a better chance out there than here at the house," Luke replied.

"I've never been quail hunting before. Not really my thing."

"Can you ride a horse?"

"It's been a long time, but yes, I can ride."

"I'll saddle a horse for you, and we'll go out after lunch." Luke looked at her business skirt and buttoned-up blouse, and slip-on shoes. "Why don't you go to Murphy's Gun and Sporting Goods on Broad Street and let Kitty help you with an outfit."

"Who is Kitty?"

"She's Murphy's wife and a good friend of mine. Tell her to put it on the Horseshoe Hill account."

"I can pay for my own wardrobe," Heather said.

"I insist."

"I have an expense account."

"So do I. We'll pay for it, and you can pay us back later."

"Okay. What about Mr. Green?"

"Maybe he'll join us. We'll go out at two, so don't be late."

Heather walked into Murphy's and found Kitty on a ladder, arranging silver bowls and table decorations.

"Hi, I'm Heather Harrison," Heather said. "Luke at Horseshoe Hill said you could help me with clothing for a quail hunt."

Kitty climbed down from the ladder and looked at Heather from head to toe.

"Luke sent you?"

"That's right."

"First time quail hunting?"

"It is."

"On Horseshoe Hill?" Kitty straightened her glasses. "You're a lucky woman. They've got the best quail hunting in the Red Hills."

"I'm not hunting, I'm riding along while I wait for a meeting with Joe Green. Do you know him?" Heather asked.

"Yes, I do. Joe Green is a man of few words. But a good man. He just doesn't socialize much."

"Apparently he's hard to find as well."

Kitty placed a red felt Barbour hat on Heather's head and turned her toward the mirror.

"I like it," Heather said. "Do you have it in a different color?"

"Red is the best color. It lowers your chances of getting shot."

"Getting shot?"

Kitty chose a quilted vest from the rack. "How well do you know Luke?"

"We've met," Heather replied.

Kitty helped button the vest. "Be careful with Luke," she said. "He's a good man, too. But be careful. He's a player and he's broken more than one heart in Thomasville."

"Are you kidding me? He's not exactly the intelligent type, is he?"

"He's intelligent about the things he wants to be intelligent about." Kitty held a pair of khaki trousers and a loden shirt with a quail print. "How do you like the shirt with these pants?"

"I love it, but it's too much." Heather took the shirt and pants and held the outfit as she looked in the mirror. "I don't like spending other people's money."

"Don't worry. Joe Green has more money than he can ever spend, and he doesn't care about money anyway," Kitty said. "And Luke might be a bit of a rascal, but he's generous, and he likes supporting local businesses in town."

"I have a question," Heather said. "If Joe Green has no interest in money, why is he selling his land?"

"I don't know why. Nobody knows. But he's Joe Green and nobody knows what Joe Green is thinking. Except Luke, and Luke doesn't say." Kitty looked at Heather's feet. "Size eight?"

"Exactly."

"Listen, don't get me wrong about Luke. He's a dear friend of mine and he has a lot of good qualities. I chair one of the less glamorous charities in town. We look after abused girls and girls who have come from broken families. It's not as popular as the arts and conservation fundraisers around here, but not only does Luke contribute through Horseshoe Hill, he also twists the arm of every plantation owner. It's just that..."

"What?"

"Luke can be quite the charmer."

Heather laughed. "I've been witness to his charm. I don't think I have anything to worry about."

"Just be careful."

Heather returned to Horseshoe Hill and met the hunting party at the barn. A matched set of Belgian mules were hitched to the wagon and Roosevelt sat on the front seat sorting the reins. Andy and another scout loaded six pointers into the dog box while Lula handed Roosevelt a jug of tea and a picnic basket covered with red-checked cloth. Three horses stood saddled and hitched to the post.

Heather, dressed in her outdoor attire, shut the car door, tied her hair in a ponytail and placed the red hat on her head.

"Well, damn," Luke said. His eyes traveled from her boots to her hat. "You look like a real plantation woman about to saddle up and hunt quail. Kitty did a fine job. A real fine job. I put a sweet little twenty-eight gauge in your scabbard. You know how to shoot, don't you?"

"Nobody said anything about shooting," Heather said. "I'll just follow along. I can't imagine getting a thrill from shooting birds."

"You eat chicken, don't you?" Luke asked.

"Yes."

"Well, we eat quail."

Andy brought a horse to Heather and helped her into the saddle. Luke mounted his horse and Roosevelt pulled the wagon next to them.

"Roosevelt, meet Miss Heather," Luke said. "She works for the company that's going to put the Red Hills on the map. Be nice to her. She has *opportunities.* She'll have you in a three-piece suit sitting in an air-conditioned office by summertime. But today, she's going to leave her briefcase in the car and watch what we do here in Disneyland."

"Don't mind him, Miss Heather." Roosevelt tipped his cap. "It's a pleasure to meet you."

Luke continued the introductions. "That's George on the wagon beside Roosevelt. He'll help with the dogs today. And that's Andy over there, riding scout." Luke removed his hat, ran his fingers through his thick wavy hair, placed the hat back on his head, then tightened the reins. "Let's go find some birds."

They stopped ten minutes from the house. George put two young pointers on the ground, faced them to the west and calmly stroked their tails. Andy gave two short blasts on the whistle, and the dogs bounded into the woods. They moved fast and steady, worked the edge of a field, then ran back into the woods under the tall pine canopy. They quartered right, and then left, and then right again with their heads high and tails twitching.

Luke and Heather rode ahead of the wagon while Andy worked the dogs with subtle commands and a low-pitched hum. Roosevelt followed in the wagon. He had shotguns, ammunition, and the basket of ham and cheese biscuits that Lula had made. The harness, couplings and spring suspension creaked and jangled as they ambled through the piney woods. Roosevelt had a thin whip as light as a feather and he tapped the mules on their backs to steer them through the trees. The well-oiled procession moved easily and blended with the hills and forest as if it were meant to be there since the beginning of time.

Heather rode her horse close to Luke. "I feel like I'm riding in a parade," she said.

"That's what it is," Luke said. "In a way."

Up ahead, Andy removed his red hat and held it high over his head.

"What's he doing?" Heather asked.

"We've got a point," Luke said. He tapped his horse with his bootheels and trotted toward the dogs. "Follow me."

The dogs stood rigid with their tails pointed at twelve o'clock and noses locked onto a patch of wiregrass. Luke slid from his horse and walked briskly toward the dogs. He slid two shells into his gun and left open the breach. He turned to Heather. "Slide off your horse and follow me," he said. "You need to be close to see what it's all about."

Heather dismounted and walked tentatively toward Luke. "I don't want to get shot," she said.

"Come closer," Luke said. "Stay right behind me and there's no way you will get shot. All the shots are in front of us."

Heather followed Luke as he quickened his pace. When he was close to the dogs, he closed his gun, raised it diagonally across his chest, and moved in for the flush. The brush rattled and shook and released a burst of brown birds streaking in all directions. Luke swung the gun from right to left. He pulled the trigger and folded a bird. He swung back to the right and folded another, then he looked back at Heather.

"Oh my God," Heather said. "Where did they come from? I didn't see a single quail, and they were right at our feet."

"There's nothing like the first time you see a covey rise," Luke said.

"Maybe cardiac arrest," Heather said.

Luke chuckled.

"Good shot, Mr. Luke," Andy shouted from his horse.

Roosevelt sent a sleek black Lab from the wagon. The Lab went straight to the first quail and delivered it to Roosevelt's open hand. Roosevelt sent him again. The Lab worked the scent, homed in on the bird, then returned with the other.

Andy held the reins and helped Heather back on her horse. "How did you like that, Miss Heather?" he asked. "Mr. Luke's a good shot, isn't he?"

"It's Heather, not Miss Heather," she said.

"Yes, ma'am."

Heather hesitated a moment. "What did you call Luke just then?" she asked.

"Mr. Luke," Andy said.

"I thought so."

Roosevelt pulled the wagon beside them. "Luke is a good shot. That's for sure. But you know the best shot to ever come down here and shoot?"

"Who is that?" Heather asked.

"None other than Annie Oakley herself. Came down and put on a show for Thomasville. My daddy was there. He said she split the ace of spades in half with one shot from her twenty-two rifle. Buffalo Bill Cody came down, too. We don't talk about him around Joe Green on account of him being an Indian fighter in his younger years."

Luke turned back to the wagon. "Come on, guys. If you get Roosevelt talking, he's never going to stop. Let's find more birds before the sun goes down."

Heather rode close to the wagon. "Can I see one?"

Roosevelt handed a quail to Heather. She turned it over in her hand and looked at the mottled brown plumage and the black-and-white face with a short brown crest.

Luke stopped next to Heather. "That's it," he said. "That's the tiny bird that's responsible for hospitals, schools, scholarships, art and lots of other things around here."

Heather looked up. "That's very dramatic," she said.

"It's true," Luke replied.

Heather opened the wings and spread the feathers. "It's beautiful," she said. "And camouflaged so well. I don't believe I've ever seen a wild one. Are wild quail good to eat?"

"They're excellent," Luke said. "For appetizers, I like a single leg wrapped in bacon. Fried is the most popular way to cook quail but tastes a little like chicken in my opinion. Wrapped in bacon and grilled is good. Sautéed in wine, or cooked Marbella style is the proper recipe for dinner parties. Guests always try to use a knife and fork, but a quail is too small for that. So nowadays, it's acceptable to pick it up and eat it with your hands. As for me...I like my quail roasted over an open fire with just a little salt. A quail deserves its own natural flavor."

"I see." Heather returned the bird to the wagon, and the hunt continued. Ten minutes later, the dogs pointed again. Luke dismounted and walked to the point with Heather close behind. The covey flushed just in front of the dogs, but this time Luke held his fire until the birds were out of range and then fired an errant shot into the air.

Heather turned to Andy, "Why did he do that? He didn't even try to hit one."

"The covey was small," Andy replied. "Only six birds. We don't want to thin a covey down too much. About eighty percent of the birds die every year whether we hunt them or not, but we try to protect the coveys. We're just one in a long line of predators. Everything eats a quail. Hawks are the main thing that gets them. And a hawk doesn't care how many's in a covey. But we do."

They found five more coveys over the next hour. Luke shot into two coveys, killing one quail out of each. At four o'clock they stopped the wagon by a small creek with sandy banks and Roosevelt opened the picnic basket. He poured tea and placed the ham and cheese biscuits on a tablecloth spread over the wagon table. Andy tied the horses and watered the dogs while everyone stretched their legs.

Luke wandered down the creek and stood on the bank at the old fishing hole where he and Eugene and Annabelle had played when they were young. On his way back to the wagon, Luke saw Heather shuffling around on the bank. He moved closer for a better look. She was squatting with her brand-new hunting trousers down to her ankles. She was talking to herself and had one hand against a tree and the other was swatting at a mosquito. Luke walked closer and leaned on a tree with his eyes to the ground. He waited until she was done, and her trousers securely buttoned.

"We have paper on the wagon," Luke said. "That way you don't have to use that poison ivy to tidy up."

"Damn it!" Heather tucked her shirt into her trousers and swept back her hair. "Did you enjoy yourself?" she asked.

"As a matter of fact, I did my best not to look, but...."

Heather, red in the face, lashed out. "I'm here to do a job, you know. I'm not here to hunt quail. I'm not here to bother you, or anybody else. I'm just doing my job. And I don't like playing games. I need to see Joe Green today. Have you even told him I'm here?"

"He knows you're here."

"But I don't know that he knows," Heather said. "I'd at least like for him to acknowledge the fact that I'm here."

"He's been riding with us all afternoon," Luke said.

Heather looked around. "Where?"

Luke pointed to the woods. "Out there. You've got to open your eyes and look. He's an Indian, you know. They don't make noise in the woods, and they mostly stay out of sight."

Heather brushed the hair from her face. "When can I talk to him?"

"I know it's hard, but you've got to be patient. Trust me. He'll meet with you. Just like he said he would."

Heather tossed one last word as she walked away. "Pervert."

They hunted to the far west side of the property. There, they came upon an opening with a wooden shed, a horse paddock, and a firepit fashioned from a circle of stones.

"We call this the Western Outpost," Luke pointed to a wooden shed with a tin roof. "That shed is a hundred years old. They used to hunt to this spot and leave the horses for the night. The next day, the hunt started here without having to leave from the barn. Sometimes we used it for picnics, or a rest stop on cold days when we needed a fire to warm our bones."

Luke pointed to a closet-sized building near the paddock. A crescent moon was carved into the door. "That's the outhouse. With all these trees out here, a man doesn't really need it. But we keep it up because most of the ladies who hunt with us like a little privacy when possible. Of course, most of the ladies who hunt with us aren't the rugged outdoors type like you. Would you like to freshen up?"

Heather ignored him. "It doesn't look like this place has been used in a while," she said.

"We don't stop here much anymore. Not now. It was the favorite place of Catherine and…other ladies at Horseshoe Hill." Luke opened his mouth to say more, but words never came.

They hunted quail until late in the afternoon. The dogs pointed and flushed fourteen coveys, and Luke shot nine birds in total. Heather kept scanning the woods, but there was no sign of Joe Green. They returned to the barn and Luke walked to the wagon, opened a leather case, and removed two bottles and two glasses. He filled the glasses with ice and poured vodka for Heather and a bourbon for himself.

"Seems like a lot of work for nine birds," Heather said.

"We could've shot more," Luke said. "And sometimes we do. But today I wanted to work a couple of the young dogs. And besides, it's not really about the numbers anyway. Did you enjoy yourself?"

"Yes, I did. Thank you." Heather rubbed her thighs. "I forgot that riding horses works a few muscles that don't usually get exercise. I might be a little sore tomorrow."

Luke raised his eyebrows into a look of deep concern. "Do you want me to check and see if that poison ivy is welling up?" he asked.

Heather glared at Luke.

Luke raised the glass to his lips and tilted his head back. The bourbon slid slowly down his throat. "Let's go meet Joe Green," he said.

"Now?"

"Yes, now. He's over at Roosevelt's cottage."

Luke nodded toward the cottage. A small-statured man with brown skin sat on the porch next to Roosevelt.

Luke cautioned Heather as they walked toward the cottage. "Remember, Joe Green is an Indian, and he still holds on to Indian ways. Try not to offend him and be careful to respect his customs. Just follow my lead."

They stepped onto the porch and Luke raised his right arm and greeted Joe Green with a somber look on his face. "How."

Roosevelt's body shook while he turned his head and choked back his laughter. Heather shot a narrowed glance in Luke's direction, and Joe Green said nothing.

"I'm Heather Harrison, vice president with Rex Corporation. Our legal team reached out to you with a message that I would be coming. We copied your attorney, Sam Horne, and he notified us that you would meet us. But we never received a reply directly from you," Heather said. She extended her hand and greeted Joe Green with a firm handshake.

"I'm Joe Green, and I got the message."

"I have contracts that our attorneys have prepared that are more detailed and binding than the letter of intent we currently have with you, Mr. Green. We have sent them to your attorney and it's my understanding that the documents are acceptable to him, and you, but he says it's up to us to get your signature. My company is making a big investment, and our stockholders would like to see something more formal for everyone's benefit. Ours and yours. I'm sure you understand."

Joe Green said nothing and showed no emotion.

Luke interrupted. "If Joe Green said he's selling his land, then he's selling his land. Indians don't lie."

Heather looked at Luke. "You mean Native Americans, don't you?" she asked. "I've listened to you using that word all day and someone needs to tell you it's disrespectful."

"It's not disrespectful. Listen, Joe Green's not offended if I, or anybody else, call him an Indian. It's just a word and we don't need your politically correct language skills around here telling us what to call our Indians. We all get along just fine without that."

"Have you asked him?"

Luke turned to Joe Green. "Joe Green, would you rather be called Indian or Native American?"

"Native American," Joe Green said. Then he turned to Heather. "You have my word. When the Cherokee Rose blooms, I'll sign your papers and my land will be your land."

"The Cherokee Rose?" Heather asked. "What is the Cherokee Rose? You never said anything about the Cherokee Rose."

"The vine growing on the wood fence at the gate is Cherokee Rose," Luke said. "It blooms in the early spring. About three months from now. Just be patient."

Heather studied Joe Green's face and it was chiseled like stone with eyes like steel. "Why?"

"When my ancestors were driven from this land and sent to the place you call Oklahoma, they planted the rose along the Trail of Tears so they would never lose their way home. When I sell my land, I will use the rose and follow the trail and I will know how my ancestors suffered. You can have my land when the rose blooms."

"Mr. Green, we have a nondisclosure agreement with you as well," Heather said. "The purpose of that agreement was to give us time to purchase properties in addition to yours at a fair price. Unfortunately, someone leaked the information and now my job as head of acquisitions has become more difficult. We can close in three months, if you insist, but I'd like to have the contracts signed before that. I have them with me if you'd like to look over them."

"I'll sign your contract when the Cherokee Rose blooms. You have my word."

She crossed her arms on her chest. "What if the Cherokee Rose doesn't bloom?" Heather asked.

"It always blooms," Luke said.

Heather looked at Luke, then she looked at Joe Green. "My company is not going to like this. I'll talk to our attorneys, but they're not going to like it. In the meantime, I guess I can stay in town, in case you change your mind. Are you sure you won't consider an earlier date?"

"I'll sign when the Cherokee Rose blooms," Joe Green said. He pointed toward the big house. "You can stay here if you wish. That way, you will be the first to see it when it blooms."

Heather took a deep breath. "That's generous of you. If it's no trouble, I'll do that. I may have some questions for you later on. Will you be around?"

"Yes."

Luke pointed to Heather's rental car parked in the driveway. "If you're going to drive on these dirt roads, you need something with four-wheel drive." He turned to Roosevelt. "Is the GMC still running?"

"It runs like a sewing machine," Roosevelt replied.

"It's got a few miles on it," Luke said, "but it's a good truck. I'll have Andy give it a wash and park it in the driveway."

"Thank you." Heather looked around the plantation grounds. "I have a question, Mr. Green."

Joe Green nodded.

"Why do you want to sell your land?"

"It's bad luck when man tries to own the land. My ancestors never owned the land, but they lived on it, and they cared for it. Then people came with a paper, and they said they owned the land. I don't want my name on the paper. It comes with a curse."

CHAPTER 14

At the Wednesday night meeting on Roosevelt's porch, Roosevelt whistled a tune as he brought ashtrays to the porch along with a bottle of whiskey and three glasses. He sat in his chair quickly and packed his pipe. "I hear there are movie stars in town," he said.

"I haven't seen any myself," said Luke. "But I hear there's quite a few stirring up the townsfolk. Imagine that, our corner of the world going Hollywood."

Roosevelt lit his pipe. "It wouldn't be the first time. My daddy used to brag about the day he watched his first Hollywood movie, *Gone with the Wind*. He watched it right down the road here. Have I ever told y'all that story?"

Luke turned to Joe Green and smiled. "Have you ever heard that story, Joe Green?"

Joe Green grunted.

"You might think that a movie as great as *Gone with the Wind* premiered in Hollywood with a red carpet full of movie stars and cigar-smoking producers," said Roosevelt. "But it didn't happen that way. The first showing of *Gone with the Wind* took place in a private theater on Cedar Hill Plantation right here in Thomasville, Georgia. And my daddy, along with other folks who tended to the plantation, were right there watching." Roosevelt took a puff from his pipe and watched the exhaled smoke rise into the night air. "It happened that one of the most prominent investors was friends with the folks on Cedar Hill, and that's where the movie was first shown to the fanciest of rich folks and poorest of plantation workers, as well."

"It's hard to imagine black people sitting in a room watching *Gone with the Wind*," Luke said.

Joe Green looked sideways at Luke and took a drink of whiskey. "Like a cowboy and Indian movie," he said.

"That too," Luke said.

"My daddy said they all laughed," Roosevelt said. "I don't think they related to the characters. They saw it as make believe. Hollywood, you know. When you work like they did back then, they enjoyed any kind of entertainment when they had it."

"I've never watched it," Luke said.

"You should watch it." Roosevelt continued. "I surely enjoyed that movie the first time I watched it, but I couldn't help but feel sad seeing folks live their dream and think it is never going to end and nothing bad will happen and believe the fruit always hangs low on the tree. But then, no matter how hard they struggle to hold on, the day comes when it's all gone. *Gone with the Wind.* That's a good name for that movie."

They sat for a few minutes in silence. Luke rattled the ice in his empty glass. "When I first came here, I thought nothing would ever change." Luke hesitated. "But things do change. Sometimes for good, and sometimes for greed."

The stories went on into the night until finally Luke stood and tapped his watch. "I'm going to turn in. I've got a big day tomorrow with your future boss-lady moving in. I'll see you fellas in the morning."

Heather parked her car in front of the big white house and walked to the front door with a suitcase in one hand and a black leather briefcase in the other. The door swung open, and Luke stood there with a smile. "Welcome to Horseshoe Hill."

Luke lifted her suitcase over the threshold and waved her inside. She stood and gazed at the grand foyer with sixteen-foot ceilings and twin staircases on each side. The house was like an abandoned movie set, with dust-covered sheets that covered hidden furniture and white cloth draped on chandeliers. The brick fireplace at the end of the open parlor was wide enough for a half dozen people to stand in front of a fire. Heather circled the room and let her hand glide along a covered sofa. "I can't imagine," she said. "It must have been something in its day."

Luke held his nose in the air and sniffed. "It's still a little musty, but I'll open some windows and air it out." He took her suitcase, and she followed him to a simple but elegant room with a tall four-poster bed, a sitting area, and a fireplace. He placed a big brass key in her hand. "If there's anything you need, just let me know."

"I'll be happy to pay for the room."

"No need," Luke replied. "We don't rent rooms. It's been a long time since anyone has stayed in the house, so I hope everything is in order. I checked the plumbing myself."

Heather held her briefcase to Luke's face. "You could be rid of me today if we could just get Mr. Green to..."

Luke cut her off. "We'll have a kitchen dinner around seven," he said. "Casual attire."

Heather's move to Horseshoe Hill was convenient. As the days went by, she became restless. Every morning, she put on running shorts, a sweatshirt, and running shoes and jogged to the front gate. When she got there, she inspected the tiny green buds on the Cherokee Rose. When they were only slightly larger than a pea, she snipped two buds from the vine and cut them open with a kitchen knife, looking for a flower inside. She secured a connection to the internet and spent hours each day on email correspondence and conference calls with her team at Rex. Most days she drove to town for coffee, and she always stopped at Murphy's to visit her new friend, Kitty.

One day, Heather stopped by Murphy's before lunch and said hello to Kitty at the register. They made small talk and Heather was about to leave when Jenny Bixler walked in, dressed in exercise clothes that showed off a perfectly toned body.

"Hey Jenny, are you on your way to exercise class?" Kitty asked. She turned to Heather. "There's a great studio downtown if you like Pilates or yoga. I'll give you the number if you'd like to take a class."

Jenny turned her attention to Heather. "How are you enjoying your stay on Horseshoe Hill?"

"I see that word gets around quickly down here," Heather said. "Actually, it's quite remote for me, but I'm getting some work done."

"Well, you are a brave woman to be staying on a place where people are less than pleased that you are here," Jenny said.

"I'm not concerned about that. Everyone has been extremely cordial, and eventually they will realize we are not the foreign invasion coming to change their way of life. We have a vigilant plan that will provide a benefit to the entire community. We are not a callous corporation."

Jenny gave Heather a silent evaluation from head to foot. "How's Luke?" she asked.

"He's a generous host," Heather replied.

"I can imagine. We should have lunch together one day. I'll show you around town and introduce you at the studio. We have an unbelievable staff of trainers for a small town."

"Hopefully, I won't be here long," Heather said. "But to be honest, that sounds wonderful. I'd love to have some activities in town. I'm not used to country life just yet."

"It's not for everyone," Jenny said.

"I know what you mean," Heather said. "But yes, call me." She handed Jenny a business card. "I would love to do lunch."

"I will." Jenny turned and started for the door.

"Was there something you needed here in the store, Jenny?" Kitty asked.

"Not now. I'll stop by later."

After she left, Kitty whispered to Heather, "She's one of Luke's old girlfriends. And don't think that figure is surgically enhanced. It's the real thing. She always wears something revealing when she comes in the store and Miles tries to act like he doesn't notice, but he's looking." Kitty paused. "But Jenny knows everything going on in town. You should go to lunch with her if you want to know what people are saying about Amadora."

After taking a couple of days off due to unseasonably warm weather, the quail hunting on Horseshoe Hill resumed. Heather joined the hunt along with Luke, Roosevelt, Joe Green, and Andy. As before, they assembled the wagon, mules, horses, and dogs beside the barn. Luke gave the signal, they were underway.

Luke rode in front and led them down the drive. He turned and shouted to Roosevelt. "Hey Roosevelt, do we have plenty of paper on the wagon today?"

"Yes, sir, Mr. Luke. We've got plenty."

"The soft kind from the big house?" Luke asked. "Not the rough, cheap kind like we have in the stable outhouse.

"Yes, sir. We have the soft kind."

Luke rode his horse next to Heather and leaned close to her ear. "We've got paper on the wagon."

Heather scoffed and pulled on the reins.

The hunt started slow and methodical. Luke rode next to Heather. He showed her things in the woods she had never seen before. There were tortoise holes, deer scrapes and Native American trail markers. There were good trees, great trees and invasive trees that were competition for the native plants. Luke had a story behind everything. "Do you see that hill over there?" he asked. "The one with the big oak on top."

"Yes."

"There's an old horseshoe hanging on an iron rod that's grown into the trunk."

Heather shaded her eyes and looked toward the hill. "Ahhh… Horseshoe Hill. Can we ride closer? I'd like to see it."

Luke glanced at Roosevelt before he answered. "Sure we can."

They rode to the top of the hill and Heather circled the tree until she found the iron spike. She leaned in and reached for the horseshoe.

"Don't touch it!" Luke shouted.

Heather jerked her hand back. "Why can't I touch it?"

"Just don't." Luke turned his horse toward the wagon. "Come on. Let's get back to the hunting."

Heather caught him on the way to the wagon. "People in town have told me about a curse on Horseshoe Hill. Most of the time they seem to be joking, but some say it's true. They say the curse is connected to a horseshoe. Is that it?"

"I don't believe in stuff like that, but some of the old-timers do," Luke said. "Legend has it that the Indians, or Native Americans as you like to call them, thought the tree was inhabited by spirits. See how nothing grows around the tree and it sits all alone on top of the hill?"

"Is that unusual?"

"Yes."

"There are two large branches on each side that look like arms," Luke said.

Heather looked back at the oak. "I see." She turned to Joe Green. "Mr. Green, do you believe there are spirits living in the tree?"

"They are the keepers of the quail," Joe Green said.

Luke continued the story. "The first settlers here bought the land through the lottery. They accused a drifter of stealing cattle, and they hung him from that oak tree. That was the way they did things back then. A couple days later, they found the cows wandering on a neighbor's land."

"They hung an innocent man from that tree?" Heather pointed to the oak.

"Yep. After that, a string of bad things happened here. The first owners abandoned the property for no apparent reason. The next owner was run over by a steam shovel. His wife went crazy and ran off leaving four kids. They were eventually adopted. Then two brothers from Virgina, planters, bought it. They were going to turn it into a cotton plantation. Never happened. They were killed by a lightning strike." Luke paused. "Guess where?"

"The oak tree?"

"That's right."

There was more to the story. Everyone except Heather knew that. But no one said anything about the fire.

Luke tapped his horse with his bootheels and rode away from the wagon. "Andy, watch those dogs on the flank," he said.

"Yes, sir."

Andy rode out on the flank, Roosevelt kept the wagon on the course, Luke and Heather rode side by side, and Joe Green disappeared. They saw three deer and the dogs pointed a turkey that Luke flushed and they watched it sail through the air and land in a distant food plot.

They continued the hunt, and the wagon and horses ascended a hill and rode down the backside into a savanna filled with mature pines and wiregrass. Heather scrutinized each tree as they passed. "There's a lot of value in these trees, isn't there?" she asked. "Aren't they supposed to be good for lumber?"

"You're right. They make fine lumber. In the old days they made ship masts and telegraph poles from the longleafs. They're tall and straight and the grain is tight because they grow slow," Luke said. "If you saw through the trunk of a longleaf pine, there's a pattern of rings. A light-colored ring for the growing season, and a dark ring for late summer and fall when the growth slows. Each ring represents a year of history around here."

"There's a lot of history here?" Heather said.

"More than most folks know about," Luke replied. "You can run your finger across those rings and count back. When you stop your finger, you are touching a living record from that year. You can find trees here that go back three hundred, even four hundred years. Most likely there were only Indians here at that time."

"Native Americans," Heather reminded him.

Luke looked at the trees and made a sweeping motion with his arm. "Thousands of trees with hundreds of rings and each one has a story. Lots of good stories." Luke hesitated. "And a few bad ones."

They rode in silence.

"I guess nothing lasts forever," Luke said after the long silence.

"Are you talking about the plantations?" Heather asked.

"Plantations, farms, whatever you want to call them," Luke said. "Plantation is only a name given to any large tract of land around here. But yes, I'm talking about the plantations and any other land around here that will eventually be stripped of life for the sake of money."

"If you are referring to Amadora, I can assure you, we won't be stripping the environment, as you say. It will be the most eco-friendly development this country has ever seen. We're committed to planting two trees for every one that is removed."

"It's not the same."

"That's right. Two for one."

"A managed forest with old growth trees conserves more carbon, which means there is less of a greenhouse effect in the atmosphere. The more trees, the better the air. You like clean air, don't you?"

"That's what we're all about," Heather said.

"You don't even know all the damage you can do," Luke replied. "Do you know that we're riding on top of an aquifer that flows into Florida's rivers? Guess what cleans that water."

Heather stopped her horse. "Maybe you're the only one who wants it to stay like it is. Have you considered that?"

"No, you're wrong."

"That's your opinion. If it's so important to everyone, then why are owners beating down the doors to sell?" Heather asked.

"There's always change. Right now, there are financial reasons and there's a watering down of ownership through inheritance. Doesn't make financial sense to have all your investments tied up in a big piece of property that costs money to operate."

"Why don't they sell the timber and replant it?"

"Sure, there's timber value." Luke rode next to a tree and placed his hand on the trunk. "Like this one here. You can sell this tree, but what happens when it's gone? It takes three hundred years to grow a three-hundred-year-old tree."

Heather looked at Luke with a smirk. "That's impressive math, Einstein."

Luke stopped his horse. "Do you know the red-cockaded woodpecker?" He pointed to a sap-lined hole high in the trunk of a longleaf pine. "They're on the endangered species list, and this is one of the last places on earth you'll find one. They like mature longleaf pine habitat and they're very specific about where they live. It has to be perfect. They like a cluster of old trees. They only use the ones that are tall but have the red fungus in the center so it's soft. It takes them two years to excavate one of those cavities." Luke pointed to the tree. "If you cut that tree, the woodpeckers disappear. Nobody knows what happens to them. They're just gone. No home, no woodpecker."

"Will we see one today?" Heather asked.

"I doubt it. But we might. I used to think it was pointless to worry about a tiny woodpecker. But if you lose just one, you're one step closer to losing them all. I think the survival of that tree and a tiny bird has an effect on us, too. They're part of us."

"Are you showing me this because you want me to feel guilty about what we're doing here?" Heather asked.

"It doesn't really matter. You have your deal," Luke said. "We're out here in the middle of the greatest place on earth and I thought you might find it interesting. But I suspect you're one of those people who only sees what they want to see."

"I think you are the same."

Luke pointed to a sun-filled meadow. "Imagine a lake over there with a golf course and million-dollar houses lining the ridge." Luke pointed in the other direction. "That fallow field is a good spot for the recycling dump or solar farm. I'm sure the deer won't mind sharing their bedding area with a solar farm."

"You're not looking at the big picture," Heather said. "We're going to have research centers that study the environment and alternative fuels. There will be specific attention given to native wildlife."

Luke scoffed. "Okay. And by the way, we already have a research center. But…"

The wagon caught up to Luke and Heather, and Roosevelt gave Luke a settle down look.

"I see Joe Green way over there on his horse," Heather said. "It looks like he's following us."

"He's watching the hunt," Luke replied. "He will lay off like that and nod his head when things go right, or when he thinks we're approaching an area where there are birds." Luke looked toward the distant hill and gave Joe Green a two-finger salute.

"Why does he stay far off in the woods? I'd like to talk with him."

Luke looked at her and smirked. "I don't know for sure, but maybe it's you. He might not like the smell of that perfume you're wearing. Joe Green likes the smell of the woods and the animals. Perfume is pollution to him. He's riding with us, but he's staying upwind of you."

Heather stopped her horse. "I see. Well, I don't like the smell of a horse's ass," she said. "Guess I'll stay upwind of you, too." She kicked her horse and trotted ahead.

In the evenings when they were at Horseshoe Hill, Luke and Heather had dinner in the kitchen, which usually consisted of something Lula had cooked earlier in the day and left in the oven. On other evenings, Luke dined with neighbors and Heather dined in Thomasville. The small town was full of fine restaurants and once the locals stopped whispering behind Heather's back, she made a few friends in town.

CHAPTER 15

Two weeks after Heather arrived, Luke and Heather received a dinner invitation to a small party on Magnolia Trace, Colonel Bronson's neighboring plantation. They accepted, and that evening, Luke dressed in blue jeans, boots, and a well-worn navy blazer. Heather wore a peasant-style cotton dress with a wildflower print that flowed to her ankles. She held the skirt out at the knee and showed it to Luke.

"Lula found this dress hanging in a closet with lots of others. I didn't pack many casual nighttime clothes and she said this would be appropriate. I hope you don't mind."

Luke swallowed hard. "It's appropriate. And it looks good on you."

Luke opened the truck door. "Listen, Heather," he began, "it's best you don't go talking to the plantation owners about how great Amadora will be, and how careful your folks are going to treat the environment and all the jobs it'll bring to the Red Hills. These people won't agree with you. Don't get me wrong, they're nice people and they'll be nice to you. But they won't agree with you."

"I've done my research," Heather said. "I know who they are."

Luke cocked his head. "Is that right? So, who are they?" he asked.

"They're old money people with more land than they need. They spend their money to hold onto the land so they can pass it on to their children who don't really want it. They are hopeless romantics in love with quail hunting and a way of life that is ending. I think they know it. I won't be pushy, but at some point, I will let them know that we can help them with a transition."

Luke ran his fingers through his hair and shook his head. "I'm sure the people you work for see themselves as generous benefactors giving the dinosaurs a way out, but I wouldn't underestimate these people. Some of these dinosaurs might put up a fight. They love the land and it's in their blood. They are better land stewards than your people will ever be. That's something I know. And they know it, too."

"They're good land stewards for the benefit of who? Themselves?"

Luke stopped smiling. "No. For the benefit of anyone who drives the dirt roads and highways around here and when they look out the window, they see something that money can't buy." Luke shut the door and walked to the driver's side. "These are nice people, and I would appreciate it if you treat them that way."

"Of course, they're nice people. They're rich. Or, I should say rich for around here. And it's easy to be nice when you're rich. But that doesn't matter anyway. I'm going to help them."

"Help them what?"

"Help them with an exit strategy. Help them with alternatives for their land. Help them see some return on their investments."

Luke hung his head as if he had accepted defeat. "Just let these people be tonight. If, or when, they sell out and go someplace else, they are going to die. This is their home and there is no other home for them. And besides, some of the people you'll meet tonight are just regular folks who worked and saved all they could so they could own a piece of land. Not all of them are rich."

"They'll make money when Amadora begins to take shape. This land is going to skyrocket in value and anybody who has land will benefit," Heather said. "The buzz has already started, you know."

"Colonel Bronson, Oscar Thornton, none of these plantation owners care about the money," Luke said. "If they did, they would have sold the timber, cleared the fields, and developed it themselves a long time ago. But they spend a lot of money to keep it like it is. A lot of money."

"A lot of money to kill a few tiny birds," Heather said.

Veins stood out on Luke's face "That's right. We kill a few birds every year. But your delusional fairytale eco-project will kill them all."

"We will have areas set aside for all the animals. I assure you."

"There will be no animals. They'll get run out and then spend the rest of their miserable lives trying to find their way home. But there won't be any home. The best they can hope for is to be put in a zoo and hand fed by humans. That's not life." Luke started the engine. "Let's go before we get into an argument neither of us will win." He glanced at the dress once more.

Luke and Heather arrived at Magnolia Trace, and Heather was swept away by Colonel Bronson. Just as Luke expected, Heather was treated like an honored guest. She drank two quick vodkas and was stopped on her way to the bathroom by Ginger Bronson, who was ahead of Heather on the drink count.

"Now tell me Heather dear, where did you grow up?" Ginger asked.

"I was born and raised in Boston."

"Oh my," Ginger said. "Another Yankee. Well, have you ever lived anywhere in the South?"

"I'm living in Southern California right now," Heather said.

"No, no, no. Oh, no. That's not the South, honey."

"Let me see..." Heather placed her index finger to her cheek. "Well, I did an internship in Dallas."

"That's it," Ginger said. "That's the South. Or, close enough, I think. I knew you had some in you. I knew it the first time I saw you."

"Is there something wrong with the Yankees?" Heather asked.

"No, honey. We like our Yankees. We introduced them to our way of life and our bobwhite quail hunting, and they came down here in droves. Now they think that they know everything. They think that their study discovered the benefits of controlled burning in our woods. But we knew all about that before they got down here. We learned it from the Native Americans. And we had a lot more quail before the Yankees came down."

Colonel Bronson stepped in and offered Heather a break from Ginger's Yankee dissertation. "Ginger, let me talk with this gal before you start another civil war," Bronson said.

He took Heather by the arm and escorted her on a tour of Magnolia Trace. The house was a modest, rambling hunting lodge, not a mansion. Each wood-paneled room was filled with antique furniture, artifacts and faded photographs of men and ladies in the field with hunting dogs and horses. There was an autographed photograph of President Eisenhower. He held a twenty-gauge side-by-side while petting a lemon-and-white pointer at his feet. There were stuffed ducks, turkey fans and mounted trout hung next to family portraits and wildlife paintings by famous artists. Bronson pointed to a yellowed map with colored blocks of land identifying each plantation in the Red Hills.

"A few have changed hands, but that's still pretty much the way it is today," Bronson said. "For now," he added.

They walked the hall and Colonel Bronson stopped at a photograph of a dozen black baseball players standing in two rows. They were dressed in crisp gray uniforms. Each player held a wooden bat. The picture was taken in a world far removed from the major leagues, but no one would have ever known looking at the photograph.

"In the old days, all the plantations had baseball teams," Bronson said. "Good teams, too. See that pudgy-faced kid standing in the middle there?"

"Yes."

"That's Roosevelt's great-uncle, Cedric. He was one of the best. He had a live fast ball and a nasty curve. Probably could have gone to the big leagues. But that was just before Jackie Robinson broke the color barrier. Did you know Jackie was born just up the road here in Cairo?"

"I know the story of Jackie Robinson, but I didn't realize he was born around here," Heather said. "That's remarkable."

"Angus's father, George Parker, hired Cedric away from us when the league got overly competitive. He said he needed another wagon driver, but George had a Horseshoe Hill uniform waiting for him when he got there. And he beat the hell out of us every time we played them."

While Colonel Bronson entertained Heather, Ginger weaved her way across the room and spoke to Luke. "Your girl's a Yankee," Ginger said.

"My girl?" Luke looked surprised. "Who are you talking about?"

"The one you've been watching from across the room all night." Ginger drank the last of the gin from her glass. "She's had her eye on you, too."

"I'm just trying to make sure she doesn't insult everybody," Luke said. "And she seems to being doing okay."

"She's an attractive woman," Ginger said. "Very attractive. But she's a Yankee. Don't forget that."

Luke sighed. "Now Ginger, tell me again what you have against the Yankees."

"I'll never get over the fact that they came down here and stole from the South. I just can't stand Yankees."

Luke looked around the room like he was taking inventory in his mind. "Here are all your very good friends in this room tonight. Eighty percent of them have Yankee roots. Now which of these are the folks you don't like?"

"Oh, Luke." Ginger rattled the ice in her empty glass. "Go and get me a gin and tonic please. Light on the tonic."

"How about no tonic at all?" Luke asked.

"Just have James fix it for me. He knows how I like it."

Luke returned with Ginger's gin. "Here you go," he said.

"I'm worried about the Red Hills, Luke." Ginger tasted her drink. "And I'm worried about her." Ginger nodded toward Heather.

Luke grunted. "I'm worried about her myself."

"What are we going to do?" Ginger asked.

"Everyone has lived this life like they thought it would go on forever. People are going to come, Ginger. People just like Heather. Or worse. Everyone who cares needs to have a plan. Do you have a plan?"

"Our granddaughter, Elizabeth, will inherit Magnolia Trace. She loves it as much as we do, or more."

"Elizabeth is in boarding school?"

"Yes."

"And her parents, Bob and Laura, are in Palm Beach?"

"Bob has a wonderful law practice there."

"But they never come here," Luke said.

Ginger huffed. "They don't love it like Elizabeth does. She loves it. Bob and Laura have their life in Palm Beach, but Elizabeth loves it here."

"And what are the chances Elizabeth will marry a man who loves it?"

"She's a beautiful girl. She can marry any man she wants," Ginger said. "The chances are excellent."

"I'd say the chances are next to zero," Luke said.

Ginger blinked her eyes and held back the tears. "Oh, Luke. You distress me. Go and get yourself another drink."

Luke backed off and Ginger socialized with guests on her way to the other side of the room.

Colonel Bronson made sure that Heather's glass was never dry. By the time dinner was served, she had lost any trace of inhibition. She talked and laughed with everyone within reasonable range of her voice. Luke was on the other side of the table and watched in awe, amused, and amazed that she was the center of attention in a room full of people with nothing in common. He said little because Heather never gave him an opening. When she recounted her first quail hunt on Horseshoe Hill, the entire room listened as if she were the expert at a dining table full of amateurs.

When the party was over, Luke and Heather said good-bye with a round of enthusiastic hugs and handshakes. They left the house and the chatter faded with each step as they walked, side by side, toward the truck parked in darkness. The air was cold and clear and the stars formed a soft blanket in the sky. The broken canopy formed by the tall pines diffused the moonlight and cast shadows along the path. They reached the truck and Luke opened the door for Heather. They locked eyes for a second before she got in.

Luke drove the truck slowly along the narrow backroads. “You should have brought a stack of blueprints and dropped them right on the table,” Luke said. “I’ve never seen anyone charm that bunch like you did tonight. Damn, that was something.”

“I wasn’t trying to charm anyone. They are genuinely nice people, and I was enjoying myself. I’m hunting with Colonel Bronson tomorrow. He invited me to the field trial too. He says you are much too serious about the field trial to have any fun. Do you have a problem with that?” Heather smiled at Luke.

“No. No problem.”

“What are you looking at?” Heather asked.

“Your dimple. I just realized that I have never seen your smile before tonight.” Luke nodded. “It’s nice.”

“Thank you.”

They finally arrived at the big house. Luke opened the door and held Heather’s hand as she stepped onto the gravel. It was a long step down and she leaned into Luke’s shoulder as she gathered her balance. Luke gently placed a hand on the small of her back.

“What are you doing?” Heather asked. She stepped back and brushed the hair from her face. “Did you have a lot to drink tonight?”

“No, I didn’t have a lot to drink. I just noticed something.”

“What?”

"You really are something else when you let your hair down." Luke paused. "And the way that dress catches in all the right places has me…well, kind of has me speechless."

"You don't sound speechless."

"Close to it."

"Are you flirting with me?"

"Maybe. But...around here, it's what we call the 'will of the wind.'"

"Will of the wind? What exactly does that mean?"

"That's an old Indian…wait, excuse me, an old Native American saying for those times when something big is about to happen and you have no control over it."

"Will of the wind?" Heather looked to the sky and repeated. "Will of the wind."

"Yes, will of the wind." Luke leaned in.

Heather crossed her arms. "That's funny," she said. "The ladies in town say that's your signature line when you want to start something." She turned, walked up the steps and opened the door to the big house. "Goodnight now, Mr. Luke."

The next morning, Luke, Roosevelt, and Joe Green stood on Roosevelt's porch and watched Heather walk from the house to the truck. She was dressed perfectly in canvas pants, tan field jacket and a green felt fedora. She gave the men a quick wave, sprung into the driver's seat, and drove off toward Magnolia Trace.

"Lord have mercy," Roosevelt said quietly, as he watched her drive away. "What have we got here?"

"I'm not too sure, Roosevelt," Luke replied. "We might have underestimated Miss Heather Harrison."

Heather was hard to dislike. Nearly impossible. She rode horses, listened to stories, and made friends wherever she went. She had a sharp wit and growing appreciation of the outdoors that endeared her to the purists. She went on hunts and attended parties. She was a fixture in town, and she dined with new friends at restaurants and attended art shows and charity dinners. But every time Heather went through the gate at Horseshoe Hill, she stopped. She searched every inch of the green vine for the smallest bit of white that would turn into the flower that would bring the deal she was sent to secure. She never forgot to look for the Cherokee Rose.

CHAPTER 16

At sunset, Roosevelt, Luke, and Joe Green sat on the porch and poured drinks. Roosevelt and Joe Green packed tobacco into their pipes, and Luke slid a large cigar from his shirt pocket.

"What are you doing with a cigar?" Roosevelt asked.

"It's not just any cigar. It's a Romeo y Julieta Churchill," Luke said. "Direct from Havana, Cuba."

Roosevelt raised his eyebrows "That's a fine-looking cigar," he said. "I thought Cuban cigars were illegal."

"They are." Luke struck a kitchen match on his pant leg and took three strong puffs on the cigar.

"Well, where did you get it?" Roosevelt asked.

"From a friend." Luke took another puff and blew a ring of smoke into the cool night air.

Roosevelt nodded. "We've got the field trial coming up," he noted. "Any big names coming this year?"

"Just the usuals," Luke replied. He paused. "Are you talking people or dogs?"

"People. Celebrities. Politicians."

"Just the usual as far as I know," Luke said.

Roosevelt looked to the sky as he pondered a question. "Who do you imagine is the most famous person to hunt quail down here?" he asked.

Luke sipped his whiskey. "Well, there were the rich industrialists back in the Gilded Age. Real-life tycoons. And I think some famous people came here without anyone knowing they were here," Luke said. "I'm talking about private people."

"That could be," replied Roosevelt. "But I can't imagine anyone more famous than President Eisenhower. He came every year to hunt quail. And he played a lot of golf, too. One of my uncles used to caddy for him. He said Eisenhower was a good golfer but a lousy tipper."

"I'd say it had to be the Duke and Duchess of Windsor," Luke said. "They stayed several times down on the Hamilton place. Duke and duchess is one step away from king and queen you know."

Roosevelt sipped his whiskey. "They were famous in England, but not as famous over here."

"You didn't say famous here," Luke said. "You said famous. You didn't say where they had to be famous."

"Errol Flynn used to come down," Roosevelt said.

"Yes, he did. I heard he was a good shot on quail."

"He made some good movies."

Luke nodded. "He was a good actor."

"How about Jackie Kennedy?" Roosevelt asked. "That's a famous lady for you. I'd say Jackie Kennedy was the most famous."

"But Jackie Kennedy didn't hunt quail. She only rode horses," Luke said. "And you said, 'the most famous to hunt quail here.'"

"She went out with the hunting party, so that means she was quail hunting. Doesn't matter if she was shooting the gun or not, she was quail hunting. You think when I go on the hunt and drive the mule wagon, I'm not quail hunting?"

"Okay," Luke said. "I guess you're right. It was Jackie Kennedy."

Roosevelt thought for a moment. "President McKinley used to come here, too. But he was one of the private ones. You don't hear much about him down here."

Luke looked toward the big house. "And now we have Princess Amadora staying right here under our roof. I've got a lot on my mind with everything going on plus the field trial, and Joe Green invites her to stay here, and I have to entertain her."

"Looks to me like she's doing a pretty good job of entertaining herself," Roosevelt said.

"Ain't that the truth."

Joe Green stood from his chair, tapped the ashes from his pipe, placed his empty glass on the rail, and left without saying a word. Luke turned to Roosevelt. "I guess it's time to turn in."

The Wiregrass Field Trial was the Kentucky Derby for the members of the club. There was a mix of blue blood pedigrees and newly established enthusiasts. In preparation for the event, there was a party for the judges, marshals, club officials and their house guests. Many of the plantations had private parties throughout the week. Each plantation picked their best dog, bathed and clipped their horses and shined their team for the competition. This year, the field trial was held at Magnolia Trace Plantation.

On the day of the trials, horse trailers, horses, dogs, and wagons transformed a remote hay field into a festival. Trucks and trailers parked side by side and anxious grooms brushed horses, hitched mules to wagons, and watered dogs. Five large tents with tables and chairs were staked on the hilltop and an empty barn was converted into a cook shed with wisps of fragrant barbeque smoke seeping from vents in the tin roof. A long wooden table sat in the open with bottles of liquor, wine, and beer. Bartenders dressed in white shirts and black bow ties waited to serve drinks after the trials.

Heather rode in the truck with Luke and Roosevelt. They parked next to George and Andy, who were busy with the horses and dogs. Luke and Heather walked to the main tent and were greeted by Colonel Bronson.

"Here's our honored guest," Bronson said. He kissed Heather on the cheek and slapped Luke on the back. "Luke, you don't mind if I steal Heather away for a few minutes, do you?"

"I'm sure she'll like that. She's been waiting for this thing for a week now. I don't know what you and Ginger have told her."

"I am grateful for the invitation," Heather said. She straightened her field jacket and brushed the hair from her face.

"How many times did you change outfits this morning while we were waiting for you?" Luke asked.

"I want to be comfortable if we're riding all day." She wore tan riding pants, tall leather boots and a white blouse with pearl buttons running down the front. She had a silk scarf with a quail print around her neck and a green felt hat on her head. She turned to Bronson. "I hope I am dressed appropriately," she said.

"Right out of the pages of *Garden and Gun*," Bronson said. "Come with me, I have some people for you to meet." He took her by the arm and led her away.

Luke mingled with the crowd until Heather returned. "There's a few dignitaries here today," she said. "And everyone I've met has room for me on their wagon."

"Don't get the wrong idea. They know about you and Amadora. They're looking to dig information out of you. I think you're safer riding with us." Luke nodded.

"Safer?"

"Yes, safer."

"Oh, Luke, I am so lucky to have you here so you can look after me." Heather batted her eyes.

The field trial began, and eighty horses, along with twenty wagons, advanced into the woods. Each brace ran two dogs while the gallery followed on horseback and wagons. Old friends, new friends, and guests rode side by side. They kept their eyes on the dogs while they chatted about the weather, the quail, and old times. Each brace lasted thirty minutes, then they called the dogs, and a new brace began.

The Horseshoe Hill draw came early in the morning. Whistling Willy ran against a sleek setter from Manchester Plantation, but when Luke turned Willy loose, he was on birds right away. He followed the scent, ran straight to a covey, and pointed before the setter had hit stride. Luke flushed the covey and Willy was off again. He patterned the wiregrass savanna to perfection. He ran through fields, down creek bottoms, jumped logs, and pointed covey after covey. Finally, near the end, the setter beat Willy to a covey and pointed. Willy saw it and froze with his tail tight as he honored the point.

After the brace, the Horseshoe Hill participants gathered at the wagon. "That Willy is some dog," Roosevelt said. "He runs just like his daddy Sam, who won all those trophies in the trophy case." He turned to Heather. "I remember my father telling me about the time they thought Sam had lost his mind."

Andy grunted, and Luke shook his head. "Here we go."

Roosevelt gathered the reins and tapped the mules. "One day, they were on an afternoon hunt, and Sam was pointing coveys right and left. Then they came up on a creek, and Sam went down to the creek bank, and struck a point. So, Angus got off his horse and went to Sam, ready to bust the covey and shoot some birds. But when he got to Sam, he saw a man. He was sitting on the bank, fishing with a cane pole. Angus didn't pay much attention to the man because he knew there had to be birds there, so he beat the bushes and waited for the covey rise."

"Sam never had a false point," Luke added.

"So, Angus beat the bushes some more, but still no quail. He tapped Sam on the head to relocate, but Sam just stood there holding tight and looking square at the man with the fishing pole. Finally, Angus asked the man if he had a quail in his pocket. The man shook his head. Angus tried to drag Sam away from there, but Sam held his point. Angus asked the man if he had been around birds, maybe picked up some scent that way. But again, the man shook his head. Finally, Angus grabbed Sam by the collar and dragged him away. Sam fought every inch of the way. And just before they got to the wagon, Angus turned and asked the man, 'What's your name?' And the man said, 'Bob White.'"

Andy grinned, Luke winked at Heather, and Roosevelt chuckled so hard that he shook the wagon.

Heather rode well at the field trial. She mingled easily with the gallery while they followed the course along with the judges and marshals. Luke never wandered far from Heather and mostly they rode side by side, or alongside the wagon with Roosevelt and Andy. They watched and talked and smiled at each other like teammates waiting for their players to take the field.

An hour and a half into the trial, during the third brace, Pat Bennet, a member of the gallery, fell from his mount while crossing a ditch and broke his arm. Moments later, Alex Britain, another member of the gallery, was bucked off. She hitched her horse to the wagon and rode there the rest of the day. Those were typical happenings during the field trial, but the most sensational event occurred just before the lunch break. And it happened to Heather.

She was riding alongside Luke on the left flank, just behind the marshals, when her horse stepped in a hole. Angry yellow jackets rose from the ground and stung her horse in the face. The frightened horse jerked her head up and down and lunged forward and dipped and bucked and made a tight circle. Then the horse broke into a frantic gallop as the helpless gallery looked on.

Luke dug his heels into Renegade and galloped after her, but she was too far ahead and moving too fast. Heather's horse ran for two hundred yards before Heather finally brought her under control. The horse stopped, and Heather calmly stroked her lathered neck, then turned around and trotted back to the gallery as if nothing had happened.

When the morning session closed, the gallery on horses and wagons and the judges on horseback with the marshals started back to the tents. The pace was brisk, and the route was direct.

Riders shuffled positions as they mingled among other riders and chatted about the morning races.

Colonel Bronson rode next to Heather. "That was some mighty fine riding," Bronson said.

"I was just holding on, but I must admit I was looking for a place to jump off if she hadn't slowed down."

"Not many of these veterans would have stayed on that horse," Bronson said. "I don't think any of them could have handled her any better than you did. I was thoroughly impressed."

"Well, I don't want to do it again," Heather said.

Everyone in the gallery had seen it. Bert Walters rode past and tipped his hat in a respectful way, then whispered something to Alan Burgess, who looked back at her. Ginger rode to the other side. "Honey, you gave us quite the scare. Will you sit with us for lunch?" Ginger asked.

"Forget lunch. I need a cocktail. Or two," Heather replied.

"That's it. We'll both have a cocktail."

After lunch, the horses and wagons reassembled, and the afternoon session began with a brace of English pointers. One of the pointers was Woodcrest Plantation's lemon-and-white male, and the other was a liver-and-white female owned by Senator Jackson from Atlanta. Both dogs were anxious but disciplined as they stood at attention with muscles twitching as the handlers mounted their horses. Then the race was on.

The dogs swung to the left, cut back to the right, and then set the pattern. The Woodcrest pointer scented birds, but Senator Jackson's dog overtook him. She ran hot and hard into the covey and the birds scattered in all directions. That ended her chance of winning the brace. Curt Lambert, the highly confident dog trainer for Senator Jackson, jumped from his horse and ran to the dog. He struck the dog in the loin with his whip and the dog yelped. He grabbed the dog by the ear and the dog yelped again. He dragged the dog by the ear back to the spot where the covey flushed and kicked the dog before he finally released her. The gallery watched the entire episode.

"Just a little correction," Curt said to no one particular.

Luke was one of the first to move. He touched Renegade with his bootheels and trotted toward Lambert.

Roosevelt watched from the wagon. "Oh, Lord," he said.

Renegade trotted faster.

Andy whispered softly to himself. "Don't do it, Mr. Luke."

It was too late. Luke caught up to Lambert's horse and slowed as he drew even. Luke and Lambert exchanged glances. Luke stood in the saddle, took his boot from the stirrup, drew his knee to his chest and side kicked Curt Lambert off his horse. Curt hit the dirt hard. He grabbed his arm and spit dirt. He rose to his knees and tried to catch his breath. Luke backed Renegade and stood directly over Lambert. Renegade stomped the dirt and Curt writhed in pain and flopped from side to side as Renegade shuffled his feet.

Luke glared down at Lambert. "There's a little correction for you."

Luke wheeled Renegade and trotted back to his position beside the wagon. Roosevelt, Andy, and Heather looked straight ahead. No one said a word.

It was close to dark, and the Wiregrass Field Trial was over, and the judging was done. Participants and guests, judges and observers gathered around the center tent for trophy awards and spoken accolades. Oscar Thornton, president of the club, called Luke aside for a private conversation.

"Luke, that dog of yours was spectacular today. Absolutely perfect. Everybody saw it." Thornton put his hand on Luke's shoulder. "But we've got to disqualify you, Luke."

Luke looked at the ground and nodded his head. "Because of that correction thing with Curt Lambert?"

"Yes, that's it."

"I'm sorry about that, Oscar. I know better, but I couldn't help myself. If he had been the least bit remorseful, I would have given him a pass. But that arrogant son-of-a-bitch needed it." Luke thought for a moment. "Actually, I'm not sorry about it. I'd give every silver cup and dog portrait in our trophy case for just five minutes alone with that jerk."

"I'm not going to disagree, but Luke, you know that's not the image we want in the club. There'll be talk about suspending you as well."

"What about Lambert?"

"He's out."

Luke glanced over Oscar's shoulder and saw Heather with Senator Jackson behind the tents. They were alone and engaged in intense conversation. Luke turned to Oscar. "Look, Oscar, maybe you could consider probation or something a little less severe than a disqualification. I don't give a damn about more trophies, and I know I can beat any of these guys on any given day, but it means something to our crew, and I don't want to be the one that cost them the trophy."

"I'll put in a good word. You know that. And by the way, that Heather can ride a horse."

"I know." Luke nodded his head. "She's fearless."

The awards presentations began with customary speeches and acknowledgments. Luke stood next to Heather while winners accepted trophies of silver for first place and colored ribbons for second and third. When the awards were over, the crowd mingled with cocktails and hors d'oeuvres. Heather smiled when she looked at Luke and Luke returned the same kind of smile. The distance between them slowly dissolved until they stood close to each other, almost touching, while they replayed the day's events.

Senator Jackson approached Luke with a drink in his hand and Heather excused herself.

"That was an offensive way to treat one of your fellow dog handlers this afternoon, Luke," Jackson said.

"He's not one of my fellow anything," Luke replied. "And he's damn sure no dog handler." Luke drank from his cup. "No offense."

"Well now," the senator replied, "Curt has his ways." Senator Jackson flashed a politician's smile. "I was watching you today, and watching that dog, Willy, too. And I tell you what, when this Horseshoe Hill sale thing goes down, why don't you come work for me on my place? Don't worry about Curt. You can take the lead position and I'll be sure you have free rein of the kennel. And I'll buy as many of your dogs from Joe Green as you like. I've got plenty of room for them in our kennel. What do you say, Luke?"

Luke crossed his arms on his chest. "Well, I appreciate the offer, Senator. But I don't think I could work for somebody who would push through a dam project down here the way you just did. And I could never work for anyone who supports the airport relocation." Luke smiled but his tone was terse. "Either you're one of those politicians who can be bought, or you really don't give a damn about the Red Hills." He drained the last of his bourbon. "But, like I said, thanks for the offer."

The field trial party lasted until dark, and the Horseshoe Hill crew celebrated until the bar was empty and the tables were put away. Luke did not seem to mind his disqualification from the cup. It was difficult to tell if he was proud of Willy, or proud of the way that Heather endeared herself to the entire Wiregrass Field Trial Club.

They returned to the big house, and Luke walked Heather to her room. They were friendly after the party and they rubbed shoulders as they walked and recounted the events of the day. They reached Heather's room and she turned and stood in the doorway. Luke leaned against the wall.

"I tried to impress you today with all our dog-handling skills and the dogs we have and everything about our place in the club. And I'll be damned if it wasn't me who got impressed."

"That's the nicest thing you've said to me," Heather said.

Luke leaned close enough that they breathed the same breath. "We shouldn't, should we?" he asked.

Heather closed her eyes and whispered, "Maybe..."

Luke stayed close. "Maybe?"

"Yes. Maybe you're right," Heather said. "We shouldn't."

Luke smiled. "Good night, Heather." He gave her a light kiss on the forehead, then turned and walked down the long hallway, out the door, and across the lawn to his cottage. Heather slipped into her room and tossed her hat onto a chair. She walked to the mirror and brushed her hair. She removed her clothes, slipped into a gown, and crawled into bed. She laid her head on a pillow, drew the other pillow to her chest, and went soundly to sleep.

CHAPTER 17

Two days after the field trials, Luke's phone rang. It was Heather. Her voice was feeble and her words barely audible. "Luke, can you come get me?"

"Where are you?"

"I'm at the hospital. I had an accident in the truck. I'm okay, but the truck is broken."

"What kind of accident?" Luke asked.

No answer.

"Are you alright? You don't sound so good."

"I've got a bump on my head. And some stitches over my eye. That's all. Just a couple of stitches. Can you come get me, please?"

"What happened?" Luke asked.

"I ran through an intersection in town. I almost hit a car broadside, but I swerved out of the way and ran over a curb. I hit a signpost and then I hit the side of a building. And my head hit the windshield. And Luke..." Heather started sobbing, "someone cut the brake lines. I had no brakes. Why would anyone do that?"

"Sit tight, Heather," Luke said. "I'm coming to get you."

That night, back at Horseshoe Hill, Luke poured a glass of wine for Heather and sat on the edge of the bed while she rested. He brought a wet cloth from the kitchen and patted the bump on her forehead.

"I talked to Sheriff Barnes on my way to the hospital, and he assured me they will find out who did this," Luke said.

"Why, Luke? Why would anyone want to hurt me?"

"I don't know," Luke replied. "I know everybody in this town, and there are a few people who are not pleased with your development, but I don't know anybody who would try to hurt you like this. It doesn't make sense."

"I feel like I'm failing at my job. Maybe I shouldn't even be here." She spoke freely as the painkillers mixed with the wine and fear. "I mean, I like this work and I know you don't wholeheartedly believe in Amadora, but I do, and I want it to be wonderful and I want everybody to see that it's wonderful." Heather raised the glass and guided it to her bruised lips with both hands. She held it there until the wine was gone. "But now I see what it will do to you, and I worry about what you will do, and this thing between us, I don't even know what this thing is." She extended the empty glass for more wine. "I should quit this job. What do you think?"

Luke looked down. "I think you should finish this job. I don't see you as a quitter. But I'm curious. Why did you choose the corporate world in the first place?"

"I don't know," Heather replied. "I'm good at it. Really good at it. I make deals happen. And this is a big deal. The biggest deal ever." Heather sighed. "I wanted to impress my father. He always said I should be in business. I was smart in school. I was smart and I studied hard too. And I knew he would never approve if I did something frivolous."

"Does he approve now?"

"He died six years ago. I spent all those years studying and working so he could be proud, and he never got to see what I accomplished. He worked all his life as a banker and moved from bank to bank, but never rose higher than mid-level. But he worked hard. Every night and weekend. He was obsessed with money and that drew him into all sorts of glorious schemes to get rich. And every one of them failed. But there was always the next big deal right around the corner."

Heather exhaled and her sharpness seemed to soften even more. "I liked other things better than math, which was the only thing he cared about. When I was in the sixth grade, I won a short story competition and I remember how I was so excited to show him. But he put it aside and never even looked at it. I wrote more and he never read anything I wrote unless it was a thesis on building wealth or some other business subject."

"Did you write anything besides that short story?" Luke asked.

"A little. I loved writing at school. But I stopped taking it home."

"You should write now," Luke said. "You should quit this project right now today and start writing. Who cares if you make lots of money?"

"Are you crazy? I couldn't do that. I can't throw away everything I've worked for and quit on people who sent me here to do a job. And besides, I make good money doing what I do. Probably much more money than a plantation manager can imagine."

"I'm going to write that insult off to painkillers and alcohol," Luke said. "But you're a smart woman. You could make it as a writer. At least you should try it."

"I can't think about it. It's a frivolous occupation, as my father used to say."

"That's a shame."

"Well, there's a price to pay for success and you can't dream about foolish things if you want to be successful. I can thank my father for the woman I turned out to be." Heather tried to drink one last drop of wine from the empty glass. "And I can blame my father for the woman I turned out to be."

Luke carefully touched the stitches on her forehead. "I think I would like you as a writer," he said.

"What?"

"Nothing."

"What did you say?"

"Nothing. Now get some rest."

The following day, Sheriff Barnes went to Horseshoe Hill and asked to see Heather in the library. "Miss Harrison, I'm very sorry about the trouble you had in town. That's not like our town at all. Not at all. Do you know of anyone who might want to harm you?" he asked.

"No, I don't."

"Have you received any threats since you've been here?"

"I've heard from some people in town and around town who are against my company's development here, but most of the negative opinions have been sort of friendly talk. Nothing angry or threatening."

"Can you give me the names of those people?"

Heather glanced through the window and saw Luke on the porch with Roosevelt and Joe Green. "I can't remember them right now. Can I think about it and give you a list later?"

"That would be helpful." Sheriff Barnes made a note in his notepad. "Has your truck been in anyone's possession besides yours?'

"I don't think so. No."

"Did you see anyone hanging around the truck? Anyone looking suspicious?"

"No."

"Can you try, to the best of your ability, to retrace your movements on the day of the accident?" the sheriff asked.

"Let's see. I parked the truck behind Murphy's."

"Start from the beginning of the day, please," Sheriff Barnes said. "Where was the truck when you woke up?"

"It was here, at Horseshoe Hill."

"Parked in the driveway?"

Heather looked out the window. "It was parked in front of Luke's cottage. I had picked up some shotgun shells at Murphy's and delivered them to Luke. I left the truck in front of his cottage so he could unload them. In the morning, I picked it up there. In front of Luke's."

Sheriff Barnes flipped the page and wrote notes. "And it had been parked there all night?"

"Yes. All night."

"And when you got in the truck, on the day of the accident, where did you go during the day?" he asked.

"I had lunch with Kitty at Brinkley's. Then I went to the Art Center to see some works by the visiting artist. I forgot her name. But I stayed there and chatted with her for another thirty minutes. Then I walked to the truck."

"About how long were you in town in total?"

"About four hours, maybe five."

Sheriff Barnes closed the notepad and put his pen in his pocket. "Okay, Miss Harrison. If I think of anything else, I'll give you a call. We've impounded the truck, and we'll dust it for prints, but we don't expect to find much. There have been a lot of folks in the truck and a lot of hands on it since they towed it in. We never expected any foul play."

Heather reached out and shook his hand. "Thank you, Sheriff. That's very thorough."

Luke walked Sheriff Barnes to his patrol car and stopped to chat in the drive.

"What do you think, Sheriff?" Luke asked. "Just an accident?"

Sheriff Barnes grimaced and spoke in a hushed tone. "I don't know for sure. But she could be a target with all that's going on."

"I don't think so," Luke said. "But I'll do some asking around."

"I'd rather you stay away and let us do the investigating." Sheriff Barnes walked to his patrol car and slid into the driver's seat. He put the car into gear then stopped and rolled the window down. "By the way, Luke, where were you yesterday?"

Luke stiffened at the question. "I was home. Right here at home."

"There are important people coming to town, and I don't want our town to look like a backwoods stepchild." He paused. "They're going to need help with security when things start moving along and I'd like them to know they can count on the sheriff here. I'd like Heather to know it, too." Sheriff Barnes rolled the window up and drove away.

Quietly, Luke called for a meeting of his plantation neighbors and local members of the Wiregrass Field Trial Club. They met at Oscar Thornton's barn so they would not be seen. When everyone had arrived, Luke began. "Gentlemen, I know most of you have heard about the accident involving Heather Harrison. There's talk and suspicion that it might not have been an accident. It appears that someone intentionally cut the brake lines. I can assure you it wasn't anyone at Horseshoe Hill and I'm fairly sure that none of you had anything to do with it. I want you all to know that we don't need anything like that happening right now."

Colonel Bronson stood and faced the room. "We need Heather. Most of y'all have the same fears about development that I've had for years now. We've seen pristine parcels of land fall to reckless development and if we're not careful, there won't be anything left in a few years. This downturn in the economy has put pressure on a lot of folks. I know that. It's time we met it head-on, or the Red Hills will shrink to nothing. Unfortunately, we've got to use the developers to get what we want."

John Pennington, owner of Sunnyland Plantation, stood in the back. "How do we know that the developers won't start building on these throwaway parcels they're buying? And what about the airport?"

Oscar Thornton stood and adjusted his shirt cuffs so that a perfect half inch sleeve showed. Then he buttoned his blazer and raised his arm for permission to speak. "Gentlemen, the airport is a grave concern. You all know, as I know, that an airport in the middle of the Red Hills means the Red Hills will fail to exist. It's as simple as that."

Someone shouted from the back, "It's already approved."

"Yes, it's been approved," Oscar said. "But it's not built. Listen, the airport location makes sense to a lot of people. It will draw people from North Florida, South Georgia, and even Alabama who currently drive to Atlanta and Jacksonville to catch flights. From an economics standpoint, it makes sense." Oscar held his index finger in the air. "But there are contingencies."

"Like what?" someone asked.

"Like the subsidy that the Rex Corporation agreed to for the funding. The bottom line is this: If there is no Amadora project, there is no airport. And if there is an airport, there is no Red Hills. At least not the one we know. And I'm not only speaking to those of us in the room. This thing is bigger than us, and it's only the start. We have to win." The room grew somber, and Oscar returned to his chair.

Luke unrolled a map onto a long wooden table. "Take a look at this," he said. "Land prices are on their way up and when more people hear about Amadora, they'll keep going up. You should consider selling tracts that are not the most desirable. I think anything will sell. There are buyers out there right now, but we need to be picky. Call Victor at Pine Ridge Realty and he can help. He has a list of buyers."

"We might have to lose a little to stop the big developers from taking it all," Oscar said from his chair.

Tom Nixon, owner of Jubilee Plantation, walked to the table and looked down. "I don't like it," he said. "It's too risky. I'll sell my wife and dogs before I sell an acre of land. All this is Joe Green's fault. I can see some of the others selling out, but I never would have believed Joe Green would."

"If it wasn't Joe Green, it would have been somebody else, sooner or later," Oscar said. "What about the damn airport? What if the airport comes anyway? Amadora or no Amadora. Can you imagine what this ecosystem will look like with an airport in the middle of it?"

Tom Nixon grunted, said a few cuss words, then leaned over the table and studied the map.

"We have to think about the future," Luke said. "You're trying to get a few more years out of something that is doomed. You're not going to live forever, and your kids don't want it. What happens next? Who is going to keep it going when you're gone? Who even cares beyond this group right here in this barn?" Luke caught his breath. "The wildlife cares, but they don't have a say. They are as good as dead." Luke paused again. "Unless we do something right now."

The meeting continued for two hours. At times there was heated debate. Fingers pointed and tempers flared. In the end, they exhausted the talk about Amadora and the airport. There was friendly talk of quail hunting and quail numbers and bird dogs, but no one walked away with a smile.

The next morning was cold, clear, and dry. Heather woke early. She was dressed, in the car, and headed out of the driveway when she ran into Luke.

"What are you all dressed up for this morning?" Luke asked.

"Jenny invited me to Brinkley's for coffee and a boatload of Thomasville gossip," she said. "Don't you know Jenny?"

"That's funny," Luke said. "I didn't know the two of you were friends."

"What's wrong, Luke? Are you afraid she will speak about you in less than flattering terms?"

"I like Jenny," Luke said. "And I think she still thinks of me as a friend."

"Oh, okay. Then why don't you join us for coffee?" A sarcastic smile punctuated the question.

"That would be nice, but I don't need to go dredging up the past. I give Jenny a wide berth since we broke up. What time are you coming back?"

"I've got some packages to pick up and I need to do some research at the courthouse, so it will probably be sometime in the afternoon," she said.

Luke leaned on the car and spoke through the driver's window. "What kind of research are you doing at the courthouse?"

"I want to look at some deeds and surveys," she replied.

"Horseshoe Hill deeds and surveys?"

"No, other documents. But don't worry, Luke. I'm not looking for anything you don't already know about."

"Alright," Luke said. "Then I'll see you later on."

Heather put the car in drive and started creeping along. She lowered the windows front and back and waved her hand in front of her nose.

"What's wrong?" Luke asked.

"This car is brand new, and it smells like someone tossed a skunk in here," Heather said. "It's horrid in here. I'm calling Hertz to bring me a replacement. Wait until you smell this."

"Drive around and air it out. Maybe a coon or opossum peed on the tire."

"That's reassuring," Heather waved her hand in front of her nose and kept driving. The car was cold and when she reached the highway, she raised the windows and turned on the heat. The smell came back strong, and she glanced around the seats and floorboard. Her eyes grew wide, and she stiffened when she saw a rattlesnake as big as her arm slowly forming a coil.

Heather slammed the brakes. Tires screeched, the car bucked, and blue smoke rose from the pavement. Her briefcase slid from the seat and landed directly on the snake, launching it into a buzzing coil with a fist-sized head that bobbed and weaved with slitted eyes and a forked tongue that went in and out. "Holy shit!" Heather jerked the wheel to the right. The car slid off the highway, caught a rut and Heather tried to bring it back onto the road but the car spun around two times and stopped in the ditch facing the other direction. Heather opened the door, ran fifty feet away from the car, fell to her knees and burst into tears.

With shaking hands, Heather called Luke, and ten minutes later his truck came sliding to a stop a few yards behind her. Luke jumped out of the truck and Joe Green calmly exited the passenger side. While Luke held Heather, Joe Green walked to the car, leaned in the door, fished around, and emerged with a six-foot rattler held just behind the head. He carried the snake to a nearby field and turned it loose.

"You aren't going to kill it?" Heather asked.

"Snakes are one of God's creatures," Luke said. "They don't hurt anybody unless somebody is messing with them. This is their home."

Heather glared at Luke. "It damn sure looked like it was about to hurt me. It was two seconds away from biting me. Coiled and rattling its tail. How did it get in my car, Luke? Tell me that. How did it get in my car? The windows were up all night, and they were up this morning."

Luke looked toward Joe Green. "Snakes crawl around. Maybe he was trying to get some warmth from the engine and somehow ended up inside."

Heather straightened her jacket and pulled her wool hat over her ears. "Can you check and be sure that was the only one?"

"Sure."

The snake incident brought Sheriff Barnes back to Horseshoe Hill. He had plenty of questions for Luke. He met him in the driveway.

"Luke, I'm not trying to suggest anything, but something is not right here," Sheriff Barnes said. "Those brake lines on the truck could have been tampered with anywhere, but from the story Miss Harrison tells me, that snake came from Horseshoe Hill. You and I both know that snakes don't crawl around here in this kind of weather."

Luke removed the cap from his head and ran his fingers through his hair. "Sometimes crazy things happen in nature."

"Not likely." Barnes said.

"It could have been a prank." Luke said.

"That's not a funny prank. Is there anyone around here who would like to harm Miss Harrison?"

"Nobody around here."

"Anybody besides the Horseshoe Hill people been out here in the last couple of days?" Barnes asked.

"Nobody."

"You keep this place pretty secure, don't you, Luke?"

"We keep the gates locked, the alarms in the house on."

"You give out the gate code to many people?"

"There are a few people who have the code," Luke said. "Not many."

"What kind of people?"

"A couple of contractors, a plumber, and a few guests. Those kinds of people."

"A few guests?" Barnes asked. "Any new girlfriend type guests?"

"Yes, a few guests. And, no, not any of the girlfriend type. Not lately." Luke leaned back and crossed his arms. "Look Sheriff, I'll get the code changed right away. I've never had any reason to worry, but I'll change it."

"That's a good idea," said Sheriff Barnes. "In the meantime, you keep your eyes open, Luke."

"Thank you, Sheriff."

CHAPTER 18

In town, the investigation into Heather's accident went on for two weeks and turned up nothing but dead ends. Sheriff Barnes called her every couple of days to let her know he had no leads and ultimately, he suggested that it could have been a natural occurrence, or perhaps some dangerous teenage mischief.

At Horseshoe Hill, Luke watched over Heather until she had settled down. At first, she continually looked over her shoulder and checked her bedroom door to be sure it was locked, but soon she was back to her usual routine. She rented a sedan from Hertz and just as before, she drove to town every day and met with investors, advertising agencies, contractors, and others who came to town with an interest in Amadora.

One afternoon, Luke walked into Murphy's and found Kitty in the back stacking briar pants on a shelf. He winked at the young cashier, strolled to the back, and tapped Kitty on the shoulder.

"Hey there," Kitty said. "What brings you to town?"

"I need to order pants for the boys. Mid-weight khakis with dark green facing. And shirts, too. With logos, please."

"You want shirts for everyone we have on file?"

"Yep, everyone."

"You want the Horseshoe Hill logo on the shirts?"

"Of course."

Kitty removed her reading glasses and looked directly at Luke. "Is there going to *be* a Horseshoe Hill anymore? Miles and I just returned from the Wildlife Arts Show in Dallas and that was the talk of the show. Everyone asked us if it was true."

"Kitty, there will always be a Horseshoe Hill in the Red Hills."

"The same Horseshoe Hill?" Kitty asked. "We love it here in Thomasville, but I'm not sure we would keep the headquarters here if all the plantations go away. So much of our business is online now and even our international sales are growing."

"Everything changes," Luke said. "We've got to have faith that it turns out for the best."

"Speaking of change," Kitty said, "how's your guest?"

"Guest?" Luke asked.

Kitty rolled her eyes. "You know who I'm talking about."

"She's fine," Luke answered, "but you probably see her as much as I do."

"I like Heather," Kitty said. She crossed her arms and waited until she had Luke's full attention. "But people are talking, Luke."

"Talking about what?"

"You and Heather. Some of the people who are supposedly on your side are beginning to wonder if you are on their side."

"Who's saying that?"

"I can't say, but Heather's staying out there on Horseshoe Hill, and people see you around town together eating lunch, having dinner, attending parties..."

"Nothing wrong with that," Luke said. "Besides, isn't there a saying about keeping your friends close and your enemies closer?"

"Like I said, I like her, Luke. She's a great girl. I'm just telling you what people are saying. Alice Thornton saw y'all touching hands at dinner."

"You know me, Kitty. I'm an affectionate guy. But I assure you there is nothing going on more than friendship. She has a job to do. Nothing else."

That evening, Luke met Heather for dinner at Griffin's Steakhouse. They had a cocktail before dinner and shared a bottle of red wine during dinner and another bottle after that one. They seemed relaxed and they talked about anything and everything that came to their minds. But they didn't talk about Amadora. They stayed until the wine was gone and the servers were sweeping the floor. No one seemed to notice.

They were quiet on the drive home. No other cars were on the dark highway, and the warm glow of dashboard lights lit the cab of the truck. When they arrived at Horseshoe Hill, Luke stepped from the truck just as a shooting star streaked across the sky. "Well, look there," he said. "I saw a shooting star."

"I saw it, too," Heather said. "Let's not waste it. We get a wish."

Luke closed his eyes and kept them closed. "I'm waiting."

"For what?"

"My wish."

Heather paused, then leaned in until her chest rested on Luke's chest. She placed one hand on the small of his back and the other hand on the back of his neck then she placed a soft kiss on his lips. She backed away, took a breath, and kissed him again. Luke's arms reached for her torso, and they kissed once more.

Heather broke away and shook her head. "I must admit it. I wondered what that would feel like."

"It felt good to me. Real good." Luke blinked his eyes. "As a matter of fact, probably top ten."

Heather smiled. "Definitely top ten."

There was a pause, then Heather walked to the door and just before she entered, she turned to Luke. "I'll see you in the morning," she said.

Two nights later, the moon was full, and a stiff wind blew from the north. A pack of coyotes howled in the distance. Luke came home late from a closed-door meeting in town and found Heather sitting on the porch of his cottage with a glass of wine in her hand.

"I haven't slept well the last couple of nights," Heather said.

"A little wine should help." Luke leaned on the rail at the far end of the porch.

"The wine does help, but I can't get used to the creaking sounds and being alone in a big house. Those damn coyotes howl every night and I hear sounds like animals scratching outside my window. I feel like something is going to crawl on me."

Luke smiled. "Well, Heather, you can stay with me in the cottage, but something is likely to crawl on you in here, too."

Heather rolled her eyes. "Sometimes you are disgustingly arrogant. And sometimes you make me so angry that I honestly hate you." She looked him in the eye. "But I always want to kiss you. Why is that?"

Luke's face lit up. "That's just physical attraction. Don't worry, it won't last. I bet if you kiss me every day for a week, you'll get over it. Done, gone, and never again. Just back to your senses."

"Really?"

Luke beckoned her with his index finger. "Come over here and let me show you."

"No."

"Come over here."

"No."

"Just one."

Heather stood and walked toward Luke. "Just one."

The kiss was soft and slow.

"There's only one bed in here," Luke said.

"That's something I'll have to deal with," Heather drank the last of her wine. "Will of the wind."

"You're right." Luke opened the door. "Will of the wind."

Luke rose from his bed early the next morning and walked to the kennels. He cleaned the concrete floors with a high-pressure hose and filled the bowls with food. Heather returned to the big house. She brushed her hair, changed into a flannel shirt and jeans, then walked outside onto the porch. White frost covered the lawn and the cold air bit into her cheeks. She breathed the cold morning air then slowly exhaled and stretched her arms over her head. She was not alone. Joe Green was standing at the far end of the porch, his arms crossed on his chest.

Heather cocked her head to the side. "Mr. Green?"

Joe Green grunted.

"Are you looking for Luke?"

Joe Green ignored the question. "Do you know the mating dance of eagles?" he asked.

"No, I don't."

Joe Green pointed to the sky. "The dance begins with two eagles circling each other in wide circles. They call to each other and ride the currents with their wings spread wide. They circle and rise all the way to the top of the sky where the spirits live. They crash together and lock their talons. They hold on and fall like fish from the heavens. They fall through clouds, past treetops and they cannot let go. Just before they crash into the earth, they let go. And open their wings."

Heather nodded her head slowly. "I never knew that," she said. "That's truly amazing."

Joe Green looked her in the eye. "Sometimes the eagles hold too tight. They crash to the ground and die."

"I see."

Joe Green stood and walked down the steps.

"Mr. Green, if you have time…"

Joe Green kept walking.

Heather stayed on the porch for a while, then joined Luke in the kitchen for breakfast. They had scrambled eggs, buttered grits, and salty ham. In between bites they sipped hot coffee from thick mugs. Luke watched his fork as he slowly guided it into the eggs. Heather picked at the ham and carefully sliced fat from the edges. They looked at their food and looked around the kitchen, and they spoke politely with Lula, but neither one looked at each other. After breakfast, they helped Lula with the dishes.

Lula stopped washing the plates. "Is there something I need to know about?" she asked.

"No, I don't think so," Heather said.

"Nothing at all," Luke replied.

CHAPTER 19

DROP A DOG HUNDREDS OF miles from home and he finds his way back. Homing pigeons have that same instinct. Salmon lay their eggs in the stream where they were born. Sea turtles, ducks and geese return to their birthplace to lay their eggs. All living things want to be home. Even humans. The scientific term is called *site fidelity.*

Luke dressed in work clothes and walked to the big house. Heather was at the kitchen table drinking coffee with Lula.

"I'm going to ride the south fence this morning and check the firebreaks," Luke said. "Are you going hunting with your new friends, or would you like to come with me?"

Heather drank from her coffee while she considered the offer. "I'll ride with you," she replied. "I'm making lots of new friends, but I think they are playing me for hunting tips. All they want to talk about is you. They ask me what's happening here and how you do things on Horseshoe Hill. Like you have secrets. Everybody thinks Joe Green is lucky to have you."

"I'm the one who's lucky to have Joe Green."

"But you're the one they talk about."

"Good or bad?" Luke asked.

"Both."

The sun was bright, and the temperature was warm for February. They saddled horses and rode a short way before shedding their jackets and rolling their shirt sleeves. They rode slow and easy and spoke little as they made their way.

"What are you going to do when the deal is done?" Luke asked.

"There are another couple of projects in the pipeline. Smaller ones. Nothing big is going to happen for me until we get this project rolling." A moment passed. "How about you? What are you going to do?"

"I've got a plan," Luke said.

"You're keeping your plan a secret?"

"It's not that hard to figure out. There's only one thing I'm good at."

Heather nodded and they rode on side by side, hips rising and sinking with the lazy gait of the horses. The crisp air and pine scent blended with the smell of horsehair and leather. The frost slowly melted in harrowed fields and pastures.

After a while, Heather asked, "What was she like?"

"Who?"

"Annabelle." Heather studied Luke's face. "I'm sorry if I'm intruding on your past, but I'm curious."

"Annabelle?" Luke shifted in his saddle. "Who told you about Annabelle?"

"Kitty said that Annabelle is the reason you act like you do."

Luke said nothing.

"She said Annabelle was the only woman you ever loved, and she doesn't think you will ever be over her."

Luke swallowed. "You want to know what Annabelle was like? She was like a princess. But the good kind of princess. She loved every minute of every day. Or at least it seemed that way. She was full of innocence and adventure. She was generous. And she could do anything a man could do around here."

"She sounds wonderful," Heather said.

"She was my best friend," Luke said. "She could ride a horse and shoot a shotgun as good as anybody. And when she talked about those things, her face lit up and her eyes sparkled, and it made everybody happy just to be around her. That was Annabelle."

"Did the two of you have a serious relationship?"

"I thought so. But she married another man. I'm not sure why she did that, and I must admit, for a long time, I wished she would change her mind. But the big fire killed that dream." Luke looked around. "When she was gone, this land held me in its arms and rocked me like a baby."

The horses stepped down into a dry creek bed and up the other side.

"Any serious relationships since then?" Heather asked.

"Relationships?... Yes. Serious?... No. How about you?"

"I'm dedicated to my job right now. Maybe someday, but not now."

"No offense, Heather, but if you wait for the perfect time, it's never going to happen."

"Then it's never going to happen."

They rode along a series of half-acre food plots.

"Are those for quail?" Heather asked.

"Mostly for quail. But deer, turkey, songbirds, and even pollinators use them as well."

"Have you lived here all your life?" Heather asked.

"Not all my life." They followed a road that skirted a cypress bottom and a wood stork rose gently from the water on wide white wings. Luke exhaled. "When I was a boy, my pa used to get drunk and beat me and my mama. There wasn't anything we could do unless we knew it was coming, and most of the time we never knew it was coming. He beat us until we couldn't fight back anymore. Then he'd leave us in the country with no food and no money. We had nothing."

"But you had friends, right?"

"When I was in school, I had a friend come to the house to play. My pa came home early that day. He had that drinking look in his eyes. He got mad over something and said some really bad things that he shouldn't have said. After that, I had no friends."

"I'm sorry," Heather said.

"Angus Parker took us in. He gave us a home and shared everything there was to share here. Sometimes, I would lie in the grass and stare at the clouds in the sky, and it felt like a dream. But it was true."

"I can see why it means so much to you," Heather said.

"I'll get by without it, but I hope that it ends up in the hands of good people. After the fire, I feel like I don't want anybody but me taking care of this place. Most people don't know what it is, or how it came to be what it is."

"You're emotionally attached," Heather said. "But you can't hold onto the past, Luke. Progress happens, and hurts heal. I know that Annabelle would want you to move on."

"I guess so," Luke replied.

Heather stopped. "I've been thinking about moving back into town," she said.

"Why?"

"Don't get me wrong, the other night was wonderful, but I want to be sure there is no misunderstanding between us."

Luke looked her in the eye. "There's no misunderstanding."

They rode trails and firebreaks until noon, then stopped for a rest. They shared water from a canteen and sat on an oak log while the horses grazed on smilax and scrub oak. After the rest, they mounted their horses and started back.

"You know all of this bottom area and half of these virgin pines will be under water when your people build the lake?" Luke asked.

"The lake may seem large, but it's only a small part of a huge project. I know you don't like it, but it'll bring so many good things to Thomasville," Heather said.

"People in Thomasville won't like it when it gets here," Luke said. "There'll be a stampede like a herd of buffalo busting into town. Taxes will go up, and nobody will recognize the people they see on Broad Street. People will move to Cairo, or Bainbridge, to get away from the new crowd. How did you manage to get a dam permit anyway?"

"We work closely with Senator Jackson," Heather said.

"I thought so," Luke replied. "From what I've seen, it looks like Senator Jackson spends a lot of time at campaign fundraisers with movie stars and rich people. I guess your folks fit right in."

"Luke, I'm sorry I have to be the one who represents Amadora. But you know if it's not me, it'll be somebody else. Amadora will surprise you, in a good way, if you give it a chance."

Luke pulled on the reins and stopped. Heather stopped, too.

"They knew what they were doing when they sent you," Luke said.

Heather did not move back to town. She stayed with Luke, and late that night, she reached across the bed, but Luke was not there. She slipped Luke's shirt around her bare body and buttoned the middle button. She didn't find Luke in the cottage, so she walked across the lawn to the big house. She saw a dim light beneath the kitchen door. She cracked the door and saw Luke at the kitchen table with a shoebox and an open bottle of whiskey.

"What are you doing?" Heather whispered.

Luke closed the lid on the shoebox. "Keeping the demons at bay."

"Are all your secrets in there?"

"Not all of them."

Heather sat in the chair next to him. "Can I see?"

Luke opened the lid and turned the shoebox toward Heather. Inside was a faded photograph of a happy couple leaning against a new Pontiac. There was an old watch, a dog collar, a gold necklace with a heart-shaped pendant, and a pistol.

"I asked my pa once why he drank whiskey," Luke said. "He was sober at the time, or I wouldn't have asked him." Luke took the bottle of whiskey and swirled the amber liquid inside. "My pa said that all the bad things that happen to a man build up in his mind. And over the years, they keep building up, turning over and over. He said they build up so bad, that a man can't take it anymore. And that's why he drank. He drank whiskey to keep all those bad things from swirling around in his head."

Heather closed the box and slid it over. "Do you have demons like that?"

"I keep them right there in that box. If I keep them there, I can deal with anything."

"You sound sure of that," Heather said.

"I am."

"Would you like to add something of mine to the shoebox?" Heather asked.

They looked at each other like two poker players weighing the next move.

"Like what?" Luke asked. "A pair of undergarments?"

Heather whispered, "I'm not wearing undergarments."

Luke put the shoebox away and never looked at it again.

Lula ran the kitchen at Horseshoe Hill like she had been running it for fifty years because she had been running it for fifty years. For the most part, she worked hard every day with no time for idle conversation. But when Lula had something to say, everyone listened. That's the way it was one morning at breakfast with Luke, Roosevelt, and Heather. Lula started talking and everyone listened.

"You fellas ought to be ashamed," Lula said. She looked at Luke and Roosevelt. "Miss Heather's been here for more than a month now and every day she eats here in this kitchen. She's our guest and she should eat in the dining room sometime, not in the kitchen like a hired man." She waited until she had everyone's attention. "Tonight, we're eating in the dining room. Invite some company too. Somebody who doesn't talk about dogs and hunting all the time. And invite somebody with a wife so Miss Heather ain't got to look at men all night long."

Luke and Roosevelt sat with their mouths open. Luke turned to Roosevelt as if Lula was not there. "What's got into Lula?" he asked.

"I don't know what's got into her. Must be something about having another woman living here in the house."

"Nothing's got into me," Lula interrupted. "It's just that you need to do something 'round here besides hunt those quail and smoke tobacco and drink that liquor on the cottage porch where you think nobody sees you."

Luke slapped the table with both hands. "Well, okay, Lula. We'll eat in the dining room tonight. That's a great idea. I'll invite Miles and Kitty to eat with us. And the Bronsons, too."

"That's good. I'll have everything served up at seven-thirty. And you men wear jackets and ties. Don't show up in the formal dining room looking like you're 'bout to go run some dogs."

"Lula, why don't you eat with us?" Heather asked. "You've been cooking for me all this time; it would be a pleasure if you would join us. I can help with the cooking."

"No ma'am, Miss Heather. I'll cook it myself. Just like we used to when Miss Catherine was here. That help I've got would make a mess trying to cook food that Miss Catherine liked. I'm going to fix it all myself."

Later that night, after cocktails, they opened the door to the dining room. Luke, Roosevelt, Heather, the Murphys and the Bronsons stood speechless. The smell of garlic and roasted vegetables and braised short ribs floated in the air. From the corner, an old phonograph played French café music that accented the room with melancholy notes drawn from accordions and clarinets.

The dining table was covered with a white cloth and set with linen napkins and polished silverware. A ceramic vase with flowers sat in the center of the table and candles burned in silver candelabras on each side. Serving dishes steamed on the sideboards and carefully selected bottles of white and red wines were on the buffet. Luke, Heather, Roosevelt, and the rest of the guests stood behind assigned chairs while Lula took one last look at her work.

"This is just the way I remember it," Lula said. "It wasn't so many years ago." Tears welled in her eyes.

"It's wonderful, Lula," Luke said.

"So beautiful," Ginger added.

After a fine dinner with lively conversation, Luke chose a bottle of brandy and escorted the dinner party into the parlor where they sat in front of a flickering fire.

"That was an incredible dinner," Heather said. She looked about the parlor. "Where has Roosevelt gone?"

"He's probably in his cottage checking his stock portfolio," Luke said.

"Funny," Heather scoffed.

"He's in the kitchen helping Lula with the dishes," Kitty said.

Heather stood from her chair. "That's not fair. He should join us."

"He likes to help Lula with the dishes," Luke said.

Heather walked through the dining room and disappeared into the kitchen. Two minutes later, she returned to the parlor. "Lula said he has gone to his cottage to read. He should be here with the rest of us. He's such a kind and intelligent man."

"If it makes you feel better, go to his cottage and ask him to join us," Luke said. "He knows he's welcomed, but you should ask him."

"I think it's the polite thing to do," Heather said. She placed her empty glass on the fireplace mantle and walked across the lawn to Roosevelt's cottage. She knocked gently on the door.

"Come in," Roosevelt said.

The door swung open, and Heather stepped inside. The pine-paneled walls were covered with bookshelves filled with rows of books that reached the ceiling. A black and white photograph of Dr. Martin Luther King, Jr. stood out on the wall. Birds and small animals carved from wood were scattered among books. Wildlife prints and oil paintings, all simply framed in wood, hung about the room and above the fireplace. Photographs of Eugene were tucked in every nook.

Roosevelt was in a leather recliner with suede slippers on his feet and a brown blanket across his legs. He placed his book on the nightstand and peered over his glasses. “Miss Heather, that sure was a fine dinner, wasn’t it?”

“Yes, it was.” Heather scanned the room. A stack of newspapers and the *Wall Street Journal* sat on a small wooden dining table. An ink pen rested on the paper and several stock quotes had been circled. There were handwritten notes in the margin. She walked over and looked at a framed diploma that hung on the wall. Thomas University. A Bachelor of Arts degree in history. Roosevelt Henry Brown was the name on the diploma.

Heather nodded toward the diploma. “That’s you?” she asked.

“Yes, ma’am. I’m right proud of that.”

Heather looked closer at the diploma. “A history degree. Have you ever thought of using it to do something other than work on a plantation?” she asked.

“No, I never thought much about it.” Roosevelt pointed to a graduation portrait on the bookshelf. “Now my son Eugene, he’s got a degree from Georgia Tech and works for a big software company out in California. He’s the smart one. But I could never leave. Eugene will do fine out there, but me, I’ve got to have this red dirt under my feet.”

“I see. What are you going to do when Horseshoe Hill is sold?” she asked.

"I guess I'll think about that when the time comes." Roosevelt removed his glasses. "But I worry about the animals. They'll move off, but they'll keep coming back to the place that they knew. Some will starve because they can't eat grass in a parking lot, and I imagine a lot of them will get run over by cars and trucks."

Heather looked as if she needed a moment to process his words. "Well, I stopped in to see if you would like to join us for a drink," she said.

"That's mighty kind. But I think I'll just sit here and enjoy a little reading time tonight. It puts me right to sleep," he said.

"Me, too."

"And that sure was a fine dinner Miss Lula fixed tonight."

"Yes, it was," she replied.

CHAPTER 20

It was another Wednesday night at Horseshoe Hill. Luke, Joe Green, and Roosevelt gathered on the cottage porch for whiskey and a smoke. They settled back in their chairs, and when they looked toward the big house, they saw Heather walking down the steps.

Roosevelt called out, "Miss Heather."

Heather turned and waved. Roosevelt waved back, beckoning her to join them. Luke and Joe Green looked at each other without saying a word.

Heather stepped onto the porch and Roosevelt pulled a chair from the far corner. "Can I get you a drink, Miss Heather?" he asked.

"Do you have vodka?"

"I believe I do." Roosevelt walked inside the cottage. Luke and Joe Green looked at each other once more. Roosevelt returned with a glass of vodka on the rocks and handed it to Heather. He settled into his chair. "Miss Heather, have you ever heard the true history of the Red Hills, and how all these plantations came to be?" he asked.

"I've only heard a brief summary."

Roosevelt stood from his chair, walked to the corner of the porch, then turned and faced his audience.

"Oh, Lord," Luke said.

Like a seasoned history professor, Roosevelt told the story of the Civil War, the demise of King Cotton, the role of the railroads, and the evolution of the sharecroppers. He knew names and dates. He told the story of Dr. T. S. Hopkins, who published a paper in 1892 praising the Red Hills climate and pine air. He explained how Hopkins promoted those factors as a cure for consumption, which brought wealthy northerners down south. Roosevelt quoted construction dates and closing dates of the resort era hotels. And he knew the names and beginnings of all the plantations. Roosevelt's dissertation lasted an hour and fifteen minutes. When he was done, the porch was quiet.

"That's quite the story," Heather said.

"We have a local museum in town if you want to know more about the history," Roosevelt replied.

"It sounds like you love it here," Heather said. "But have you ever considered that it could be more?" she asked. "You know, expand on it so more people can enjoy it."

Luke cut his eyes toward Joe Green.

Roosevelt nodded his head. "I leave all that up to the Lord, Miss Heather."

After a kitchen breakfast the following day, Heather and Luke walked to a pasture near the barn. A young colt trotted to the fence. Roosevelt was outside the barn with a water hose, a five-gallon bucket and a pile of towels. His forehead was beaded with sweat as he washed a bright yellow '53 Cadillac convertible.

Heather waved to Roosevelt, then turned to Luke. "This is what I don't understand," she said. "The man has a college degree, and he washes that car every Monday. I've never seen it leave the barn. It comes out clean and goes back clean. Isn't there someone else who could wash the car? Maybe one of the young guys around here?"

Luke watched Roosevelt circle the car with a towel as he rubbed a spot here and there. "Roosevelt never lets anyone wash that car."

"Why not?"

"It's his car."

Heather watched Roosevelt remove a spot from the fender. "Why doesn't he drive it?" she asked.

"He drives it around the plantation occasionally. But it's never been off Horseshoe Hill since it got here from Magnolia Trace. It was his daddy's car. His daddy bought it brand-new in 1953, but I don't believe it's got five hundred miles on it."

"His father bought a brand-new Cadillac in 1953. Where did a mule driver get the money to buy a car like that?"

"He was a smart man. He drove the mule wagon on Magnolia Trace plantation for Colonel Bronson's grandfather before he came to Horseshoe Hill." Luke leaned on the fence and watched the colt trot around the pasture. "They called Roosevelt's daddy Big Robert because he was a big man. Big and round, and he knew those mules like they were his brothers. So, Bronson had connections up North, and he had very wealthy guests come down and hunt. Once they started hunting quail and riding through the woods with coffee and biscuits on the wagon, they relaxed. During the breaks from hunting, the conversation usually migrated to business and that led to bragging about making money with stocks."

"Sharing insider information I presume," Heather said.

"Call it what you want, but Big Robert saw the private railcars arrive, and he watched brand-new automobiles coming off the train. He saw kids dressed in fancy clothes. And he knew there had to be opportunity for him somehow. There used to be a saying in Thomasville back then, 'A Yankee is worth two bales of cotton, and twice as easy to pick.'" Luke turned to Heather. "And Big Robert picked quite a few. Anyway, Big Robert got his nerve up and asked how he could buy a little stock for himself. Big Robert had timed it just right because Colonel Bronson's grandfather and his guests were a little sauced at the time. So, they tried to out-do each other and each one of them anteed up the best stock they had and put shares in Big Robert's name."

"Did he sell it?"

"No. He kept it. Big Robert learned to read the stock pages and when he saw it going up, it almost drove him crazy. He had to stop looking at the price because it was all he could think about."

"How much money did he make?"

"Quite a bit. Enough that he could talk stocks with any of the guests."

"That's quite a story," Heather said.

"That's not all," Luke said. "There was a banker from Quincy, Florida on the wagon one day. He told Bronson about an Atlanta stock that was just coming out and sure to go up. Well, Big Robert paid attention and he used his stock dividends to buy a few shares himself. He bought ten shares. And that stock kept rising and splitting and paying dividends that he reinvested and before long, Big Robert was a rich man."

"What was the stock?"

"Coca-Cola. Do you know what that stock is worth today?"

"Quite a bit, I'm sure. He made enough money to buy a Cadillac?"

"He bought the nicest Cadillac in Thomasville. It's only been on the highway once and that was when he and Roosevelt moved here from Magnolia Trace. It stayed in the barn except for Sundays when Big Robert would load up all the ladies on Horseshoe Hill and drive down the old stagecoach road to the church for worship. He would load eight women in the car and drive real slow so the wind didn't blow their Sunday hats off."

"And Roosevelt?" Heather asked. "Did he inherit the stocks from his father?"

"That Cadillac is the only money Big Robert ever spent and when Big Robert died and they opened his estate, Roosevelt discovered he had inherited a fortune." Luke turned to Heather. "Things aren't always what they look like."

"How much is he worth?" Heather asked.

"Millions."

Heather looked toward Roosevelt and lowered her voice. "Roosevelt is a millionaire?"

"Many times over."

Heather paused in thought. "If he has that much money, why does he stay here and drive a mule wagon?" she asked.

"You should ask him," Luke replied.

"I think I will."

Luke drove into town that night. Heather stayed at Horseshoe Hill and shared a kitchen dinner with Lula, who had prepared a small dish of hunter's pie made with venison, garden peas and carrots. After dinner, she walked to Roosevelt's cottage and knocked on the door.

"I hope I'm not disturbing you," Heather said.

"Not at all," Roosevelt replied. "I like my quiet reading time, but I like a little company from time to time as well. Come in and have a seat." Roosevelt placed his reading glasses on the side table. "Are you enjoying your stay here at Horseshoe Hill?" he asked.

"I've learned a lot, and actually, I'm not here to enjoy myself as much as I'm here representing the Rex Corporation. I'm not making as much progress as I'd like with land acquisitions, but some people have been very helpful. And kind."

"Don't pay much attention to the things Luke says out there," he said. "He's not a bad man, but he's not very good with change. He thinks things should stay the way they are. It's nothing personal."

"Luke doesn't bother me. Not much, anyway."

"That's good."

"However, there is something I am curious about."

"And what's that?"

Heather glanced around the room. "I see the diploma and the books, and I saw you yesterday with the car. Luke told me the story."

"Let me tell you," Roosevelt said. "Luke likes to think I have a whole lot more money than I have. Don't listen to everything he says."

"Oh, I don't. Don't worry about that. But…" She hesitated. "It seems that you have sufficient money to do something else. Why haven't you left here?"

Roosevelt smiled. "You see, Miss Heather, this is my home. My roots are here. Most people who grew up here have left. Almost all of them, as a matter of fact. Most went on to a better life, but back in my granddaddy's generation, this was a black community, and everybody helped each other out. There weren't many opportunities for rural blacks back then, but they made the most of what they had. I remember the struggle." Roosevelt paused. "But they had a church, doctors, and even a school right here on Horseshoe Hill. That was more than most rural communities back then."

"Who paid for those things?"

"The Parker family paid. That was their part. Everybody had a part."

"Where are all the people now?" Heather asked.

"Most have moved on. Miss Marjorie Parker sent a lot of young people to college and most of them turned out to be successful at whatever business they went into. Some stayed around. They were mostly the ones who worked with the dogs and horses and other stuff to do with quail hunting."

"And you? What are you going to do when this is part of Amadora?" Heather asked.

"I'll let the Lord decide that for me. Right now, the Lord is telling me this is where I need to be. So, this is where I am."

CHAPTER 21

THREE DAYS LATER, OSCAR THORNTON and eight core members of the Wiregrass Field Trial Club arrived at Horseshoe Hill. Luke and Heather had just finished lunch in the kitchen when the group arrived. Luke greeted them on the front lawn.

"Luke, we've got to talk with you," Oscar said. "Alone, please."

"Sure, Oscar. Y'all step into the library."

As soon as they entered the library, Colonel Bronson shut the door and unfurled a large map on the conference table.

"Sanderson sold Sassafras," Bronson said. He pointed to a large tract of land on the map and the others gathered around the table.

"Son of a bitch," Luke said. "I thought he was putting it in a conservation easement. I know he never gave a damn about that place like his daddy did."

"He always said he was putting it in an easement, but he's ninety-two. Never got around to doing it," Thornton said. "I don't know for sure how much they got, but I heard it was more than seven thousand an acre. Dirk put the deal together, and hotel people bought it."

Luke stood back and studied the map. "That's okay. The rest of you guys need to stay calm."

"I don't know about that, Luke. Things are so tight at my place now," Oscar said. "I've had some good offers lately. So has the Colonel and Pine Ridge. You know that some of the family want to sell Pine Ridge."

"How much have you been offered?" Luke asked.

"Six thousand an acre for it all."

"I've been offered sixty-five hundred," Bronson said. "Most of mine is wrapped up in a trust and my kids don't give a damn about it. They're pushing me like hell to sell it and buy a place in Palm Beach so they can shop and sail on the yacht. They haven't been down here in two years. Not one of them."

"Look," Luke said, "you've got to hold out a little longer. You should be able to get seventy-five hundred or eight thousand for the worst of it. The stuff that's surrounding the lake is what they want and it's poor land anyway. Just stick together and land prices all over the Red Hills will increase. They have to."

"I've got shingles falling off my roof and paint peeling all over the place," Oscar said. "Not to mention, I've got fences falling apart. It looks like bloody hell."

Carl Spencer spoke up. "If we can't keep the prime longleaf habitat together, the Red Hills is gone forever. Gentlemen, that would be a shame."

"Listen," Luke said. "If you want to test the market, carve out a couple of tracts of hardwoods, the scruffy stuff that's no good anyway. Put it on the market for an outrageous price and see what happens. But whatever you do, let Victor list it."

"I want to sell some now," Oscar said. "I'm afraid there won't be enough buyers to go around."

"Call Victor. He has buyers waiting. Plenty of buyers."

Oscar pointed to a block of land on the map. "I've got some around the lake plan that's pretty rough. I'd be happy to sell that."

"Me, too," Bronson said.

"Okay. Call Victor and get it listed. He'll know how to handle it," Luke said. "Now, who needs a drink?"

The library turned quiet. Then Colonel Bronson blurted, "My God. Look at us. I never would have believed we would be standing here talking about how much land each of us will sell to developers. What have we gotten ourselves into? I think someone knows something that we don't know and we're the only people who think our plan is a good plan. The people we're up against make us look like a bunch of fools. WE better have it right, or we're screwed. One way, or another, I think we're screwed, anyway."

CHAPTER 22

THE BLACK HANDLER'S FIELD TRIAL. That was the name given to the annual competition sanctioned by the Wiregrass Field Trial Club. It was held at the end of each season, just before the weather turns warm and just before the blooms appear on the Cherokee Rose. The Black Handler's trial was a competition for black scouts, grooms, and wagon drivers who worked hard and put in long hours during the season. It was their chance to run the dogs. It was fun and competitive and displayed some of the best dog work of the year. That year the competition was held at Oaky Sink Plantation.

Two days before the Black Handler's Trial, Luke and Heather sauntered into the kitchen for breakfast. A few minutes later, Roosevelt walked through the door. He poured a cup of coffee and sat down. He had a grin on his face and a twinkle in his eye.

"Good morning, Miss Heather, Luke. Do you know who's coming to the Black Handler's this year?" Roosevelt asked.

"I don't know," Luke replied. "Who's coming?"

"Eugene's coming. He's flying into Tallahassee tomorrow evening."

Luke's face lit up. "Damn, that's good news. I haven't seen Eugene since he graduated from Tech. He's making so much money, I thought he lost his way home." Luke turned to Heather. "Eugene and I grew up together. Now he works for one of the big technology companies in California. Drives a BMW and wears Italian loafers."

Roosevelt chuckled and Luke went on. "We ran around barefoot when we were kids and now he's wearing those fancy loafers. I saw them in a picture he sent Roosevelt."

"Roosevelt told me about Eugene," Heather said.

Luke drank his coffee and nodded his head. "I have an idea. Let's run Willy. He's never lost a field trial and he's rested up good. I can just imagine Eugene's face when he sees that dog on point."

"You're the only one who has ever run Willy."

"Doesn't matter. Willy knows what to do."

"That would be mighty fine. And Eugene said he wants to ride a horse," Roosevelt said. "I think I might like to ride along with him."

"Hell yeah," Luke said. "I'll drive the wagon. Heather can ride the wagon with me. You run Willy, and Andy can ride scout too. That'll be a good day. It's supposed to be perfect weather for the trial." Lula walked into the kitchen. "Lula, did you hear that? Eugene's coming tomorrow night and we're going to the field trial on Wednesday."

"I heard it. I ain't seen that boy in a long time," Lula said. "I'll fix a great big basket for the wagon on Wednesday. I'll put biscuits and fig preserves out for breakfast. That boy loves my figs."

"We can make a batch of Bloody Marys to take on the wagon, too," Luke said. "Damn, I haven't been this excited for a field trial in years."

It was half past midnight when the last plane landed at the Tallahassee airport. Eugene was dressed sharp in a blue suit with an open collar, and he carried a slim briefcase in one hand and a folded magazine in the other. He walked out of terminal B and spotted Roosevelt in the waiting area. They hugged each other tightly while the crowd of passengers passed them by.

Eugene looked at Roosevelt's overalls. "You didn't have to get all dressed up to meet me," he said.

"We'll have you out of that fancy suit soon enough," Roosevelt replied.

After several minutes of looking, they found Roosevelt's truck in the parking lot and drove north toward the Georgia line.

Roosevelt slapped his son on the shoulder. "Lord, it's good to see you, but my goodness, looks like you don't eat anything out there in California. You've grown tall and skinny. You don't look anything like the Brown family."

"I work all the time, but I get outside and exercise every chance I get," Eugene said. "Everybody in California does. I work twelve or fourteen hours a day, but I still find time for the outdoors every chance I get. We've got hiking trails, beaches and the hilliest bike trails you've ever seen running through the valley."

"I spend all my time outdoors, too, but I'm not skinny like you," Roosevelt said.

"You're exercising now?" Eugene asked.

"Of course I'm exercising," Roosevelt replied. "I'm driving that mule wagon every day."

"Driving a mule wagon is not exercise."

"It is, if you do it right." Roosevelt glanced over at Eugene. "All the menfolk in the Brown family were big. Your granddaddy was a mule driver too, and he was a big man. Even your great granddaddy who liked to have worked himself to death as a sharecropper. He was a big man. It ought to run in the genes."

Eugene looked at Roosevelt's stomach straining the buttons on his canvas work shirt. "Maybe you shouldn't blame it on the genes. I expect it's got something to do with Lula's cooking," Eugene said. "Miss Lula's cooking is the thing I miss the most about South Georgia."

"I imagine she'll have something a little special cooked up for you over the next couple of days. She asks about you all the time."

Eugene's face lit up with a big smile. "I can't wait for Lula's grits. You know, you can't find grits anywhere in California. Not good grits, that is."

They drove the two-lane road that led them from the airport, then merged onto a six-lane interstate for five miles. They exited the interstate onto a four-lane road and slowed down for a long stretch of retail businesses and traffic lights. Roosevelt's truck crossed the centerline, and an annoyed driver blared his horn.

"Would you like me to drive?" Eugene asked.

"Of course not," Roosevelt replied. "It's all these lights down here in the city. Everything's a blur at night and I can barely see at all. That's why I like it out where we live. Not a light in sight except the moon and the stars."

"That's going to be a change for me for sure," Eugene said. "We've got lights. Lots of lights. Twenty-four hours a day."

They drove past strip malls, fast food restaurants and gas stations. The Ford truck moved from red light to red light to red light until finally they reached the north side of Tallahassee. The road narrowed and the city lights faded into the rearview mirror. The highway turned dark, and they settled in for a long, quiet drive on the Plantation Parkway.

Eugene looked out the window. "There's something about this land in the Red Hills," he said. "I try to explain it to my friends in California, but I don't think they understand. I wonder what folks think when they see this place of ours for the first time." He folded his arms and looked out the window. They passed mile after mile of pine forest on both sides of the highway. "There's so much history here," he said.

"I think about the history all the time," Roosevelt said. "And I feel good every time I drive on this stretch of road. I don't have deed to a single acre of land, but it's home and I feel like I own a piece of it all."

They rode in silence for several miles. "How's Luke?" Eugene asked. "I've heard rumors that Horseshoe Hill is going to sell. Is that true?"

"He'll tell you about it."

"Does it have anything to do with the fire?"

"He's just now getting over that fire, but he's been through a lot."

"We talk on the phone all the time," Eugene said. "But he's never said a word about the fire." Eugene swallowed. "And he never talks about Annabelle."

"None of us talk about Annabelle."

Luke, Roosevelt, and Eugene had dinner in Roosevelt's cottage that night. They stayed up until early morning telling stories and catching up. The next morning, they stumbled around like they had never run a field trial in their lives.

They finally managed to hitch the horse trailer to Luke's truck and load the horses and wagon. Fifteen minutes down the road, Luke slammed on the brakes. He looked in the back seat at Roosevelt.

"Roosevelt, did you get Willy?"

"I thought you loaded him."

Luke turned the truck around, drove back to Horseshoe Hill and loaded Willy into the dog box. When they got to the trial, Roosevelt fell while trying to mount his horse. Luke got the harness crossed up on the wagon and ran over Ginger Bronson's ice cooler, causing a jug of sweet tea and ice to spill on the ground. It was Andy's first field trial for the black handlers. He left his saddle in the tack room and had to borrow one from one of the competitors. Finally, the Horseshoe Hill team successfully mounted their horses and positioned the wagon for the start of the trial.

The awkward beginning did not escape Eugene and he let them know. He looked at Luke. "How'd you get all those trophies in the trophy case?"

Luke laughed. "We're so nervous having you here, we forgot how to run dogs and hunt quail." He turned to Heather. "Can you pour me a Bloody Mary? You might want one yourself. It looks like it's going to be a long day." He punched Eugene in the shoulder. "I've missed this man."

The trials began. Thirty black men ran the show and a gallery of forty men and women followed on horseback and in wagons. Roosevelt and Eugene rode close to the wagon. They watched each dog in every brace and analyzed their performance while judging their chances of winning. Luke, Heather, and Eugene told stories and drank Bloody Marys.

When it was Roosevelt's turn to run his dog, Willy knew what he had to do. Willy hit the ground, Roosevelt hit the whistle and Willy was off. While the competing dog scratched dirt and squatted, Willy pointed quail. Roosevelt flushed the covey, fired the obligatory shot in the air and two minutes later, Willy was pointed again.

Luke drove the wagon with one hand, drank with the other and nodded toward a man on horseback riding the far side of a fallow field. "Look who's here. I knew he wouldn't miss this."

"It's Joe Green," said Eugene.

The thirty-minute brace ended, and there was no doubt that Willy had won.

Roosevelt circled his horse back to the wagon and broke out in a wide grin. "Yes, sir. That Willy can hunt. Did you see that dog when his competition slowed down in front of him? Willy jumped right over him. Didn't even slow down, just jumped right over his back, and then found the covey before he went another fifty yards."

"You ran him good, Roosevelt. Real good," Luke said.

"That was something to watch," said Eugene. "Sure was."

They returned to the big house, where Lula had prepared a beef tenderloin. They dined by candlelight in the dining room and Lula played the French café music the way she liked to on special occasions. And for the first time ever, Lula joined them at the table. She sat next to Eugene and asked everything about California. She wanted to know if he had spotted movie stars on the street but was disappointed he had met none. She wanted to know how the fishing was, but he had never been fishing in California.

"Well, what in the world are you living out there for?" Lula asked.

"I guess because they pay me a lot of money, Miss Lula."

"Ain't worth it if you've got to work all the time. If you ask me, that is."

"Maybe you're right, but I don't work all the time."

"So, what do you do with your time?"

"I spend four hours every day driving back and forth to work."

The morning after the field trial, Lula made breakfast in the kitchen for Roosevelt, Luke, and Eugene. They had fresh eggs, venison sausage, Henry's country ham, cathead biscuits with butter and mayhaw jelly. The breakfast lasted two hours and Lula watched over them while they ate every bite.

In the afternoon, Luke, Eugene, and Heather rode horses to the old fishing hole. They tied the horses to branches and walked to the creek bank.

"It sure looks much smaller than I remember," said Eugene.

"Yep, it sure seemed like an ocean that time you fell in, and I pulled you out with a cane pole," Luke said.

Eugene laughed. "I remember that."

"So, who was the best fisherman when you two were boys?" Heather asked.

Luke and Eugene looked at each other and answered simultaneously, "Annabelle." The answer was awkward, but it was said, and it was true.

"When Eugene and I were about fifteen years old, we used to sneak beer from the refrigerator by the gun room and put it here in the creek to keep it cold. I think that's the best tasting beer I ever had," Luke said.

"I have to agree," said Eugene.

Heather leaned on Luke and slipped her arm inside his. Eugene saw it out of the corner of his eye.

"Tell me the truth, Eugene," Luke said. "This has been a great day. Isn't this better than anything you have in California?"

"It has been a great day," Eugene replied. "One of the best days I can remember." He shrugged. "But this is your thing, Luke. You were born for it. My dad, too."

"I know you're banking money, but I can't imagine anything better than this."

"I love the IT world, but it was a lot more exciting in the early days," Eugene said. "Right now, we're in a transition. When it was new and we had stuff nobody had ever seen, it was fun. But now, it's all about the money. There's a push to get things out before somebody else does. Everybody watches the stock. We're hiring overseas staff for chicken scratch money. They find smart people in poor places. Real smart. They fast-track visas and bring them here to work too. I don't blame the company, but it's not as fun as it used to be."

"You should talk to us," Heather said. "Our major investors are names you would recognize in the technology business."

Eugene bobbed his head and smiled. "I think I'll stay where I am for the time being."

"Hey," Luke said, "tomorrow is Eugene's last full day here. Why don't we go on a real quail hunt, shoot a few quail, and have Lula fix a quail dinner?"

Eugene and Heather exchanged glances. "That works for me," Eugene said.

"I was going to do some work tomorrow," Heather said. "But, why not? Count me in."

In the early afternoon, they met at the barn where Roosevelt stood by the wagon while Andy loaded the dogs. Luke had the horses groomed and saddled.

Who's shooting today?" Luke asked.

"I'm only here to watch and enjoy the day," Eugene said.

"I'll carry a gun," Heather said.

Luke slid a twenty-eight gauge over-and-under into the scabbard strapped to Heather's saddle.

"Where's your gun?" Heather asked.

"It's all you today," Luke said. "No quail, no dinner."

"That's a lot of pressure," Heather said.

"I'm not worried," Luke replied.

They started from the barn. Luke, Heather, and Eugene rode horses. Roosevelt drove the wagon with six English Pointers in the dog boxes and an overly excited black lab rode up front. As they covered the course, Luke and Heather rode side by side. Eugene rode next to them, but sometimes broke away and joined the wagon where he chatted with Roosevelt.

Thirty minutes into the hunt, the dogs locked on a point. Luke, Heather, and Eugene slid from their saddles. Heather broke the shotgun and dropped two shells into the barrels. Luke and Eugene stopped at the backing dog and Luke gently stroked his tail into the twelve o'clock position.

"Move up, Heather," Luke said. "The cover's thin so you can flush the covey yourself. We'll stay back here."

Heather closed the gun and walked past the pointed dog. The covey jumped and exploded in all directions. Heather swung to the left and dropped a bird, then swung back to the right and dropped another. Both birds hit the ground stone dead.

Eugene whistled low and slow. "Damn."

"I told you she was a fast learner," Luke said.

"There's my dinner," Roosevelt shouted from the wagon as he sent the lab for the retrieve.

The rest of the afternoon went much the same way and by the end of the hunt, they had a dozen quail for dinner. Luke cleaned the birds while Heather, Eugene and Roosevelt put away the horses, mules, and wagon. Lula fried the quail and added roasted potatoes and green beans to complete the informal kitchen dinner. After dinner, Heather went to her room to answer work emails and Luke, Roosevelt and Eugene met Joe Green on Roosevelt's porch for drinks.

The men poured their drinks, sat in their chairs, and looked at the stars. Joe Green was quiet, Luke was quiet, Eugene was quiet, and even Roosevelt had nothing to say. Finally, Eugene broke the silence, "Luke, you've got to tell her."

CHAPTER 23

It was a blustery winter day with heavy gray clouds pouring waves of rain. The weather was unfit for hunting quail or working dogs. Luke woke early and drove his truck to the barn. He checked on the horses, then walked to the kennel and saw that the dogs had water and warm bedding. When he returned to the cottage, Heather was awake and dressed in warm clothes.

"I'm going into town," Heather said.

"It's a nasty day to be going anywhere," Luke said. "What's your hurry?"

"The company is on my back. I need to go to the courthouse and look at some deeds. I feel like I'm wasting time here waiting for that damn bush to bloom." She ran a brush through her hair for a few quick strokes. "They think it's ridiculous that they are paying all that money and I'm here waiting for a flower."

"You seem to be in a big hurry to get this project done and over so you can leave town."

"I am."

"I love it when you are sweet and romantic in the morning."

"I'm sorry, Luke. There's so much to do right now and people are looking to me to get it done. I love being with you, and maybe there will be something for us when this is done. I really don't know."

"I do."

Luke drove back to the barn after she left. He walked by the stalls and spoke to the horses, and he acted like a man who was looking for an answer when he did not even know the question. He left the barn, went to town, and stopped by Murphy's for shotgun shells and hunting supplies.

Kitty greeted him at the checkout counter. "I've been spending time with Heather," Kitty said. "Seems like things have gotten cozy between you two. She's popular around town and some people are saying that she might be the one for you."

Luke looked down and thumbed a stack of jeans looking for his size. "There's nothing serious going on," he said.

"Are you sure about that, Luke? She has a twinkle in her eye when she talks about you. And she talks about you all the time."

Luke pulled a pair of jeans from the stack and handed them to Kitty. "She's not going to be around much longer anyway," he said.

"I'm not so sure."

"Oh, I'm sure."

"Whatever you say. You better be careful with her, Luke. She's a looker. And a smart one, too."

"You know something, Kitty? Sometimes I think I was better off when I lived in a two-room shack, just me and Momma. Back then, I didn't have so many people paying attention to everything I was doing. I'll just take the shells and the jeans. I don't need any life advice today."

Kitty gave Luke a hard look. "What's gotten into you today?"

"Nothing."

Luke walked next door to the pool hall, ordered a beer and had a seat at the bar. He stretched his arms across the bar and planted his forehead on the beer-stained wood. He lifted his head and looked into the mirror. Dirk Thompson stood behind him.

"Rough day, Luke?" Dirk asked.

"Just a day like any other."

"That Cherokee Rose is going to bloom before you know it, Luke." Dirk ordered a beer and sat on the stool next to Luke. "That's right. It's going to be a big day for a lot of people around here. A few more weeks I figure. Where are you going to go when most of Horseshoe Hill is under water?"

"Your momma's house. Where else?"

"I'm glad to see you still have a sense of humor."

Luke looked into the mirror and rubbed the stubble on his chin. "Say, Dirk, I think I saw a couple of nice tracts around Horseshoe Hill that just came on the market. I see that Victor listed those. I guess somebody forgot to give you a recommendation. I think he's already sold one tract and there are several buyers looking at the other one. Pretty big commission on those tracts."

Dirk grunted and lowered his voice. "You need to act nice, Luke. I can get you a job with Amadora if you think you can get cleaned up every day. After work, you can get into the park for free with one of your girlfriends. Yep, you'll be eating blue cotton candy and spinning around in a pink teacup before you know it. Right there where you used to hunt quail."

At that moment, Luke's phone rang. It was Sheriff Barnes. Luke walked outside to take the call.

"Luke," Barnes began, "I've got a solid lead on the Heather Harrison incidents. I need to ask you some questions."

"Sure. What do you need to know?"

"How well do you know Jenny Bixler's brother?"

"Carl?"

"Yes."

"I don't know him at all except to know that he's been in trouble before. Spent a little time in jail, I think."

"That's right. He's back in town. We picked up one of his friends on a drug charge a couple days ago, and this guy is telling us that Carl is the one responsible for the brake lines and the snake."

"That doesn't make sense," Luke said.

"The man says that Carl did it for his sister. He says Carl's sister wants Heather Harrison out of Thomasville."

Luke was silent.

"We don't have enough evidence to pick him up. But if you know anything, you need to tell us."

"I don't know anything," Luke said.

"Well, if you hear anything, you let us know."

"I will."

Luke ended the call and called Jenny. "Hey Jenny, do you want to meet me for a drink at Griffin's?"

"That sounds perfect on a rainy day like today. What time?"

"Now?"

"Now is a good time, and I'm already downtown. I'll see you in ten minutes."

Luke walked back inside the pool hall, chugged his beer and threw a couple of dollars on the counter. Then he turned to Dirk. "Well, it's been great to see you as usual, Dirk, but I've got to go."

Luke left and walked three blocks in the rain to Griffin's Steakhouse. Jenny was alone at the bar with a glass of Chardonnay in front of her. Luke took the empty seat next to Jenny and she wrapped her arms around his neck and gave him a solid kiss on the cheek. Luke noted Jenny's wine then ordered a bourbon for himself.

"Tell me it's not true, Luke. Tell me you don't have a new girlfriend." Jenny edged close to Luke and rubbed her shoulder against his.

"You better ask your friends around town. It seems like they know more about that than I do," Luke said.

Jenny tossed her hair, moved her hand to Luke's thigh and whispered in his ear, "I don't care anyway."

Luke sipped his bourbon and cracked a smile. "I'm not sure which way to interpret that."

"We dated a long time, Luke," Jenny said. "I think I still hold the record for that, don't I?"

"Yes, I think you do."

"So, how have you been, Luke?"

"Oh Lord, Jenny. I have more spinning plates in the air than a circus clown. But I'm doing alright. I guess."

"Alright. So, how about Joe Green? I can't believe he is selling Horseshoe Hill and pulling the rug out from under you. I always thought the two of you were close and would be there forever."

"I've got no problems with Joe Green."

"I don't see that half-cocked grin on your face," Jenny said. "I haven't seen it in a while."

"I'm okay. But how about you? I hear that Carl is back in town."

The smile faded from Jenny's face. "That's right."

Luke rattled the ice in his glass and pushed it toward the bartender for a refill. He looked Jenny in the eye. "Did he have anything to do with the brake lines on our truck that Heather was driving?"

"No."

"The snake?"

"Of course not." There was a long silence. "Luke...she's using you. All she cares about is bringing that development here. On your land. She doesn't care about you. She's fooling around with that Dirk Thompson."

"She's working with him."

"Is that all? People in town have seen them together and it looks like more than work."

"She's the new girl in town and people love to talk. Don't believe those things you hear on the street."

"I hate to see you get hurt."

"I know what I'm doing."

"Oh, Luke." Jenny leaned her head on Luke's shoulder. The bartender filled their glasses, and neither Luke nor Jenny noticed Heather when she walked in the door.

"Would you like a table, Miss Harrison?" the hostess asked.

Heather looked toward the bar and for several seconds she watched Jenny massage the shoulders of the man she was sleeping with. "No. No, thank you. I don't care for a table because I'm leaving. I'm sorry."

Heather was asleep in Luke's bed when he came home late that night. He crawled into bed and leaned over to kiss her. His breath smelled of bourbon, and Heather pushed him away.

"What's wrong with you?" Luke asked.

Heather didn't answer. They slept back-to-back that night with Heather as close to the edge of the bed as one could sleep without falling off. She woke early in the morning, just before sunrise and turned on the nightstand light and began rummaging through the top drawer.

"What are you doing?" Luke asked. He held his hand to his face and shielded his eyes from the light.

"I'm looking for the pocketknife you keep on your dresser."

"Pocketknife?" Luke asked. "What the hell?"

"Yes, pocketknife. I'm going to carve a notch in the bedpost with a pocketknife," she said. "Isn't that what we're supposed to do after a good romp between the sheets?"

"Did I miss something?" Luke asked. He rubbed his eyes. "I don't seem to remember us having a romp between the sheets last night."

"You're right," Heather said. "This notch is for the night before last. I want to be sure and carve a good one because it's going to be the last. A good notch for a good romp."

"Well, if you're talking about the night before last..." Luke sat up in bed. "By my count, you better carve three notches."

Heather threw the knife back in the dresser drawer. "I'm moving to the big house." She walked out and slammed the door behind her.

A few minutes later, Luke, dressed in pajama bottoms, went to the big house, and knocked on Heather's door. She let him in and then went to the bed and lay on top of the covers.

"Is something wrong with you?" Luke asked.

"Do you think something is wrong? What would that be?"

"I have no idea."

"I saw you at Griffin's last night," she said. "Sitting with Jenny at the bar."

"Oh..." Luke pulled over a chair, sat down and crossed his arms. "That was nothing. I had two drinks with her and some innocent conversation. Maybe a little bit too friendly, but it was innocent." Luke nodded his head as he recounted his actions from the night before. "Maybe it was inappropriate. I honestly don't know. I was having a bad day, and she was a friendly face. Nothing happened."

"Nothing happened?" Heather asked. "You came home late. Long after Griffin's closes."

"I stopped by Roosevelt's cottage, and we spent a couple of hours talking on the porch." Luke put his hand on hers and she pulled it back. "I ran into Dirk in the pool hall yesterday. He reminded me that everything I live for is going to be gone someday. It's hard for me to imagine, and I try not to think about it. But sometimes I do."

"It may change, but it won't disappear," Heather said.

"When it changes it will be gone for good. I truly love this land. It's not just dirt to me. It's living earth and it saved my life. Twice. I just feel...I feel like I owe it the same."

CHAPTER 24

Perhaps Heather was still angry with Luke, or maybe she felt guilty for having the affair that she knew was unprofessional. Whatever the reason, Heather moved her things back into the big house.

Two days later, Luke walked into the kitchen for breakfast, and found her seated at the table. She twirled a spoon in her coffee and barely acknowledged his presence after he sat down. Luke watched her for some time before he spoke. "That's not the look I'm used to seeing in the mornings. You got something on your mind?"

"I'm going to move into town for a few days." She looked up from her coffee. "My brother Robert is driving to Maine from Sarasota and he's stopping in Thomasville. It's been two years since we have seen each other, and our relationship has always been somewhat confrontational. Well…very confrontational."

Luke drank from his coffee. "Never too late for a new beginning."

"The last time we saw each other was at Mother's funeral and it didn't go well. He is always such the ass."

"You've never mentioned your mother. Mind if I ask?"

"Our relationship was complicated. We had lengthy periods of time when we didn't speak to each other." Heather placed her spoon on the table. "She was always sick with something. She had been ill for some time and Robert kept telling me I should visit. He's the baby and I thought he was exaggerating her condition. The two of them were inseparable. I was always criticizing him because he lived on her money. He always said he had some secret job that he couldn't talk about. He would disappear for weeks at a time and then come home with a tan saying he had been working at some grand location, but he never divulged any details. The only home he's ever had is the garage apartment at Mother's house."

"Sounds like it was probably a good thing she had someone close by," Luke said.

"Looking back, it was a good thing. But it kept me from visiting her like I should. She called for me when she was on her death bed, and I was out in San Francisco on business. By the time I got there, she was gone."

"I'm sorry to hear that."

"Anyway, I thought that we could stay at Slater House until I find out what he is up to." Heather sipped her coffee. "But I'm not looking forward to seeing him."

"Listen, why don't you bring him here and he can stay at Horseshoe Hill? We've got plenty of room."

Heather laughed. "You don't know my brother. Robert is a different character."

"Different how?"

"Different like he'll take over. Like always. He'll spin his fascinating stories and charm the pants off everyone. And the next thing you know, everyone is doing what Robert wants them to do."

"I guess that runs in the family," Luke said.

Heather shot Luke a stare.

"He's more than welcome here," Luke said. "Besides, you make him sound somewhat interesting."

Heather turned to Lula. "Is that alright with you, Lula?"

"Yes, ma'am, Miss Heather. We'll roll out the red carpet for your brother. Don't you worry about that."

Robert Harrison had never hunted game in his life, but he was pleased when Heather informed him he would stay on a hunting plantation. He walked through the front door wearing spanking new canvas trousers, a safari jacket fastened with a wide belt, a skinny tie, and tall leather boots. With his tall frame and wavy black hair, he was as dashing as any diplomat or celebrity who ever set foot in the Red Hills. Luke hugged him like they were long-lost brothers.

"Robert, can you ride a horse?" Luke asked.

"I've always had great affection for the equestrian lifestyle," Robert said. "And I've never met the horse I couldn't ride."

Heather raised an eyebrow. "Really?" She turned to Luke. "We have plans in town today. We're going to the historical museum and then we're going to browse around the downtown shops. I want Robert to see the art galleries here. He's going to love Thomasville."

"I'm giving him the option," Luke said. "We're quail hunting this afternoon, and if Robert wants to go, we'll show him what we do around here in the Red Hills. How about it, Robert?" Luke slapped him on the back.

"That sounds fantastic," Robert said. "You don't mind do you, Heather?"

"No, but I'm still going to town," Heather said. "You manly men go and shoot your birds. And be sure to put Robert on a spirited horse and let him take the first shot at a quail. I'm sure Robert is an expert with a rifle."

"Shotgun," Luke corrected.

"Yes, shotgun, Heather," Robert said.

Heather rolled her eyes. "Of course. Shotgun."

"Perfect," Luke said. "We'll meet on the side lawn in about thirty minutes."

The hunting party assembled at the barn, and Andy walked out leading a black-and-white Tennessee Walker named Rebel.

"That's your horse there, Robert," said Luke. "He's a tall one, so be sure you don't fall off. It's a long way to the ground."

Robert approached the horse and ran his hand from the rump along the flanks and caressed his forehead. He looked at Roosevelt, who sat alone on the wagon. "Is anyone riding with this gentleman?" Robert pointed toward Roosevelt. "That looks like the stylish mode of transportation out here."

"Climb on board," Roosevelt said. "We'll tie your horse on the back in case you want to ride a little later. It's a fine ride on this wagon, but you can get closer to the birds riding on a horse."

Robert bounded onto the wagon and gave Roosevelt a light pat on the back. "Let's go hunt some quail."

Late that afternoon, Heather came back from town. The hunters were still out. She paced back and forth and occasionally glanced out the window. As twilight darkened the sky, the hunt party appeared on the driveway. Robert was on a horse fifty yards ahead of the wagon. He kicked the flanks of the tall horse and galloped onto the lawn with the reins in one hand and a silver flask in the other. He came to an abrupt stop and slid out of the saddle.

Heather and Lula walked onto the porch.

"Come take a look, Heather," Robert announced. "We killed us a mess of birds."

Luke and Roosevelt arrived with the wagon. "I don't know where he learned to shoot," Luke said, "but ol' Robert here is a hell of a shot. He did all the shooting and we just sat back and watched."

Heather stood stiff and crossed her arms. Lula walked to the wagon and inspected the pile of birds in the bird box.

"Tell her about the doubles, Luke." Robert took a pull from the silver flask.

"That's right," Luke said. "Two doubles. Robert, you can go inside and get cleaned up and we'll put the dogs and horses up. Lula's going to show you what we do with these birds tonight."

For dinner that night, Lula prepared fried quail and grits for Robert, Luke, Heather, and Roosevelt. Robert chose two bottles of Chenin Blanc from the cellar, and when they sat at the dining table, Robert dominated the conversation. He talked about horses, the synchronized pointers that crisscrossed the field, and the thrill he felt at each covey rise.

Lula brought a platter of quail and served the plates one by one. Three sets of silver candlesticks lit the dining table and soft music played in the background.

"Robert, this sure is a special occasion here, tonight," Roosevelt said. "But you notice that, while you all have two quail on your plates, I only have one. Things have not changed much over the years, and it looks like the mule driver still doesn't eat like the important folks. Yes sir, one quail is all a mule driver gets."

Robert dropped his fork and looked at Roosevelt's plate. One quail. He glanced around the dining table, and no one seemed to care.

"Here Roosevelt, you can have one of my quail," Robert said. He offered his plate.

"Don't you dare," said Lula. She crossed her arms and stared at Roosevelt. "You wait just a minute. I'll be right back."

Lula marched into the kitchen and came back in a matter of seconds with a platter full of quail. She stopped at Roosevelt's chair and piled fried quail high on his plate until it could hold no more. "There you go," Lula said. "A whole plate full of quail and cholesterol like your doctor told you not to eat. You eat all you want. And if you have a heart attack at this table, I'm going to stick two more birds in your pockets for the ride to the hospital."

Roosevelt grinned. "Well, thank you, Miss Lula. That's mighty kind."

The kitchen door swung open again and again with dishes from the kitchen. Robert poured wine while Lula served green beans, field peas, steamed carrots, and a bowl of mashed potatoes made with six sticks of butter.

Robert took a sip of wine and raised his glass toward the chandelier and looked closely at the color as he tilted the glass back and forth. "How do you all like this wine?"

"That's one of the bottles Miss Catherine ordered years back. We have a whole cellar filled with wine like that," Lula said. "Mr. Robert says there is some fine wine down there."

"Heather, would you like to take a look at the cellar?" Robert asked.

"That's your passion Robert, not mine."

"Okay, maybe tomorrow."

They were nearly done with dinner and five bottles of wine, when Robert pushed back from the table and wiped his chin with a napkin. "Heather, are you still in love with that married professor in Chicago?" he asked. "What's his name? Stephen Darling?"

Heather gritted her teeth, and everyone stopped eating. "No, that's over, but thank you for reminding me," she said.

Robert went on. "Then have you gone back with one of the others?" he asked.

Luke's eyes widened. "There was more than one?"

"She has a thing for intellectuals," Robert said. "The older the better." He lifted his glass as if to offer a toast.

"Stop it, Robert," Heather said.

"Okay, I was only teasing. Now, who wants more wine?" Robert waved his hand in the air as if it were nothing. "I'm sorry, Heather. I almost forgot about your sensitive side."

Heather addressed the table. "Maybe Robert is jealous because my boyfriends have been more handsome than his." She glanced around the room and waited for a response. None came. "His *boyfriends*," Heather said. "He's gay." She waited, but still no response. "Didn't you tell your hunting buddies you're gay?" she asked.

"He did," Luke said. "It just slipped out. He wasn't bragging or anything like that."

Roosevelt nodded his head in the affirmative. Heather stabbed three green beans with her fork and shoved them in her mouth.

"I've got an idea," Luke said. "Let's take Robert downtown and shoot a little pool. Drink a couple of drafts. How about it, Robert?"

"Perfect," Heather said. Her face was still red. "Robert, you, and your hunting buddy go downtown and shoot some pool."

"Oh, no. You're coming with us," Luke said. "You've got to help us show your brother a good time while he's here. Right?"

"I insist," Robert added. "I came all this way to see you and we've barely spent any time together. Be a sport. Let's go shoot pool."

They arrived at the pool hall, and Luke held the door open for Heather and Robert. Smoke poured out the door and inside four regulars sat hunched over beers at the bar while others played pool in the back. Hank Williams Jr.'s "Honky Tonkin" played on the juke box.

Luke leaned on the bar and ordered. "Three PBRs please, Chuck." He turned around and looked to the rear of the pool room where a boisterous group of three played pool. One was fat, one was tall, and one was bald with a red beard.

"God damn it!" One of the men in the back shouted when he missed an easy shot.

"Look, Heather," Luke said. "Some of your Rex colleagues are playing pool in the back."

"Funny," Heather replied.

"Those fellows are developers from Central Florida looking for land to build an RV park," Chuck said. "There will be more of those soon, I guess. Everybody's showing up to cash in on the boom town."

Luke, Heather, and Robert turned around and drank their beers. Heather sat on one end, Luke on the other, and Robert sat in the middle. Heather and Robert carried on a quiet, but intense, conversation as if Luke was not there.

"Anybody play pool?" Luke asked.

Robert jumped off his barstool. "I do."

Heather rolled her eyes. "Of course, you do."

"The only table open is the one next to the yahoos back there," Chuck said. "They've been looking for trouble for three nights running."

"We'll be alright. Follow me." Luke led them to a table in the back where cigarette smoke filled the air and empty beer bottles were scattered around. Luke racked a set of balls on the table next to the three men.

"Ladies first," Luke said as he handed a cue stick to Heather. She aimed her shot and sank two balls while the others scattered around the table.

The fat man noticed. "She breaks pretty good for a girl." He diverted his eyes to Robert who removed his safari jacket and hung it on a coat rack. "That's a fancy jacket you have there, buddy. Did y'all kill any elephants out there today?" The three men laughed out loud.

Heather had not smiled since dinner. "He's actually a good shot with a rifle," she said.

The bald man lined his shot and slammed the six ball into the corner pocket. "This place might be too fancy for us," he said. He drank his beer with his pinky held high like an aristocrat sipping from a teacup.

Luke smiled. "Hey. Ease up, friend."

The fat man glared at Luke and as he lined his shot, Robert accidently backed into him. The man turned and poked Robert in the chest with his cue. "Watch out, Jungle Jim."

Heather's face turned red, and her lips grew tight. She set her beer on the table and approached the man. "His name is Robert, not Jungle Jim. And you're an asshole."

Luke pulled Heather from the man's face. "Gentlemen, it was an accident," Luke said. "We're just trying to play pool. Nobody meant any harm."

The meanest looking of the three men stepped forward. His red eyes peered out of thin slits and his breath smelled like beer and cigarettes. It was a look that Luke knew well. "Your boy there has been crowding us all night," the man said. "Why don't you take Jungle Jim and that foul-mouthed lady and find another place to play pool?"

Luke laid his cue on the table. "Okay, gentlemen, we're going. We were about to leave anyway." Luke shouted out to the bartender. "Chuck, buy these men a beer and put it on my tab. We're leaving."

They climbed into the truck and Heather sat with her arms crossed. "I must tell you, Luke, I'm somewhat disappointed you let them say those things. But I'm happy to know that chivalry is finally dead in the Deep South. I guess a southern gentleman doesn't defend a lady's honor anymore."

"I did you a favor," Luke said.

"Really?"

"Really. Those idiots were looking for trouble and they're not the type you want to waste your time with. Besides, it wouldn't look very professional for the vice president of Rex Corporation to get arrested in a pool hall."

Luke drove eighty miles an hour back to Horseshoe Hill and not another word was said. He drove to the front of the house, and everyone got out except Luke.

"Aren't you coming in?" Heather asked.

"I'm going back to town. I left my hat at the pool hall," Luke said.

"Your hat is on your head."

"I'm going back anyway."

Robert shot a look at Heather, then looked at Luke. He jumped into the front seat. "Me too."

Luke slammed the truck in reverse, turned around and headed back to town throwing a cloud of dust and gravel as they left.

Luke and Robert returned to Horseshoe Hill at daybreak and Heather met them in the driveway. Luke's hair was disheveled, and Robert's jacket was torn at the sleeve. He had a cut with six stitches above his left eye.

"What happened?" Heather asked.

Robert jumped in before Luke could answer. "A bar fight. A God-almighty bar fight. The sheriff came and we were all carted off to jail." He slapped Luke on the back. "God, I love this place."

"It wasn't much of a fight," said Luke. "Chuck called the sheriff when we walked in the door and there was some pushing and shoving, a couple of punches, but nobody got hurt."

Robert leaned in and whispered in Heather's ear, "He drug the nasty one outside by his collar."

"What about Robert's eye?" Heather asked.

"Your little brother took a big swing, lost his balance, and fell into the corner of the pool table. He has six stitches, but he'll be alright." Luke reached into his shirt pocket and unfolded a crumpled sheet of paper. "Here's your written apology."

"Did you beat it out of them?" Heather asked.

"We didn't need to. Sheriff Barnes gave them the option of writing an apology or spending a couple of days in jail."

Robert had planned to stay only four days in South Georgia, but he extended his stay for another week. They hunted quail during the day and in the evenings, Lula invited Robert into the kitchen where they cooked together. Lula taught him a few tricks to Southern cooking such as using lots of butter, plenty of salt, and the proper use of hog jowl. She also showed him how much sugar goes into sweet tea. When Robert ran out of things to do in the kitchen, he and Lula rearranged every piece of furniture in the big house.

On the day that Robert's stay ended, Heather asked Luke a favor. "It's Robert's last day here," she said. "Would you mind if we saddle a couple of horses and go for a ride?"

"Help yourself," Luke said. "I'll have the boys saddle the horses and you can ride as long as you like. The sun's shining and it's a great day to be in the woods."

Heather and Robert rode slowly down the drive then turned off on a firebreak that led to the fishing hole. They arrived at the creek, climbed from their horses, and sat on the bank.

"There's something I need to tell you, Robert," Heather said. "I feel guilty for failing to visit Mother before she passed away. I had no idea she was that sick and I was so buried with work that every time I planned to go, something came up." She took a deep breath. "And I must be honest. I really didn't want to go. I dreaded seeing her in that condition."

"She understood, Heather. Me, too. You probably don't know this, but she idolized you. She kept up with everything you did, and she talked about you all the time. She was so proud."

"I was always jealous of the two of you," Heather said. She placed her hand on Robert's shoulder. "The way you two seemed to have your own world and I was always on the outside." Heather sighed. "Maybe I was wrong."

"It's okay, honey. She said some bad stuff to you, but you said dreadful things to her, as well. She never understood why you blamed her for Dad leaving."

"I never blamed her when Daddy left. I only said that she could have tried a little harder to make the marriage work." There was sharpness in Heather's tone.

"He had an affair. Multiple affairs. How was she supposed to make it work when he was never there? And you treated him like he was a god, even though he acted as though you never existed. I'm sorry, Heather, but you must know that's how it was. It was all about Dad for you. And Mom tried so hard to keep you from knowing the terrible things he did."

Heather started to cry. "I loved him, Robert. I couldn't help it. I loved him so much."

"It's alright, Heather." Robert put his arm around her and held her close. "Go out this summer, put flowers on her grave and talk to her. It will do you good, honey."

Heather wiped the tears from her eyes and leaned her head on Robert's shoulder. They sat there on the bank of the creek where the only sounds that could be heard were squirrels scratching in the leaves, quail whistling, and crows calling from far away. They watched the stream flow into the fishing hole, circle around the hole and then go out the other side.

"I hope we can see each other more often, Robert. Really, I do."

"I do, too," Robert replied. "And by the way, your man's a little rough around the edges, but I can't imagine that old married professor at Northwestern fighting three drunken hillbillies for your honor."

Heather chuckled. "I can't imagine you fighting three drunken hillbillies for me, either. But you did."

Robert rubbed the stitches on his head. "Yes, I did."

CHAPTER 25

LUKE DROVE TO THE AIRPORT and parked his truck beside the dark runway. Joe Green sat in the passenger seat beside him. It was late evening, and the small airport was deserted and dark except for the runway lights that stretched far to the north and faded in the distance. A low-pitched hum broke the silence and grew louder. Over the end of Runway 19, a Gulfstream G150 dropped out of the clouds and glided into position above two rows of runway lights. Tires screeched and the jet streaked by. It slowed at the end of the runway and taxied to a discreet section of the tarmac.

A small light came on and stairs unfolded from the belly of the plane. A tall man in a pin-striped suit slowly and deliberately descended the stairs and met Luke on the tarmac. The man embraced Luke with a strong hug. Luke took the man's duffel bag and briefcase and they walked to the truck. When they reached the truck, the man peered in through the passenger side window.

"It's good to see you, Joe Green," the tall man said.

Joe Green nodded. "Hello, Angus."

Angus climbed in the back seat and the three men drove away in the darkness. Thirty minutes later, they arrived at Horseshoe

Hill. Luke walked Angus to his bedroom and dropped his luggage inside the door. They said good night and Luke went back to his cottage.

In the morning, Luke woke Heather before sunrise. "Do you have anything you need to do in town today?" Luke asked.

"I have some documents to print at the library, but that's it," Heather said. "Why do you ask?"

"Angus is here."

Heather sat up in bed. She rubbed the sleep from her eyes. "Angus Parker?"

"Yes. He flew in for one day only. We're going to hunt quail and then he's flying back to New York. It's kind of a special day—just me and Angus with Roosevelt and Joe Green. After the hunt we're having a few of the old guys over to the big house for drinks and a sort of reunion. I don't know what to expect. Angus has been gone for a long time and it was a hard day when he left."

"And you want me out of the way?"

"He's only here for a day and I don't want to spend time with introductions and polite conversation. It's nothing personal. He's a gentleman and would treat you accordingly…but today is not the day."

Heather rose from bed and slipped into a terry cloth robe. "I can spend the day in town, I guess. I'll stop by the art center and see what's happening there. And maybe I'll have lunch with Kitty."

"Thank you. I'll take Angus back to the airport around seven. I can meet you for dinner at Griffin's at seven-thirty if you'd like."

"That sounds good." Heather stopped Luke before he walked out the door. "Luke, why did Angus come back?"

"He's eighty-one years old, Heather. This is where he spent a big part of his life. I think he wants to be sure he has one more hunt before it's too late. It's as simple as that."

The day was cold and gray, and the forecast called for rain. It was the only day they had. Before they went out, Roosevelt inspected the wagon. He checked the leather straps, tightened the bolts, oiled the springs and couplings, and wiped the morning frost from the seats. The day before, he and Andy had washed it and polished the brass as bright as it had ever been. Lula packed a basket of homemade biscuits stuffed with salty ham and a dozen bran muffins. She filled a brass urn with hot coffee and placed two wool blankets on the wagon to keep the hunters warm. Luke retrieved Angus's Merkel side-by-side with custom engraving. It was oiled and clean as if Luke had known that Angus would return.

Luke put five of his best English Pointers on the wagon and closed each compartment. The last compartment was saved for Whistling Willy, who was standing attentive at the kennel gate. Luke opened the latch and kneeled as he clipped a leather lead to Willy's collar. "This is a big day, Willy," Luke said. "Bigger than any trial we've ever run. Don't let me down, ol' boy."

Nature is the great equalizer. An old man, a young man, a black man, and a Native American. They had different faces and different bloodlines but love of the land made them brothers. Roosevelt drove the wagon, Angus sat next to Roosevelt, and Luke worked the dogs from horseback. Joe Green tied Dancer behind the wagon, then sat on the front seat between Roosevelt and Angus. Andy was out on the flank riding scout.

The scouts and the wagon loaded with dogs and provisions set out toward the best course they had. They rode by a weed field that had once been a sharecropper's field. It had recently been turned with a harrow, leaving a five-acre patch of raw dirt filled with deer and turkey tracks. Angus reached over and touched Roosevelt on the shoulder. "Let's stop here for a minute," Angus said.

Roosevelt stopped the mules, and Angus stepped from the wagon and walked into the field. He looked around and then reached down and cupped a handful of dirt. He held it to his nose, closed his eyes and smelled the dirt. He held it there, then let the dirt fall from his hand before slowly returning to his place on the wagon. "I think about the smell of this dirt all the time," he said. "And the pine in the air."

Roosevelt nodded. "It's fine smelling dirt, Angus." He tapped the mules with the reins and the wagon lurched forward. "It sure is."

The weather turned bitter cold and the wind burned the cheeks and ears of the men as they rode. But, as if the gods had willed it, the hunting was as good as it had ever been on Horseshoe Hill. The dogs found covey after covey and the birds held tight. Angus was slow and rigid, but his aim was true, and he took one bird or two from every covey. They followed the course through pine meadows, scattered food plots and the edges of hardwood bottoms. Along the way, they scattered flocks of turkey, flushed deer, and spotted rabbits as they ducked into brush piles. It was as if every creature on the plantation was aware that Angus was back.

At noon, they broke for lunch and returned to the big house for venison pie and buttered biscuits with cane syrup. In the living room, a fire crackled in the fireplace and the men stood close and turned from side to side to warm their waxed field jackets and leather boots. Lula brought a fresh pot of hot coffee, and they drank to warm their insides.

They rested for an hour then saddled the horses and hitched the wagon for the afternoon hunt. They started at the edge of the old ball diamond. Years before, the field was the site of Sunday baseball and picnics on the grass. It was converted into a prime brood field long before Luke's time.

"No stories about the baseball team today?" Luke asked Roosevelt.

"I think Angus has heard them all," Roosevelt replied.

Angus laughed. "At least once."

Andy brought out a pointer named Cindy Sue and held her by the collar while Luke unlatched the untouched box and brought the handsome male pointer to the front of the wagon and showed him to Angus. "You're in for a treat, Angus." Luke held the dog on a lead and waited for Angus to notice.

Angus studied the dog through squinted eyes then stood and stepped from the wagon for a closer look. Angus looked at Whistling Willy as if he had found the Holy Grail. He bent down and placed his gloved hands on each side of the dog's head. "It can't be," Angus said. He turned the dog's head and studied the markings. He ran his hand down the dog's loin and lifted his paw from the ground.

"Same big, tough feet. And look at that head. I've seen only one pointer with a noble head like that. He has the same color and ticking of..."

"That's right, Angus. Ol' Sam sired a litter before he died. Nobody knew how that bitch got bred. We thought we had her shut up while she was in heat, but when I saw this one, I knew Sam had bred her. I watched him for two years, and he was sure enough the spitting image of Sam, but he acted like he had no idea what a quail was. He almost had me convinced he didn't care about quail." Luke stroked Willy's head. "Turns out he was just taking his time to catch on. Just like Sam. I never pushed him because I knew what was inside of him. Just the way you worked with Sam. I never gave up. Do you remember how we thought Sam would never amount to anything?"

"Yes, I do." Angus's eyes filled with tears, and he could barely speak. "Let's watch him run," he said.

"I'll try to keep him close in, but he runs big, Angus. And fast."

"That's okay. That's the same way Sam ran."

Andy turned Cindy Sue loose. She jolted ahead, broke to the left and then angled back to the right. Luke let Willy go. Willy caught, then passed, Cindy Sue in what seemed like three long strides. Luke tapped his horse with his bootheels and called to Willy. The big dog with an easy gait and thundering paws hurdled a pine log, topped a ridge, ran down the other side, and finally doubled back on Luke's whistle. He made a wide circle, then disappeared over the hill as if he ran for show.

Luke skirted the wagon as he set out on the course. "Sorry, Angus. He likes to go big. But he'll hold a point when he finds birds."

"Let him run, Luke," said Angus. "Don't hold him back for an old man like me. Let him run."

Angus climbed aboard the wagon and Roosevelt tapped the back of the mules with the reins and they were off.

"Not many dogs run the woods like Willy," Roosevelt said.

Luke followed Willy over the crest of the hill, and when he reached the other side, he stopped abruptly and raised his hat high over his head.

"He's on point," Roosevelt said. "It doesn't take Willy long to find birds."

Luke dismounted and disappeared into tall cover. Two shots came from the cover and moments later, Willy was casting the left flank with his head held high. Luke rode by the wagon, reached in his vest and pulled two quail from the pocket, tossing them into the bird box.

"He's got another point," Angus said.

"You're down this time," said Luke.

Angus took two birds from the covey rise, and for the next half hour, it seemed that every time a bird was tossed on the wagon, another covey was pointed. Angus's aim was true, and they gathered birds from every covey rise. Gray clouds descended from the heavens and settled among the treetops. A light rain began to fall, and the men donned rain jackets to keep dry.

They hunted for another half hour and the rain came harder. Luke rode to the wagon. "Should I pick him up, Angus?"

"Is he tired?"

"He's like Sam. He can go all day."

"Then let him run. But have someone else do the shooting. I'll stay here on the wagon."

Luke handed the leather lead to Andy. "Let's put Cindy Sue up and we'll keep Willy out."

Five minutes later, Willy slammed to a stop and threw his tail straight and hard into the air. He was barely visible in the rain. Luke slid off his horse, removed his gun from the scabbard and walked to Willy. He walked past Willy's nose and a cloud of birds burst into the sky. Luke held his gun at his waist and fired a token shot into the air. He tapped Willy on the head and Willy circled the pine meadow. He found another covey and then another.

Time after time, Willy pointed, and Luke fired into the air. They were done taking birds, but they could not quit.

The rain came hard in a steady pour and the men held their jackets close to their throats and leaned forward into the driving rain. The rain was cold on their faces, but they did not quit. Puddles formed on the ground and ran in the ditches, and they could only see flashes of white as Willy quartered back and forth through the pines. The four men were cold and wet, but they were home and they continued as if they knew it would be the last time.

They returned to the big house and chased the cold with whiskey and warm towels. Angus Parker wore the bittersweet smile of a man who had returned home from the war. Colonel Bronson, his wife Ginger, Oscar Thornton, and several other plantation neighbors drank cocktails in the parlor while the hunt party changed into dry clothes.

Angus changed into dry clothes and walked to Roosevelt's cottage. "Roosevelt, I'd like for you to join us for drinks."

Roosevelt smiled. "I appreciate that, Angus, but I'm mighty comfortable right here. I just got the chill off me, and I poured myself a brandy. I'm going to sip on that and enjoy reading by the fire."

"I wish you would change your mind," Angus said.

"It was a mighty fine day out there today," Roosevelt said.

"It was a fine day," Angus agreed. He put his hands in his pockets while he stood in the doorway. "I'm leaving later on tonight," he said.

"I know."

"That was a good hunt to quit on," Angus said. He stood in the open doorway and looked down as if there was something that he needed to say. "This is not the way I dreamed things would turn out," he said.

"Things don't always turn out the way we hope for," Roosevelt replied.

"I know that, but I feel like I have failed. I feel like I let people down."

"You did the best that you could, Angus."

"I tried."

The men stood in awkward silence.

"I had planned on leaving the Brown Place to you in my will," Angus said. "But I changed my mind."

"I wasn't counting on anything like that, anyway," Roosevelt replied.

"I'm deeding that property to Eugene."

Roosevelt took his time while he thought about what Angus had said. "That's mighty generous, Angus, but I'm not sure he wants it."

"That will be up to him. He can sell it if he wants, but we need our young people if there is any hope of salvaging this mess."

"You need to think about it, Angus."

"I already have. There are two good homes there. I hope you put them to good use." Angus put his hands in his pockets. "Goodbye, Roosevelt."

"Goodbye, Angus."

Angus left Roosevelt's cottage and joined his guests inside the house. They made small talk and recounted the dog work and covey rises. There was also talk about Heather—a subject that Luke tried to avoid. They grazed on Lula's jelly biscuits, salted pecans and assorted cheeses and they sipped bourbon cocktails and coffee that warmed them from the inside out.

When the hunting stories were done, Angus Parker invited his guests into the library and closed the door behind them. Two hours later, Angus Parker walked out and said goodbye to the guests. He gathered his duffel and briefcase and took one last look at the big white house that had once been his home. He carefully placed his bags in the back seat of Luke's truck, and they started for the airport.

They passed the front gate, and tears came to Angus's eyes. "Luke, it's been a hell of a day. A lot of years have passed, but it's as great as I remember it. If it weren't…we couldn't do what we have to do."

"Angus, what did you really come for?" Luke asked.

"To tell you the truth, I had a moment of guilty conscience. This plan, my actions, everything that is going on, I fear that it's all for spite and it's wrong to live a life filled consumed with those feelings. I saw Charles with the investors a few weeks ago. He had his mistress clinging to him like he was the king of England. I despise those greedy bastards." Angus exhaled. "I came to be sure what we're doing is a good thing. I had to be sure that what is here now is worth saving."

"What do you think now?" Luke asked.

"It's worth it a hundred times over."

Luke stared straight ahead as he drove. "I know it was hard to come back, but you did it. You survived the worst of it. You can make this your home again. You're the one who made Horseshoe Hill what it is today and what it was back then. Come back to it."

"I can never go back to where I was before. It's too painful and I'm an old man." His lips trembled. "I need to tell you something else. My doctor has diagnosed me with the early stages of dementia. It's in check at the moment, but I'm afraid I don't have long before it sets in."

Luke turned to Angus with his mouth open. "You seem good to me."

"That's good, Luke. I wouldn't want you to remember me any other way." Angus paused. "I'm not the same man I was when I was here. I was a better man then. But now I belong to a different ecosystem where everything is driven by money and that's what I'm good at now. I have forsaken so many good things and that's who I am today."

"I see the same man I've always known," Luke said.

"I'm not the same. I've made more money than a man can spend, but I'm not proud of it."

"Angus, I want to thank you for everything you did for me and my mother," Luke said. "I'm not sure I have ever thanked you."

"Both of you have thanked me plenty already. Now, listen," Angus said. His eyes were steel. "We need to buy as much land as we can. You find it and I'll have Sam Horne—he's a good man, and a good lawyer—set up corporate names for titles. Start with small parcels and let's drive the price up. Then see if we can land the bigger stuff. You know the ones we want. The guys we are up against have unlimited resources, but I haven't done bad myself the last few years, and I don't mind spending every penny of it."

"What are you going to do with all the land when you're done, Angus?"

"We'll put it all in conservation easements, and then sell it to people who will keep it like it is." Angus paused. "I see the way you look at the land. You'll know what to do when the time comes."

"Conservation easements will help with the taxes," Luke said.

Angus looked him in the eye. "At my age, I don't need tax credits, but devaluing the land will be a good thing in the long run. And the same goes for the other landowners."

They rode the dark highway for the next ten minutes before Angus broke the silence. "Luke, it's been long enough."

"Long enough for what?"

"Long enough for you to stop grieving over your loss. I know you've suffered the same as I've suffered. But son, I don't have the time left that you have. You need to start living like you have a plan for the future."

Luke looked over at Angus, studied his face for a second, then looked back to the road. "I feel pretty good about my future."

"That womanizing behavior of yours will catch up with you one day. You've got talent, Luke. A talent like I've rarely seen." Angus looked at Luke's face. "You need to pass it on. Just like one of those rare bird dogs that has the whole package. You've got good genes. Don't waste an opportunity to leave your mark."

"Angus, that womanizing is not as bad as you've heard."

"That woman, Heather," Angus said. "I've heard talk."

Luke did not answer, and Angus finally broke the silence. "I did you wrong and now you're the only one I have left. Don't die a lonely man."

When they arrived at the airport, the Gulfstream was waiting on the tarmac with the engines idling and navigation lights flashing red and green. Luke drove the truck onto the tarmac and parked next to the plane.

"Don't get out, Luke," Angus said. "I don't want to say goodbye."

"At least let me help you with..."

"I've got it. But one last thing..."

"What's that?"

"I'm going to deed the Brown Place to Eugene."

"That's a beautiful place, but are you sure he wants it?"

"Maybe not now, but his family has a lot of history here. Perhaps he has it in his blood."

"He's the smartest person I know," Luke said. "He'd do well in the Red Hills."

Angus nodded and Luke watched as Angus Parker walked slowly to the plane. A man dressed in a white shirt and black tie stood at the foot of the stairs. The pilot sat in the cockpit and ran the instrument checklist. Angus limped as he walked and there was tightness in his joints. He ascended the stairs slowly and did not look back.

Luke went straight to Griffin's from the airport and found Heather waiting for him at the bar. As usual, she had a martini sitting in front of her. Vodka, straight up, extra dry, with a blue cheese olive.

Luke winked at the blonde behind the bar, and she smiled back at him. "Jim Beam on the rocks, please," he said.

Heather gave Luke a small kiss on the cheek. A friendly kiss. "How did Angus enjoy his visit?" she asked. "I wish I had been able to meet him."

"Coming back was hard for him," Luke said. "But it was something he had to do. Something we both had to do...but it was hard."

"Seemed like a lot of whispers and secrets surrounding his visit, but I guess you would tell me if there was anything I needed to know."

"Just people who love to hunt doing what they love to do," Luke replied.

Heather took a drink from her martini. "I've been sitting here tonight thinking about the last time I saw you in here. With Jenny. You remember that night?" she asked.

"I seem to recall something like that," Luke said.

Heather set her glass on the bar. "Well, guess what?"

"Tell me."

"I've been invited to Chicago for my birthday tomorrow."

"I had no idea it was your birthday."

"Actually, it's not tomorrow, it's Saturday. But I'm going up for a long weekend." The smile went away from Heather's face. "I'm going to see Stephen."

Luke was stunned. "The married English professor you were in love with?" he asked. Luke drained his bourbon, rattled the ice, then tapped his glass for a refill. "I thought you were done with him."

"I don't know what to say. You know it would never work out for me and you. We are only good together because we know we will never be together."

Luke said nothing.

"Stephen and I never had a chance before because he's married, but he's getting divorced for sure this time. He and his wife have separated, and the papers have been filed. It's what we wanted for years, but he couldn't leave the children."

"I guess he changed his mind about that," Luke said.

"It's a hard decision for him, but now he's sure." Heather ordered another martini. "You probably wouldn't like him at all, but he's brilliant. One of the most intelligent men I've ever met. His classes are so popular it's nearly impossible to get in. Of course, that probably has something to do with the fact that he is very handsome. You know, he has that sexy college professor look. Lots of female students take his classes."

Luke tossed back the last of his bourbon.

"I wish you would say something cocky," Heather said.

"I'm all out of cocky," Luke replied.

Heather looked him in the eye. "This thing between me and you has gotten out of control, Luke. I'll never be able to look you in the eye when this deal is done. I feel guilty already."

"It's not your fault. As a matter of fact, I'm going to go ahead and forgive you right now."

"Are you going to try to stop me?"

"Sounds to me like you have made up your mind. Like you said, this thing has gotten out of control. It's going to end badly, one way or another. So, I'm leaving it to fate. Will of the wind."

They clinked glasses.

"Will of the wind," Heather said.

CHAPTER 26

HEATHER'S PLANE TOUCHED DOWN IN Chicago, and she took the train downtown. She checked into the Drake Hotel where Stephen had reserved a room for her. She placed her suitcase on the king-sized bed and opened it. There was a light blue present inside with a handwritten note attached. *To be opened five years from today. Not before. Happy Birthday, Heather.* It was signed *Luke.* She gave the present a shake and held it as if she contemplated opening it. Instead, she tossed it on the dresser, arranged her clothes into drawers and took a shower.

When Heather was dressed, she looked into the mirror and turned from front to back, side to side. She took off the red dress and put on a blue one. She changed that one too and finally decided on a simple black dress and matching high-heeled shoes.

She took a taxi to the Metropolitan, a clubby steak place where she and Stephen often met for special occasions when she was in school. She surveyed the room and saw Stephen seated at a table in the rear coddling an Old Fashioned. Heather followed the hostess to Stephen's table. "Waiting for someone?" she asked.

Stephen rose from his chair and gave her a kiss on the lips. "Only you, my dear," Stephen said. He pulled a chair for her. "Does this place bring back memories?" he asked.

"Yes, it does. And I need a drink, please."

Stephen motioned the waiter over and ordered a cabernet for Heather.

Heather stopped the waiter. "I'd like a vodka martini," she said. The waiter looked at Stephen and waited for confirmation.

"I'm going to order a great bottle of wine with dinner, dear. And we're ordering steak. Don't you want a cabernet?"

"You're drinking a cocktail," Heather replied. "I'd like a cocktail as well."

"I know, but you get tipsy when you drink liquor and I want this evening to be special. Wouldn't you rather have wine?"

Heather managed to smile. "Okay, the cabernet."

The waiter left and Stephen reached across the table and took Heather's hand. "Now that the divorce is nearly done, I feel like I'm more alive than I've been in years. I feel like I'm reading Shakespeare for the first time." He kissed her hand. "And whenever I hear one of our songs over the radio, I tear up like a schoolboy."

"Which one of our songs?" Heather asked.

"Any of our songs. We had so many."

Heather drew her hand back and crossed her arms.

"Melissa is killing me with this divorce," Stephen said. "My attorney is supposed to be the best around. He's an alumnus and we communicate very well, but Melissa has a bulldog for an attorney, and they want everything I've got—including the girls. But that's not going to happen."

"How are the girls taking the news?"

"They're doing okay, but they don't understand what's going on. Melissa is trying to sway them against me, and she has asked for full custody. She's being real nasty about the whole thing."

"I thought the two of you had been living separate lives for a long time now. Has something changed?"

"She accuses me of having an affair with every attractive student in my class. She listens in on my calls, checks my texts and reads my mail." Stephen let go of Heather's hand and drank from his glass.

Heather leaned across the table. "*Are* you having an affair with every attractive student in your class?"

Stephen stiffened. "Of course not. Don't be silly."

"You were always a big flirt with your students," Heather said. "At least the attractive ones."

The waiter returned to the table. "Would you like to order now?"

"Yes," Stephen said. "I'll have a New York strip medium rare, and she'll have a medium rare filet."

"I'd like mine medium," Heather said.

"Heather, no one in a fine restaurant orders their steak cooked medium. That hides the flavor of good steak. It should never be any more than medium rare."

"Okay, medium rare," Heather agreed.

Stephen reached across the table and again took Heather's hand. She tossed her hair with her free hand and smiled at Stephen while he talked about the old times. Again, the conversation turned to his divorce. He ordered another cocktail for himself. His eyes were laser focused and he spoke at a rapid pace as if he were speaking to his divorce attorney rather than someone he was supposed to adore.

"Please, Stephen. Relax," Heather pleaded. "Can't we talk about something else?"

Stephen agreed and did not talk about the divorce again, but he appeared anxious, and he fidgeted during dinner. He ordered a bottle of cabernet and then another. Stephen ate every morsel of his strip steak while Heather picked at the outer edges of her filet. The minute they were done with their food, Stephen paid the check and stood from the table. Heather took one last drink of wine and followed him outside.

Heather stopped outside the revolving door and waited until she had Stephen's attention. "You must have a lot on your mind," she said.

"What?" he asked.

"You barged out of the restaurant like I wasn't even here," she said. "You used to have impeccable manners. That's one of the things I've always loved about you, your manners. But you seem to be off tonight."

Stephen smiled and placed his gloved hands on each side of her cheeks. "You're right. I am off tonight. I should have known you would be looking for a break from those hillbillies you've been stuck with." He kissed her on the lips. "I promise I will make it up to you." Stephen fastened the buttons of her coat. He handed the ticket to the valet and stood nervously while the car was parked.

Heather slid into the passenger side and removed a pink blanket and toy lion from her seat. "For me?" she asked.

Stephen did not answer, and Heather placed the blanket and toy lion into the back seat. When they arrived at the Drake, Heather waited beside the car while Stephen handed the keys to the valet and started toward the door.

She stopped the valet. "Wait a minute." She turned to Stephen. "I'm really tired from the flight, and I have to get some sleep tonight," she said. "What do you have planned for tomorrow?"

Stephen arched his eyebrows. "I haven't seen you in nine months and you're sleeping alone tonight?"

"Yes, we can play tomorrow. All day," Heather said. A moment passed. She cocked her head to the side. "You do know it's my birthday tomorrow, don't you?"

Stephen's mouth fell open. "I knew it was this month, but I didn't know it's tomorrow. That's great. We'll do something fabulous. Melissa has the girls and I'm free all day long. We'll paint the town. We'll make this the best birthday ever. Call me in the morning, okay?"

"Sure, I'll call you in the morning."

Heather walked into the cold hotel room with the king-sized bed and placed her purse on the dresser next to the blue package. She picked up the card and slowly read it aloud. "Five years," she said to herself. She shook the gift and held it to the light. Then, she gently opened the package as if she would wrap it again in a way that appeared it had never been opened.

Inside the box was a writer's pad, a Mont Blanc pen and a framed quotation that read, *The person born with a talent they were meant to use will be happiest in using it.* It was signed by the writer, Johann Wolfgang von Goethe.

Heather smiled and placed the framed quotation on the dresser so that it faced the bed. She fluffed a pillow, took her phone from the dresser, and called Luke.

"Heather? What time is it? Are you alright?"

"It's eleven forty here in Chicago," she said. "So, that makes it about twelve forty where you are. Were you sleeping?"

"I was." Luke sat up in his bed and turned on the nightstand light. "How's your weekend going?" he asked.

"I have a confession to make."

"You have a confession to make?"

"Yes, I opened your gift."

"Damn," Luke said. "I knew I shouldn't have wrapped it in Tiffany blue paper. You couldn't wait, could you?"

"Tiffany blue." Heather smiled. "How do you know about Tiffany blue?"

Luke laughed. "Lula once told me that if a man wants to give a special gift to a woman, it should come in a Tiffany blue box. She learned that from watching Catherine unwrap presents from Angus over the years. The best ones always came in Tiffany blue."

"Lula is a smart woman. And very observant I would say. I love the package and I love the gift." Heather said. "I'm curious about the note. Why did you want me to wait five years to open it?"

"I figured that in five years, you would be ready to write if you weren't writing already. But mostly, I hope in five years you will remember me kindly. No matter what happens between now and then, maybe you can give me a call, or something like that."

"Or something like that?" Heather asked. "Okay, something like that."

"How's your weekend going?" asked Luke.

"Tell me something, please," Heather asked. "How do I like my steak?"

"Let's see...you order your steak medium, but most of the time, if there's too much pink in the middle, you send it back to the kitchen. So, you like your steak medium-well," Luke said. "But you order medium."

"And what do I drink?" Heather asked.

"You like a Tito's vodka martini, straight up, extra dry with a blue cheese olive. You'll drink Grey Goose if they don't have Tito's."

"How many martinis do I usually drink?" she asked. "At dinner."

"One, sometimes two," Luke answered. "When the meal comes, you like wine. A glass or two, and sometimes three glasses of wine. Usually a Cabernet, but Pinot Grigio if you're drinking a white wine."

"Am I obnoxious when I'm drunk?"

"I don't know," Luke said. "I've never seen you drunk. A little tipsy, but never drunk. And you are charming when you're tipsy. That's when you take your foot off the brake and let it ride."

"Luke, I made a mistake coming here."

"I know," Luke said. "But I wasn't sure you were going to figure that out."

"Why didn't you stop me?"

"Maybe it was best if I didn't."

"Are you going to be around Horseshoe Hill tomorrow?" Heather asked.

"Of course. I'll be around tomorrow."

"Can we ride horses in the afternoon?"

"Yes, we can ride horses in the afternoon."

"Okay then, I'm changing my flight and coming back tomorrow. As early as possible. It's cold up here and nothing feels right. I just want to be there, and ride horses all day."

"I'll have them saddled and waiting."

When Heather arrived at Horseshoe Hill, Luke was in the drive with a suitcase and duffel bag. He was sitting in a Jeep with the top down.

"Are we riding horses today?" Heather asked.

"We have a change of plans," Luke said. "I haven't slept in a week. You're carrying a boatload of stress. And there are so many things happening around here, I think we need to forget about Amadora, Horseshoe Hill, the Rex Corporation and all that other stuff. Do you like oysters?"

"I happen to love oysters."

"Good, I've been craving oysters lately," Luke said. "We're going to the coast to eat oysters. I know a great place, and the drive there is just as good as the oysters."

Heather returned from the big house and placed her bag beside the Jeep. Luke packed cans of beer in a cooler and nestled it in the back seat along with the overnight bags and a heavy blanket. Roosevelt and Joe Green shuffled around the Jeep with their heads hung low like two bird dogs left in the kennel when the hunt wagon left them behind. "You're going to bring back some oysters for us, aren't you?" Roosevelt asked.

"A whole bushel," Luke replied. "And smoked mullet, too. If I can find it."

"Alright," Roosevelt said. "Don't you forget."

Luke helped Heather into the Jeep and handed her a field jacket with flannel lining. "It's warm now, but it's going to be twice as cold as you think with the top down," he said.

Heather brushed back her hair and secured it with a blue headband. Luke pulled a pair of aviators from his shirt pocket and snugged them onto the bridge of his nose. It was nearly noon, and the sun was high, and the cloudless sky was brilliant blue.

They drove down the Horseshoe Hill drive and turned south on the Plantation Parkway. They wore their sunglasses and they smiled, and the wind tousled their hair. Luke reached over and took Heather's hand, and she drew his arm to her chest. Five minutes down the highway and they were people without a worry in the world. They said few words as they passed through mile after mile of plantation piney woods. They crossed the state line into Florida and drove for miles more and it seemed the pine woods would go on forever.

The pines thinned and buildings began when they reached the north side city limits of Tallahassee. On the side of the road two bulldozers toppled trees and moved dirt on a vacant lot. Luke hit the brakes and pulled over.

"What are you doing?" Heather asked.

"Wait here," Luke replied. He jumped from the Jeep and walked onto the lot toward a small object moving slowly on the bare ground. He picked up the object, examined it, and brought it back to the Jeep.

"What is that?" Heather asked.

"A gopher tortoise. She's the lucky one," Luke said. "There are probably others buried in their burrows by those damn dozers. It's not a good way to die."

"And what are we going to do with your turtle?"

"Relocate it." Luke turned and smiled.

They kept moving south through the heart of downtown Tallahassee where the pace slowed with mile after mile of stoplights and four lanes of cars and trucks merging on and merging off the busy road. South of Tallahassee, the road narrowed, and they passed through sleepy towns with bait stores and filling stations. Luke stopped the Jeep on a bridge crossing the Wakulla River.

"Have you ever seen water so clear?" Luke asked.

"It's beautiful," Heather replied.

"Do you know where the water comes from?" Luke asked.

"Tell me."

"It comes from an underground aquifer that flows through limestone caverns. And the aquifer extends all the way to the Red Hills. It runs right underneath the land where you're going to build your eco-resort. Everything that passes through that red dirt ends up in this aquifer."

Heather cast her eyes on Luke. "You promised we wouldn't talk about work today."

"Yes, I did. Sorry." Luke started the Jeep, and they continued the journey. They came to another bridge that spanned the Ochlocknee Bay. Gradually, the crisp air turned to heavy air, and it was warm, and the feel of the salt air clung to their skin.

When they reached the Gulf, they turned west on Highway 98 and skirted the coast on a two-lane blacktop. They meandered along the Forgotten Coast, and Luke reached into the cooler and plucked a can of Budweiser from the ice. He popped the top and offered the first drink to Heather. "Beaches and beer," he said. "Welcome to Old Florida."

"It's so pretty."

"Beauty is in the eye of the beholder. But I think it's pretty, too," Luke said.

On the north side of the coastal highway were tall pines, magnolias, and moss-draped oak trees. The south side had the bay with islands on the horizon and sawgrass flats near the shore. The smell of salt and sea grasses and fish and crabs was strong and when they passed a concrete shack with oyster shells piled outside, the smell was stronger.

Luke asked a casual question. "What did he do that made you come back?"

"Stephen?"

"Yes."

"Nothing."

"Nothing?"

"Nothing at all."

"Then why did you come back?"

Heather relaxed in her seat. "You." she said without turning her head to look at him.

"Me?"

"Yes, you. I was cold and irritated and somewhat sad in Chicago. Then I opened your present."

"I figured you might."

She turned and smiled at Luke. "I see the way you look at your dogs. And the way you look at the land. The way you watch the covey rise, the horses, Roosevelt, Joe Green, Lula. I see the way you look at all those things." She paused. "And you look at me the same way."

"I didn't think it was that obvious."

"It's nice."

On a long stretch of road with pine forest, Luke stopped and freed the tortoise. They passed through Carrabelle, and Luke pulled to the side of the road. He parked at a white sand beach that had a dozen concrete pads with concrete tables and a tile roof over each one. The quarter-mile stretch of beach was empty except for a cluster of terns that shuffled back and forth and dipped their beaks into the sand as the waves advanced and retreated. Overhead, seagulls chattered, and pelicans glided along the coastline on set wings with only the occasional wingbeat to hold altitude.

Luke and Heather walked along the beach at the edge of the waves that splashed on their ankles and sometimes reached their thighs. They gathered empty shells and kept some in their hands and tossed others into the water. They reached a wide stretch of beach and Luke spread the blanket in soft sand between two dunes. He took off his flannel shirt and undershirt and rolled the cuffs of his jeans to his knees. Heather rolled the cuffs of her jeans and lay on the blanket next to Luke. She raised the hem of her cotton sweater and exposed a winter white tummy and navel.

Luke sat up and looked at Heather from head to toe. "I guess a bikini could be better, but that's a pretty good look for you," he said.

"I can't remember the last time I was on a beach."

"Well, it's not Miami Beach, but I like it here."

"Me, too."

They closed their eyes and lay in the warmth of the sun. Heather plucked a sprig of sea oat from the sand and tickled Luke on the nose. "What are you thinking?" she asked.

"Nothing. Absolutely nothing. It's perfect here when you're thinking of nothing."

After a few minutes in the sun, they fell asleep and slept for almost an hour. When they woke, they left Carrabelle Beach and drove west to Apalachicola. Luke parked outside a ramshackle wood building with a screen porch and a weathered deck overlooking the marsh. "Here's where you will find the best oysters in the world," Luke said.

"The whole wide world?" Heather asked.

"Yes, the whole wide world. Come on, you'll find out."

They sat alone at the bar and ordered a dozen oysters and two glasses of draft beer. The first dozen went down easy along with the beer and they ordered another. The oysters were bright gray with a briny taste and just the right size on a saltine cracker. Heather ate hers on a cracker with homemade cocktail sauce and Luke ate his straight from the shell with a couple drops of Tabasco sauce.

"Okay, you are right," Heather said. "These are the best oysters I have ever eaten." She rested her hand on Luke's thigh. "A dozen more?" she asked.

Luke and Heather ate six dozen oysters and drank a beer with each order. They finished their oysters and beer and held hands while they walked along the river. They peered into windows of small shops filled with seaside treasures and junk. Strewn about the sidewalks were nautical antiques scavenged from sunken shrimp boats and battered buildings that once shined in the affluent days when Apalachicola was a bustling cotton port.

When the sun went down, they checked into the Rusty Oyster Inn and finished the day with two cocktails on the wide wooden porch that overlooked the marsh. After drinks they walked hand in hand to their room and lay on the four-poster bed. A ceiling fan over the bed turned slowly and air from the open window filled the room with the salt smell of the sea. The night passed slowly, and the tide came and went, came and went, and then came again just before dawn.

Sunlight through the windows woke them the next morning. Luke went to the window, pulled the curtains tight, and returned to bed. The room was dark, their skin was warm, and the scent from their bodies clung to tangled sheets. They stayed that way until noon.

They checked out of the Rusty Oyster, tossed the luggage in the back seat, shared a quick kiss, put sunglasses on, and set out on the road back home.

"I wish we could keep going west," Heather said. "Just like this. With the top down. And we could eat at all the oyster places and think of nothing else."

"All the way to California?"

"Yes, all the way to California."

"What would we do when we got there?"

"We'd turn around and come back, and we'd stay in our same room, and we'd act like the best lovers ever. We'd eat oysters and then we'd go back west so we could do it all again."

"Maybe there's hope for us after all," Luke said.

Luke and Heather bought a half bushel of oysters and packed them in a cooler for Roosevelt. They left Apalachicola and drove east along Highway 98. A few miles down the road, they turned north at a sign welcoming them into the state forest known as Tate's Hell. They passed a fire station and Luke turned left onto a sand road and drove a few hundred yards until they reached a long wooden boardwalk extending into a vast sawgrass marsh.

"Come look at this," Luke said. He walked around the Jeep and opened the door for Heather. They walked to the end of the boardwalk and watched tannin-stained water flow beneath the planks. In the distance a fish rose and plucked an insect from the surface. Overhead, osprey, eagles, egrets, and grackles filled the sky and on occasion they swooped low and settled in the grass. "Now, this is a wild place," Luke said. "Tate's Hell. The short version of a long story is that Tate went off hunting in the forest and got lost. He showed up seven days later, snake bit, briar-clawed and starving. The last thing he said before he died was, 'My name's Tate and I just came from Hell'."

"It looks so endless," Heather said. "It seems like it goes on forever."

They stayed at the end of the boardwalk and watched the birds and the fish and the swaying sawgrass until Luke said finally, "It's time to go home."

They started back along the sand road, but before they hit the highway, Luke stopped. "You have a look in your eyes. Is everything okay?" Luke asked.

"Yes. It's just that, well…I feel free," Heather said. "It's a strange feeling, but I like it."

"I feel the same way."

Luke jammed the Jeep into gear and scattered gravel with the tires when they lurched onto the paved road. Heather held onto her hair and smiled. They drove north through the Apalachicola Forest with mile after mile of pine and palmetto. Luke looked from side to side as they passed the wilderness. Heather looked at Luke and placed her hand on his arm.

"You love this, don't you?" she asked.

Luke smiled back at her. "They call this area the flatwoods. The name is obvious. And yes, I love it. All of it."

"I haven't seen another car for miles," Heather said.

"I always think of this drive as a big nature park," Luke said. "You don't have to leave the car to see egrets and the ospreys and the swamp flowers and trees. It's all right there and I hope it never changes."

CHAPTER 27

LUKE, JOE GREEN, AND ROOSEVELT sat on the front porch of Roosevelt's cottage. They drank whiskey and smoked tobacco in the cold winter air. Orion, the hunter, hovered in the Western sky. Coyotes howled in the distance and disrupted the calm.

"The coyotes are restless," Joe Green said. "Not good."

Luke turned his head toward the sound. "Don't start with your Indian ways Joe Green. I've had enough of the curse."

"It's not the curse," Joe Green replied. He stood and gazed into the darkness. "The coyotes know something."

In a far-off city on the West Coast, the sun slipped below the horizon. Eugene sat in his tiny cubicle hunched over a keyboard with two large monitors above. He was used to working late and he was thankful that he was one of the lucky ones spared the termination letters that had filled mailboxes the previous day.

Eugene jerked his head from the keyboard as multiple shots rang out in the hallway. He ran to the doorway and looked first right then left down the empty hall. He walked swiftly toward the exit and when he rounded the corner a stray bullet from a disgruntled employee hit him just above his left eye. He hit the floor, flinched twice, then shut his eyes and lay still.

Back at Horseshoe Hill, Luke turned out the lights and crawled into bed. Just as he fell asleep, someone pounded on his door.

"What the hell?"

"It's me, Luke," said Roosevelt. "Open the door."

The door swung open and there stood Roosevelt. He was out of breath and his eyes were as wide as saucers.

"What the hell, Roosevelt?"

"They shot him, Luke. Out in California. They shot my boy." Tears rained from his eyes, and he broke down.

"Is he dead?"

"He's shot in the head. They wouldn't tell me anything else. I think they didn't want to tell me he's dead. Nobody will tell me anything. He's at the hospital and they won't tell me if he is alive or dead."

"Okay. Okay. We've got this, Roosevelt." Luke scrambled for his clothes. "Do you have the number to the hospital?"

"Yes. I wrote it on a piece of paper in the cottage."

"Go get it. In the meantime, I'll call Angus."

When Roosevelt returned, Luke was on the phone with Angus. Luke took the scrap of paper and read Angus the name and address of the hospital along with the phone number. They talked for several minutes then Luke hung up the phone and turned to Roosevelt.

"Go pack a bag, Roosevelt. Angus is picking you up in the Gulfstream. They'll be here in three hours and then y'all are flying to California. You'll be there by morning."

The Thomasville airport was dark and deserted except for security lights and the blue and orange lights on the runway. Luke and Roosevelt sat on an iron bench at the edge of the tarmac. Luke had his arm around Roosevelt, who sat with his head buried in his hands. "I should have never encouraged that boy to leave, Luke."

"He would have gone anyway."

"I've seen him two times in the last two years. Two times, that's all. I never thought about it being like that. I missed all that time while he was growing into a man and now, he's gone."

"You don't know that for sure, Roosevelt. There's a whole lot of people who will be praying for you. You know that. Think about your church and how much praying that's going to be happening as soon as they get the news. And I'll let them know as soon as I'm home. Don't think about things you could have done differently. That doesn't help anybody."

Roosevelt sat and his body shook, and the tears came in waves. Out of the darkness, a set of blinking lights dropped from the western sky and descended onto the runway. Tires screeched and the jet streaked by.

"There it is," Luke said.

The G150 slowed at the end of the runway, then taxied back to the tarmac. The whine of the engines quieted, and stairs emerged from the belly. A tall man with kind eyes waited at the top of the stairs. Roosevelt walked to the plane and grasped the handrail. He pulled himself to the top of the stairs and handed his suitcase to Angus. Before closing the door, the tall man with kind eyes looked at Luke. He raised his hand as if to say he would take care of it all.

The next morning, Luke fed the dogs, brushed the horses, and rearranged tractor implements in the barn. He walked into the kitchen at the big house and sat down for a late breakfast with Lula.

"Has anybody called?" asked Luke.

"Not yet," Lula answered. "I told you I'd get a hold of you when they call. Walking around fretting like you're doing isn't doing anybody any good."

"I know." Luke broke a biscuit in half, smeared one half with butter and laid it on his plate. "I swear, Lula," he said, "I feel so bad for Roosevelt."

"He's a good man," Lula said. "The good Lord ain't got no reason to put a burden on him like he has."

"It breaks my heart to see him suffer like this," Luke said.

"Go get your Bible and say a prayer. The Lord will look after Roosevelt."

"I'm not too good at praying, Lula."

"It's never too late to start."

Luke stood by the phone all day and the call finally came late at night. It was Roosevelt. His voice sounded far away. "Luke? Is that you, Luke."

"It's me. I can barely hear you, Roosevelt." The phone went dead and then it rang again. "Roosevelt? Roosevelt?"

"It's me, Luke. Lord Almighty, I never in my life thought I would be proud of having a hard-headed boy," Roosevelt said. "But that hard-headed boy of mine is going to be alright. They told me he was dead when we got here, but it wasn't him. They got so mixed up here they didn't know who was killed and who wasn't killed. Eugene's going to be alright. Going to be just fine. He got hit in the head, but the bullet bounced right off. It cracked some skull all around, but the bullet bounced right off. Right off."

Luke collapsed into a chair. He clutched the phone so tight that blood vessels stood out in his arms. "That's good news, Roosevelt. Real good news."

"I've got to stay out here a few days. The doctor wants to be sure his brain doesn't swell. Angus left already for New York, but I'm staying here until Eugene is out of the hospital."

"Take all the time you need. And tell Eugene to call me as soon as he can. Damn it, Roosevelt, I was scared."

"Me too, Luke. Me, too."

Roosevelt stayed in California for a week. When he came home, he brought Eugene with him. Eugene was fine, but his doctors recommended a steel plate and reconstruction surgery to clean up the wound. The surgery was scheduled in Thomasville.

Land started selling at the highest prices ever seen in the Red Hills. Colonel Bronson sold a thousand acres for seventy-five hundred an acre. He divided a piece of future lakefront and listed it for nine thousand an acre. Oscar Thornton used the same strategy and got eight thousand an acre for seven-hundred and fifty acres. That tract sold so fast he listed a hundred acres of swamp land for ten. Attorneys in Thomasville were busy closing deals and investors from all over the country came to town looking to buy land.

Victor at Pine Ridge Realty handled most of the sales, but Dirk Thompson brokered a few. Dirk strolled around Thomasville in a Barbour field jacket and Russell boots like he had just stepped off the hunting wagon. Around town, when he had a prospect with him, he pretended he was old friends with everyone in Thomasville and he shook hands and slapped the backs of people who despised him. But he didn't slap Luke on the back when he saw him at Edwin Quick's Cheese Shop and Deli.

"It looks like Heather is domesticating you, Luke. Look at you eating fancy cheese and drinking wine at the wine bar instead of your usual chilidogs and beer at the pool hall. By the way, how is Heather?" he asked.

"She's fine, Dirk," Luke said. "Just hanging out in the Red Hills, day after day, waiting to get Joe Green to the table and get on with the closing."

"Me, too," Dirk said. His eyes got shifty, and the fake smile went away. "Luke, do you have a second? I need to ask you about something."

"Sure. I've always got time for someone important like you."

Dirk sat across the table from Luke. "Listen to me Luke, land is selling right now, and I've been closing deals, but there's still a core group that's not giving me any listings. Most of them are listing with Victor. You know the ones I'm talking about. Listen up, if you refer sellers to me, I could throw a little something your way. What do you say?"

"Isn't that illegal according to Georgia real estate law?" Luke asked.

"Not if nobody knows about it."

"I'd rather stay out of it," Luke said. "But I don't mind passing the word around if you've got qualified buyers willing to spend top dollar."

"I've got buyers alright."

"Developers?"

"You know I avoid developers as much as I can, Luke, but it's going to happen."

At that time, Heather walked through the door and sat at the table just as the waiter brought a cheeseboard with three cheeses, Spanish ham, and raspberry jam. Luke ordered a beer and a glass of white wine for Heather.

Dirk stood. "I'll leave you two alone. But don't forget—I've got buyers, and it could be beneficial to you." He winked at Luke.

As Luke and Heather picked from the cheeseboard, Oscar Thornton walked in and scanned the busy restaurant. He had a concerned look on his face and when he saw Luke, he shoved his way to their table. "Luke, we've got a big problem." He glanced at Heather. "It's a private matter. Can we go somewhere to talk?"

Heather rolled her eyes. "You can talk here at the table," she said. "Ginger just walked in with the Colonel. I'll go say hello. But be quick, I'm starving."

When Heather was safely out of hearing range, Oscar started talking. "I heard that Carrington is selling Prima Luna to one of the Amadora group. Did you know that?"

"Are you sure?"

"Yes, I'm sure. They've got the contract at Lyle Satterfield's office, and they're supposed to sign it sometime in the next couple of weeks. Lyle told me, but he told me to keep it quiet."

"Damn Carrington. He swore to me he wouldn't sell. He's over ninety years old."

"He's a greedy bastard. He's always cared more about money than anything. Now he has one of the kids helping him. They're cutting longleaf and replacing it with the fastest growing, cheapest trees they can find. No thought at all about the habitat."

Luke drank from his beer. "Are you sure about this?"

"I'm sure. The kid got power of attorney and signed the contract. Engineers have been working on it for weeks. They want to dam the water flow and extend the lake down there. They're going to have a golf course and four hundred home lots. It's one of the prettiest pieces of land in the Red Hills. And that's not all," Oscar said.

"What else?"

"His nephew is shopping Quail Creek to developers, and so are a couple of neighbors with smaller acreage. They could sell it all."

Luke shook his head from side to side. "With that location it would bring big money as a residential development. Lake or no lake. Almost all of it is on the Florida side of the line. And that's what people want. They want Florida residency to avoid state income tax. Damn. Carrington swore to me." Luke took a big swallow of beer. "You know, Angus tried to buy it from him years ago. He always wanted it. And I thought we had an understanding that he would give Joe Green the last right of refusal if they decided to sell. Son-of-a-bitch."

"What are we going to do, Luke? Even if the big lake is scrapped, that property makes sense to developers. Think of the waterway that runs through it. They could dam the Georgia side and go on with the project before anything is done. It would spoil everything from here to the Gulf of Mexico. This is bad news, Luke."

"Just relax." Luke leaned back in his chair and crossed his arms. He cast his eyes toward the floor. "I'm sure there are contingencies in the contract. I'm good friends with Satterfield. He'll share the details with me. Maybe there's a way we can delay it a little. All we need is a little time."

"We don't have any time, Luke. Why don't you go talk to Carrington?"

"He probably won't talk to me since he already knows he lied to me." Luke looked around the room. "We need to toss a cat in the pigeon coup. Cause some commotion and slow things down a bit."

"But how?"

Luke nodded his head as his mind gathered an idea. "What if we let people know that the largest, most significant colony of red-cockaded woodpeckers is right there on Prima Luna?"

"Red-cockaded woodpeckers? Carrington always said he doesn't have woodpeckers. I figure he has plenty, but he says he doesn't. He's probably been saying that just in case a time like this came along."

"It doesn't matter if he has them or not as long as people *think* he does. I can get Arnold at *The Tribune* to run the story. And we'll contact the environmentalists at Florida State. Hell, we'll get the Audubon Society down here."

"That sounds good, Luke, but where are we going to find the woodpeckers if he doesn't have them?"

"Remember our friend who we hired to help when they wanted to run the pipeline through that tract of virgin timber?"

"Kellogg?" Thornton choked on his tea. "He's an idiot. And a drunk. I'm not sure we can even find him again. I don't know about this, Luke. I just don't know."

Someone tapped Luke on the shoulder. He turned around and saw Ginger with a half-empty wine glass in her hand.

"Luke, can I have a word with you?" Ginger asked.

"I need to finish with Oscar. Can it wait, Ginger?"

"This will only take a minute." Luke grunted and Ginger kept talking. "I want to tell you—I'm not saying they're bad, but I want to tell you, I have done some research, and I have found the biographies of the investors who are building the resort. I've read every word I can find about those people, and I've researched them and their families, and, Luke, every one of them is a Yankee."

Luke took a deep breath. "I know, Ginger. We are going to deal with them the same way we've always dealt with the Yankees. Don't worry about it. Everything will work out alright."

"But they're Yankees, Luke. Buying up all the valuable properties around here. We're going to be stuck with another round of Yankees."

"It's going to be alright, Ginger. I'm talking with Oscar about something important right now. Can we please talk about this later?"

Ginger lowered her voice to a whisper. "The Colonel told me you have a plan. Do you have a plan, Luke?"

"I can't talk about that right now."

"Just tell me about the plan so I can sleep. I'm not sleeping at all these days, Luke."

"We'll talk later, Ginger. I have to talk with Oscar right now. Don't worry."

"Call me later, okay Luke?"

"Okay. I promise."

Luke watched Ginger walk back to her table then he turned to Oscar. "Anyway Oscar, it'll cost us some money, but we don't have time to shop around. I got to know Kellogg pretty well and he's not as bad as you think. He's motivated by money and that's good to know."

"I don't like it," Oscar said.

"I know, but we've got to do something quick, or they'll turn that beautiful property into urban sprawl that will keep growing. I still have Kellogg's number. I'm calling him as soon as I leave."

"Oh God," Oscar said. "The more I think about it, the more I remember what a disaster he really was. Didn't he hold us up for all kinds of bogus expenses when he was done? He had us over a barrel and we had to pay him."

"That was our fault. We'll have a better understanding this time. Now what do you say I get ahold of Kellogg? We need to throw some controversy into that land sale. And fast. We'll have an upfront understanding with Kellogg, and I think he'll deal straight with us if it's in his best interest. Do you have a better idea?"

"I guess not, but you better watch him, Luke. We're dealing with the devil."

"Like I said, I got to know him pretty good. He's okay when he's sober. And we don't have any other options anyway."

When Doctor Kellogg arrived in town, no one doubted his qualifications because he looked exactly like you would imagine a man who had studied birds all his life to look. The middle-aged ornithologist had a nose like the beak of a quail and a tuft of unkempt hair on the top of his head like a cock's comb. He wore horn-rimmed glasses that made his eyes look like an owl's, khaki pants, a khaki vest with eight pockets, and a pair of battered binoculars around his neck.

As soon as he dropped his bags at the Slater House Bed and Breakfast, Doctor Kellogg went straight to Horseshoe Hill and met Luke in the barn. He concocted a plan for any red-cockaded woodpecker colonies that would need relocation due to Amadora. According to the plan, he would mistakenly wander onto Carrington's property where he would locate the most prolific yet sensitive colony of endangered woodpeckers in the entire world. True or not, Doctor Kellogg would leak the news to environmental groups, newspapers, and anyone else who could create an issue for the Prima Luna sale.

After only three days, Doctor Kellogg had pages and pages of notes, diagrams, and maps. He had a slide show of colored photographs, and he showed them to anyone who cared about the environment. The only problem was the fact that he couldn't take anyone there.

The *Thomasville Tribune* picked up the story and ran a series of articles on the red-cockaded woodpecker. The articles were careful to point out that there were solutions for Amadora, but no plans were in place to protect the newfound colony on Prima Luna. Doctor Kellogg was quoted often in the articles, and he became something of a celebrity with his gawky style and willingness to share knowledge at local schools, civic organizations, and any bar he happened to accidentally stumble into.

Enamored townspeople paid for his drinks and settled his dinner tab on a regular basis. All Doctor Kellogg had to do was push those horn-rimmed glasses back on his nose and start reeling off Latin names of birds and such, and he had everyone in the Red Hills grateful for his presence. In addition, he graciously posed for pictures with dignitaries, accepted invitations to lecture school children, and he never refused a cocktail.

Doctor Kellogg was too busy in the field to discuss facts and studies with other ornithologists and conservationists who were interested in investigating the environmental impact of that particular tract of land, but he caused enough controversy and negative impression to delay the closing for a six-month study.

CHAPTER 28

THE WILL OF THE WIND brought many changes to the people in this story. Good and bad. For a time, it brought a life of tranquility to Angus Parker. It brought riches beyond dreams to a humble mule driver. It brought Luke and Grace to a new home. And it stoked a fire that nearly ruined them all. Perhaps there was a curse on Horseshoe Hill. Perhaps not. Curse or no curse, the will of the wind was not done yet.

It was late morning, and Luke was at the kennel watering the dogs when a car came to a stop and Heather stepped out. "Luke, come here." she said. "I've got something to tell you." She kept walking toward Luke. "Guess what?"

"What is it?"

"It's bloomed. The Cherokee Rose has bloomed. White blossoms all over. I had begun to wonder, but it's here." Her voice was happy, but her expression was guarded. "I've called the attorney and he's preparing closing documents for me to pick up tomorrow."

Luke picked up the water hose and turned back to his dogs. Heather stood behind him. She wrapped her arms around him and pressed her forehead against his back. "I'm sorry, Luke. I shouldn't expect you to be happy. I know that. It's just that I've been so nervous with Joe Green and his Indian ways."

"Native American," Luke said.

"Please don't make me feel like I ruined it for you. For all of you. You and Roosevelt and Joe Green. I'm sorry. You know if it wasn't me, it would be somebody else. Luke, look at me. Don't make me feel this way. You've got to give it a chance."

"You should be happy," Luke said. "You worked hard for this, but you know..."

"What?"

"This means that you'll be leaving soon, and I never thought I would say this, but I'm going to miss you."

"I'll miss you too," she said. "Of all the preposterous things that could have happened to me here, I've grown quite fond of your company."

Luke turned off the hose and looked at Heather. "Why don't we take a drive. There's something I've got to show you."

In the truck, Heather sat close to Luke and held his hand. The sky was clear, the weather was cool, and Luke drove slow on the backroads. They drove for eight miles, then crossed the river and turned onto a dirt road. They drove another two miles and came to a patch of scrub oaks with a dozen trailer homes spread throughout. Lying in the dirt at the side of the drive was a sign that read Plantation Village. There were four abandoned cars and two golf carts with flat tires. A fifty-five gallon burn barrel was smoldering with trash beside one of the homes. Luke slowed the truck and came to a stop in the middle of the property.

"Is this what you want to show me?" Heather asked.

Luke said nothing.

"What is this place?"

"This is what happens when a man is uprooted from his natural place in nature," Luke said. "See that boy sitting at the picnic table with rotting teeth and a beer in his hand?"

"Yes."

"That's Joe Green's nephew. His family sent him here from Oklahoma thinking Joe Green could help him with some problems. Now he smokes meth all day and lives off a monthly check from the government," Luke said. "Spends most of the day inside playing video games."

"I never knew Joe Green had a family," Heather said. "He can help them when he gets his funds for the land."

"I'm sure he will. He has before," Luke said. He turned and looked directly into Heather's eyes. "There's something we need to talk about."

Heather stopped him. "Maybe we shouldn't talk about anything," she said. "I don't want to be sad today, and I don't want to be happy either. I'm leaving Horseshoe Hill and going to the Slater House tomorrow. We're meeting with Joe Green's lawyer tomorrow to review the documents and I'll be done with my part here when everything's in order." She leaned toward Luke, so their faces were close. "Let's have this day. Can't we? Just one day when we think of nothing else. Like our trip to the coast."

Luke sat silent.

"Let's go, Luke," Heather said. "I want this day to be beautiful and this place is depressing. Please, Luke. Let's go."

"Alright," Luke said. "We'll go. And we'll pretend like there's not going to be any tomorrow. Just me and you and today."

Luke and Heather returned to Horseshoe Hill and saddled their horses. They rode along a ridge overlooking a pine meadow and a tiny gray bird with red cheeks flew to the tallest pine and disappeared into a hole. They rode down to the creek, climbed down from the horses, and held hands while they watched the creek flow. Heather looked straight ahead when she broke the silence. "You look sad now. Are you thinking of Annabelle?" she asked. "I sometimes think you're thinking of her when you look sad."

"No, I'm not thinking of her," Luke said. "I don't think about Annabelle when I'm with you."

"But you think about her when you're alone," Heather said. "Do you miss her?"

"Sometimes, I do. She was a big part of my life," Luke said. "I think about my pa, too. But I don't miss him."

"Why are you sad now?" Heather asked. "Are you going to miss me?" She forced her mouth into a smile. "You know we disagree on everything. You should be relieved."

"I'm sad because everything will be different tomorrow. It's too late. I can't stop it now."

"What's that thing that you and Joe Green say all the time?"

"It's the will of the wind."

"That's it. The will of the wind."

It was Heather's last night at Horseshoe Hill and Luke took her to Griffin's for dinner. They sat close together in a dark booth in the corner. They promised each other there would be no talk of Amadora and no talk of Heather moving away. They smiled and laughed and touched each other's legs beneath the table. At the end of the dinner, Luke reached for his wallet to pay the check, but Heather already had her credit card in hand. "I want you to owe me one," she said.

When Luke and Heather returned to the cottage, they undressed and went to bed. Luke turned off the nightstand light and they found each other in the dark. Sometime, late in the night when they had both fallen into a deep sleep, they untied the knot. When Luke woke, Heather was gone.

CHAPTER 29

HEATHER PULLED INTO THE PARKING lot at Sam Horne's law office and nearly ran over Dirk Thompson. He was pacing back and forth, chain-smoking cigarettes, and he had his hand on her door handle before the car came to a stop.

"What's wrong, Dirk? You look like you've seen a ghost."

"I've been looking into something for a few weeks, and I just found some answers," he said. "You know all that property that has been sold around Horseshoe Hill and I never heard a word about it until it was done?"

"Yes, the pieces were bought by our people. What's wrong with that?"

"I've been looking at the deeds. All those parcels were bought by a company named Sugna Forestry Corporation."

"So?"

"So, I'm not sure they're your people."

"Our people are still being secretive. No one is supposed to know. We don't want to look like we are buying it all. You know, it's a public relations thing."

"Well, I can trace the Rex purchases back to Rex. But not these. These are shady. There's a tangled web of shell companies. Somebody has put in a lot of effort to hide it."

"And?"

"I found it." Dirk took a long draw on his cigarette and flicked the butt in the parking lot. "It's Angus Parker. Angus Parker bought every one of those tracts I didn't sell."

Heather crossed her arms. "Angus Parker is not coming back," she said. "Luke has assured me of that."

"Luke has assured you?" Dirk glared at Heather. "Maybe you've been spending a little too much cozy time with Luke Walker."

"I resent that."

"Well, look at this." Dirk reached into his car and pulled out a crumpled map. He spread it across the hood of his car. "Here's a map of everything that has sold lately. Several of them haven't even closed yet. The yellow tracts are the ones that I sold."

"Okay. I see that."

"And..." Dirk lit another cigarette. "The red ones are the ones that lead back to Parker. Do you see a pattern?" he asked.

"No."

"The only viable access to the pieces I sold is through Horseshoe Hill. If Horseshoe Hill doesn't close, Sugna Corporation has everything landlocked."

Heather leaned over and studied the map. "Dirk, you're panicking over nothing."

"Nothing? Well, look at this." Dirk circled the name *Sugna* on the map. "What does this spell backwards?" he asked.

Heather looked at the map. "Let's see. Sugna backwards is... Angus."

"Exactly."

Heather looked at the map again. "Your imagination is running wild. We're closing the deal now and Amadora is a sure thing. My people get more excited every day. Trust me, it's going to happen." Heather retrieved a briefcase from her car. "Now, let's go in here and get this deal done."

They waited in the reception room of Sam Horne's office, among the antique furnishings and wildlife prints on the heart-pine paneled walls. The appointment was set for two-thirty, but at three o'clock they were still waiting. They drank coffee and whispered over soft music. Dirk walked outside and smoked half a cigarette. Again and again.

Finally, a clerk walked in and directed them to the conference table where Joe Green and Sam Horne sat while a paralegal stacked documents in front of each chair.

Sam pressed the blinking red light on a phone in the center of the table. "I have Mr. Kaminsky, counsel for Rex Corporation, on the line from New York," Sam said. "Lidia, could you fax a set of documents to Mr. Kaminsky, please?"

After the introduction, Sam Horne adjusted his glasses and picked up a stack of documents. "Now, people, as I have been told, and according to this letter of intent, Mr. Joe Green here has agreed to sell the plantation, and all improvements to the plantation, to the Rex Corporation for the sum of fifty-five hundred dollars an acre." Sam Horne shuffled the papers and brought out a survey. "Now, according to this survey, Mr. Joe Green's Plantation Village consists of exactly seven point two three acres." He looked at Heather. "Do you all have a copy of the survey? It's there in front of you."

Heather and Dirk exchanged a look of disbelief then rifled through a stack of papers and pulled the survey. Their jaws tightened and they turned the single paper back and front looking for more.

"Where's the rest?" Dirk asked.

"It's all there," Sam Horne replied.

Heather stood up. "Plantation Village? Why the hell are you talking about Plantation Village? That's a trailer park. We're talking about Horseshoe Hill. Thirty thousand acres. That's what Joe Green is selling us. We have the letter of intent right here, and you have had it for months." Heather slapped a one-page document on the table. She was red in the face and veins pulsed on her forehead. Dirk rifled through papers with shaking hands. Joe Green sat calmly and looked out the window.

"No, ma'am." Sam Horne spoke calmly. "Joe Green doesn't own Horseshoe Hill. He is selling *his* property. Plantation Village. Seven point two three acres and twelve manufactured homes. Eleven and a half manufactured homes if you count the one that was fifty percent consumed in a kitchen fire. That one is in bad shape. Joe Green wasn't carrying any insurance on it. Is that correct, Joe Green?"

Joe Green nodded in the affirmative.

Dirk's lips quivered. "What?"

"Eleven and a half manufactured homes," Sam repeated.

"I don't give a damn about a trailer park. What did you say about Horseshoe Hill?"

"Joe Green doesn't own Horseshoe Hill."

"If you say Joe Green doesn't own Horseshoe Hill, who owns it?" Dirk demanded.

"If you look it up on the tax card..." Sam turned to his paralegal standing near the door. "Lidia, bring us a copy of the tax card on Horseshoe Hill. It looks like we've got a discrepancy here."

Dirk stood up and started yelling. "We don't have a discrepancy, what we have is god-damned fraud!"

"It seems pretty simple to me," Horne said. "You agreed to buy all of Joe Green's real estate holdings for fifty-five hundred dollars an acre. At seven point two three acres, that comes to thirty-nine thousand, seven hundred and sixty-five dollars you owe Mr. Joe Green for his property. If you don't care to proceed with the purchase, I suppose Mr. Joe Green will have the option of claiming breach of contract."

Lidia brought copies of the tax card into the room. She handed them to Heather, but Heather would not look at them.

"We don't need the tax card," Heather said. She stuffed papers into her briefcase and slammed it shut. "I know what it says."

Lidia handed a copy of the tax card to Sam, and he interpreted the document aloud. "It says here that Joe Green Enterprises owns thirty-thousand acres that make up Horseshoe Hill plantation and it says here that the mailing address is Horseshoe Hill Drive, Thomasville, Georgia." He went on. "Now there might be some misunderstanding here because Joe Green does not own Joe Green Enterprises."

"What?" Heather's face was bright red.

Sam Horne repeated himself. "Joe Green does not own Joe Green Enterprises."

"Who *does* own Joe Green Enterprises?"

"I'm not at liberty to divulge that information since that is not the property we are closing today, but I will say that Angus Parker arranged all that twelve years ago, when he left after that tragic fire incident. Nobody knows exactly what Angus was thinking, but I can tell you that he buried the ownership so deep that no one would know the true owner unless he told them. I'm sure he had his reasons for doing that."

"That's fraud." Dirk pointed his finger at Sam Horne. "We'll have your ass for this. We'll have everybody's ass." He glared at Joe Green. "You're going to prison. And you have no idea who you are stealing from. Like it, or not, we'll get the land. And you will get nothing." He slammed the door and left.

Heather sat stunned. She gathered the papers, closed her briefcase, and left without a word.

Heather drove onto the Horseshoe Hill lawn and stopped within inches of the steps. She marched up the stairs, through the door, and into the living room. She glared at the mixed cast of characters.

Andy came in behind Heather. "She drove through the gate, Mr. Luke. I changed the code like you said, but she drove right through."

"It's all right, Andy."

"A trailer park?" The veins in Heather's neck and forehead pulsed with every syllable. "You made a fool out of me."

The room was silent. In the far corner, Colonel Bronson poured a drink at the bar. Ginger sat in a wing chair. Dr. Kellogg stood in the middle of the room as if he had been entertaining everyone before Heather arrived. His thick glasses were gone. The unkempt hair was slicked back on his head and held in place with just the right amount of gel. He wore a velvet blazer with a white silk pocket square. Oscar Thornton stood fidgeting by the fireplace. Each of them had a cocktail in their hand. Only Luke looked directly at Heather as she spoke.

"I've been waiting patiently to put this deal together according to your wishes and this was going on behind my back the entire time." She looked at Oscar Thornton. "I guess you want to buy your swamp land back. At a reduced price, I'm sure."

"Sixty cents on the dollar sounds reasonable," Thornton said.

She turned to Luke. "And what is Angus Parker going to do with all that property he bought?"

Luke hung his head. "He'll put it in a conservation easement and preserve it from development for good." Luke kept talking as if he needed to get it all off his chest. "He'll get a tax break and then sell it back to the original owners, or someone who appreciates it. I'm sorry, Heather. Nobody wanted you to get hurt."

Heather's chest heaved with every breath. "Who actually owns Horseshoe Hill?" she asked.

"Angus," Luke said.

Heather breathed deep. "Angus Parker is an old man. Who will own Horseshoe Hill when he is gone?"

There was a long silence. "I will," Luke said. "Except for the small parcel that he is giving Roosevelt."

No one moved and Heather looked at Luke with hurt in her eyes. She caught her breath and shook her head from side to side with her mouth open wide. "You don't know what you've done," she said. "You think you won, but you have screwed everything. Everything. You had the chance to be something, but you're... blind. Just plain blind."

Ginger stood and walked toward Heather. "Heather, dear..."

Heather held her hand out and stopped Ginger from saying anything more. She straightened her jacket, put her hair into place, and walked away from Horseshoe Hill and Thomasville and the terrible mess in which she had somehow played a starring role.

CHAPTER 30

In the end, Amadora was nothing more than a grand scale model stashed away in a dusty basement. Joe Green once said the land could never be owned and there was a price to pay when someone tried. The price had been paid at Horseshoe Hill. No one knew that better than Luke. He wasted no time. He established a conservation easement on all thirty-thousand acres. It was the best he could do. Amadora was gone, and it seemed to Luke that the worst was over. But Luke was wrong.

Angus called and asked Luke if everyone was doing alright. His voice was slow and low, and Luke barely heard the words, but they talked for a long time. At the end of the conversation, Luke pleaded with Angus to come back to Horseshoe Hill. Angus said no.

Later that night, Angus took a taxi to his high-rise office in the financial district. He sat at his mahogany desk and pulled a pen and stationery from the drawer. He wrote a two-page letter and folded it. He placed the letter in a sealed envelope and printed a name on the front—LUKE—before he locked it away in the safe. Angus Parker opened the bottom drawer of his desk and took his father's thirty-eight revolver. He opened the cylinder, counted the cartridges, then closed it again. Without hesitation, he placed the cold barrel beneath his chin and pulled the trigger.

All members of the Parker family had been buried in the north—New York, New Jersey, and Connecticut. But not Angus Parker. He chose a pretty hillside overlooking the old baseball field. Through the tall pines you could see the big house on Horseshoe Hill almost a half mile away.

A small gathering of old friends and family attended the graveside funeral. Colonel Bronson and Ginger were there along with Miles and Kitty and the Thorntons. Grace and Randolph were there with Luke, Lula, Roosevelt, Andy, and a half dozen men who worked on Horseshoe Hill. In the middle of the field, away from the crowd, a brown-faced man sat on a horse that shuffled back and forth.

The preacher said a few simple words. A bobwhite quail whistled from afar, and the story of Angus Parker was done. As two men lowered the casket into the red dirt, Joe Green rode to the grave. He got down from his horse and parted the crowd as he walked slowly to the casket. He held his sweat-stained hat in one hand and a twisted clump of green vine with a white blossom in the other. He laid the Cherokee Rose on top of the casket and knelt on one knee. He spoke in a graveled, deep voice, "This will lead you back home."

Luke's eyes were heavy with tears. He stood close to the red clay hole as the casket was lowered into the earth. Grace reached out and placed her hand on Luke's shoulder when he leaned over as if he wanted to pull Angus back from the hole. He stayed there by the grave while the rest of the crowd went back to the big house.

After the funeral, Luke worked like a madman at Horseshoe Hill. He rose before the sun and did not return to the house until after sunset. In the evenings, he joined Grace, Randolph, and Lula for dinner at the long dining table with four place settings and eight empty chairs.

One evening, Luke drove to Roosevelt's new home with an apple pie that Lula made. He found Roosevelt on his porch with Joe Green and Eugene. Roosevelt and Joe Green each smoked a pipe and all three had a glass of whiskey in their hands. When Luke approached the porch, Joe Green said nothing, Eugene drank from his glass, and Roosevelt tapped ashes from his pipe.

"Lula sent this apple pie over for Eugene," Luke said. "You fellows are lucky it made it over here all in one piece. There's nothing makes my mouth water like the smell of Lula's apple pie." Luke tried to smile.

Eugene set his glass on the porch rail and took the pie. "We were going to call you to join us, Luke. But I guess we all thought you'd know, or maybe one of us had already invited you. We're just trying to get the porch broken in on this new house."

"Well, it looks like you all are breaking it in pretty good by yourselves," Luke said.

Roosevelt stood up. "You know we wouldn't leave you out of anything, Luke. We didn't plan anything ahead. We just kind of came together at the last minute."

"I know, Roosevelt."

"Then sit down and have a drink with us. Help us break in this porch."

"I best be getting back to the house," Luke said. "I've got a big day tomorrow and the farrier is coming early in the morning."

Luke turned on the radio when he sat in the truck. He drove slowly and when he arrived, he walked into the living room and took a bottle of bourbon and a glass from the bar. He left the big house, walked across the lawn to the old cottage where Roosevelt lived for most of his life. He sat in a rocking chair, poured two fingers of bourbon, and looked to the sky. He was alone with his whiskey and the porch was quiet. The darkness was close. Luke finished his drink and poured another. He stayed there until the moon and the stars faded and the tall pines emerged with the dawn and stood silhouetted in the pale pink sky.

The next day, Luke received a call from Andy.

"Hey, Mr. Luke," Andy said. "I'm down here at the kennel, and Whistling Willy doesn't look too good."

"What do you mean he doesn't look too good?"

"I mean he's not eating his food, and he's laid back in the kennel and won't move at all. I tried to pick him up, but he doesn't want to get up."

"Alright," Luke said. "We're about to break for lunch. I'll come get him and run him into town to see the vet."

When the vet returned from the examination room with Willy, he wore a stern look on his face. "I'm afraid I have bad news,

Luke," he said. "Willy has cancer, and it doesn't look good. It's spread into his liver and lungs."

"He's never been sick a day in his life. Is there any way to treat it?"

"No. It's spread too far, and it's overly aggressive. I can run more tests, but the results will be the same. You need to take him home and make him as comfortable as possible."

Tears welled in Luke's eyes. "Is this something we should have noticed a long time ago?"

"It wouldn't have mattered."

Luke looked down and shook his head. "How long do we have?"

"I would say it's a matter of days."

The vet brought Willy out and Luke looked at the dog with drooping eyes and a tear rolled down his face. "I don't want him to suffer."

The vet placed the dog in Luke's arms. "Then take him home and make him comfortable."

Luke called Roosevelt as soon as he got home with Willy.

"Roosevelt, I need a favor. A big favor."

"Sure, Luke. What is it you have in mind?"

"It's Willy." Luke's voice trembled. "He's dying. He's got cancer real bad."

"Oh God, no."

"I have to put him down." Luke paused until he regained his speech. "I want to take him out in the field. One more time. He's too weak to run so I was thinking we could take him in the wagon. Just me and you and Willy."

"I'm on my way," Roosevelt said. "Have Andy hitch the mules and I'll be there as quick as I can."

Roosevelt climbed onto the wagon and took the reins while Luke stepped up on the opposite side. Luke held Willy in his arms, wrapped in a brown blanket. They rode slowly through the pine meadows and over the hills. Tears filled Luke's eyes and rolled down his cheeks. He gently stroked Willy.

"This dog is more than a dog to me," Luke said.

"I know."

"I feel stupid for loving a dog like this," Luke said.

Roosevelt stopped the wagon and looked at Luke until he had his full attention. "This dog doesn't feel like you are stupid."

Luke wiped a tear. "I used to take Willy and run him out here when nobody else was around."

"It wasn't any secret," Roosevelt said.

"I just felt like I had to run him here. I told him about Annabelle and the dream of a picture dog that filled the house with trophies." Luke brushed the hair from his face. "It was like he understood every word I said. He ran like there were a thousand dogs trying to beat him to the birds. I could hardly keep up with him. I could feel her watching." Luke patted Willy's head.

"There might never be another dog like him," Roosevelt said. "Look around at all these tall trees that are hundreds of years old."

"I see them."

"The old ones are bent over with crooked branches and scars from storms way before our time. And look where they have fallen, you see young trees growing where the old trees fell and opened a place where the sun warmed the ground and seeds took hold. It's regeneration and that's the way the good Lord planned it."

The wagon rolled along for several minutes, and Luke looked around and spoke. "I remember the first time we came out here alone. It felt like the animals and these trees, and this land didn't want us here." Luke took a deep breath. "But this dog ran and ran like his life depended on it. It changed everything. After a while, it was like the quail waited for him to find them, and the squirrels watched from the trees and every hill had a deer watching. Everything wanted us to win."

"Win what?" Roosevelt asked.

"I don't know, Roosevelt. I really don't...know."

Roosevelt stopped the wagon. "Listen to the words you just said about the woods and the animals and everything watching you. That's the Lord talking to you, Luke."

Luke drew Willy closer and stroked his ears. The wagon jangled and creaked and they rode down the slope of a big hill and then climbed another.

Roosevelt clucked at the mules. "The Lord has put a lot on you, Luke. That dog was here for you, and now I'm here for you. And Eugene is here for you. But we're nothing compared to the Lord. You've got to give that pain to him. The good Lord wouldn't bring you to it if he was not going to see you through it. Good dogs will come and go, but the Lord will never leave you."

They rode on for a while. "I remember the first time I saw you as a scared boy sitting on your momma's porch," Roosevelt said. "I knew right then that the Lord sent you here. He has plans for you. You might not know it now, but he is looking over you. And he has a plan."

"I just wish he didn't have to take this dog," Luke said. "Not now."

Roosevelt looked to the sky. Neither he nor Luke had noticed that the gentle breeze had turned into a sturdy wind that swayed the tops of the pines. Roosevelt nodded and pointed his finger toward the sky. "Wind from the east, prepare for a feast," he said.

Luke studied Roosevelt's face. "I've never heard that saying before. Is that one of Joe Green's sayings, or did you make it up?"

"Well, maybe I made it up. But the Lord is going to send good things your way, Luke. I know it."

They rode beside a hardwood thicket and a covey of quail flushed beside the wagon. Willy lifted his head, and his tail tapped against the wooden seat.

"That's it, boy," Luke said. He stroked Willy's head. "That's what it's all about. I hope there's a whole lot of quail for you in heaven's woods."

They stayed out on the wagon for a long time. Time passed slowly. At the edge of the pine meadow, a watchful doe stood over her fawn hidden in the tall grass. Across the way, a family of tiny woodpeckers came and went from a sap-lined cavity high in the pines. Shadows grew long and the sunlight turned to dusk.

"Let's go, Roosevelt. We're done here."

Luke requested beef tenderloin for dinner that evening, but he did not eat with the others in the dining room. He took his plate from the table and carried it to his room. He cut small pieces of steak and placed them in a dish beside Willy. The frail dog lifted his head and slowly chewed the meat piece by piece. Luke placed Willy at the foot of his bed and covered him with a blanket.

Luke woke up at dawn and when the veterinarian arrived, he carried Willy outside and laid him on the tailgate of his truck. Luke rubbed Willy's eyes and stroked the bridge of his nose as the veterinarian eased the needle into his vein. Willy closed his eyes and then he was still.

Randolph returned to New Jersey, and that evening, at dinner with Grace and Lula, Luke sat with swollen eyes and his head hung over his dinner plate. He gathered food on his fork and put it in his mouth.

"Maybe you should go into town and look up some of your friends," Grace said.

Luke carved a bite from his pork chop. "Don't worry about me. It's been a real hard day, but I'll be fine. I have the best company a man could have, right here at this table."

"You sure smiled a lot more when you used to bring all your lady friends around here for entertaining," Lula said.

Grace cut her eyes at Lula and frowned.

"I'm all done entertaining the ladies." Luke set down his fork. "Sometimes it seems like the more you've got, the more you have to lose."

Grace stopped eating and placed her hand on Luke's arm. "Sometimes you must appreciate what you've got, whether you lose it or not. Y'all have that saying, 'will of the wind.' I hear it all the time. That's just another way of saying that life has ups and downs. I know you hurt. Everybody does at one time or another. It's part of life, and that's the way you know you are alive. If you aren't hurting now, you're not living." She paused. "You have a good heart, Luke. Good things will come to you, and when they do, you're going to feel it. Besides, you've got plenty to be thankful for already."

"Yes, I do."

"You can't live in fear," Grace added.

CHAPTER 31

Sometimes life comes at you hard, and everything is bad, and the more you have lived, the more bad things you know. A friend is sick, a relative has died, a dog is lost. A storm destroys something you loved. These things add to the weight that crushes your soul and you struggle to rise from your knees because you have forgotten the good.

Luke buried Willy near the stables in the dog cemetery, shaded by a ring of oak trees. The wind was gentle and cool and kind, and peacefulness seemed to surround the small granite stone that covered a red dirt hole that held the dog that meant so much to him.

The following day, Luke called Eugene then went to the equipment shed, hitched a bush hog mower to the tractor and headed west. He passed the big house where gardeners planted rose bushes, and painters on tall ladders brushed fresh paint onto the pine siding. He tipped his hat at the workers and continued to the main road that ran down the spine of Horseshoe Hill. It was summer and green grasses covered the blackened ground where fire had run in the spring. He stopped often and listened to the bobwhite whistle. He tried to count the coveys, but there were too many to count.

He stopped at the scar. At the edge of the opening, Eugene sat on the tailgate of the old GMC with a Coke in one hand and a ham sandwich in the other. An open laptop sat next to him.

Luke walked to the truck and ran his hand across the hood. "The body shop did a pretty good job on this old truck. And looks like it fits you just right."

Eugene chewed on his sandwich. "How about the brakes?" he asked.

"We fixed the brakes."

"That's nice to know."

"What are you working on?" Luke pointed to the laptop.

"I'm making a spread sheet that shows the amount of carbon sequestered by trees during each stage of growth. I think it will help with our timber plan."

Luke nodded.

Eugene sighed and took a swallow from his Coke. "What are you going to do about Heather?"

"What do you mean?"

"I mean you've been moping around with your head hung low and working like there is no joy in life. Even when you and Heather were on different sides of the big issue, there was something that radiated from you two like I have never seen. You need to call her."

"I have called her. Many, many times."

"What did she say?"

"She never answered." Luke started toward the tractor. "Come on and I'll show you how to operate this tractor."

They climbed into the cab and Luke lowered the mower and cut a swath through the briars and brambles and vines that covered the ground. Then he turned the tractor over to Eugene who cut another swath, and another, until the land was clean and new.

Eugene was admitted for surgery a week later. He was a celebrity in his third-floor room, which seemed to fill with nurses night and day. The celebrity status was not due to his time in California, but due to the never-ending supply of baked goods sent by Lula.

Eugene's surgery went well, and Luke stopped by his room the following day and checked on his recovery. He opened the door and saw a woman sitting on the edge of the bed. She had her back to Luke, but Luke knew who it was.

The woman turned around. "Hello, Luke," Heather said.

Luke took a breath and searched for words. "I never expected to see you here. I don't know what to say."

"I was just having a conversation with Eugene about his carbon sequestration model." She smiled. "So, you are running dogs and Eugene is saving the world."

Luke relaxed. "Don't let him fool you. He is running dogs, too. He needs the scientific explanation for everything."

Heather turned to Eugene and patted his leg. "I'll leave you two fellows to talk about the nurses." She stood and smoothed the wrinkles from her skirt. "Luke, I'd like to talk with you if you have some time."

Luke's eyes darted back and forth between Eugene and Heather. "Now is as good a time as any."

"Not now. How about tomorrow?"

"I have some errands, but I'll be home at five. How about today?"

"If you're sure it's no bother," Heather said.

"No bother at all. I'll see you at Horseshoe Hill at five."

"Five, it is."

Heather stood and walked to the door. She stopped, smiled, and gave Luke a nervous kiss on the cheek. "I'm sorry about Angus," she said. "Really, I am."

"Thank you."

Eugene sat wide-eyed on the bed through it all. "Man, I would get up and walk out of this hospital right now if I could be there for that conversation. Man, oh man."

Later that afternoon, right at five o'clock, Heather arrived at the big house. The live oaks with hanging moss brought a smile to her face. When she got there, Grace and Lula were sitting in rocking chairs on the porch. They were drinking lemonade and fumbling with chocolate chip cookies on a silver platter.

Heather stopped at the foot of the steps and directed her attention to Grace. "Hello, I'm Heather Harrison," she said. "I came to see Luke."

"I thought that was you, I'm Grace." She took a moment to look at Heather from top to bottom. "It's a pleasure to meet you."

They looked at each other in awkward silence until Grace finally spoke. "You won the heart of a good man. Will you do me a favor?"

"I will, if I can," Heather replied.

"If you came here to give my son a piece of your mind," Grace said, "you give it to him hard. Make sure he knows that it's all over between the two of you. Don't let him hold on to anything. That boy has had a whole lot of hurt in his life. He doesn't need any more. Not right now."

Heather stood quietly. A gentle breeze blew warm air across the porch and the wind chimes jangled together. Grace rocked slowly in the white chair. "He's down at the fishing hole where he and Eugene played when they were little boys."

"I know the place," Heather said.

At the fishing hole, Heather found Luke sitting on the bank, resting his back on a hickory tree. His eyes were red and swollen. "I never imagined this place without Angus," he said. "I never imagined my life without him being a part of it." He paused. "I'm glad you're here."

"Actually, I've been in town for a couple of days. I just couldn't see you right away." Heather sat next to Luke. "I said some pretty mean things when I left."

"I know you didn't mean them."

"I meant some of them."

Luke smiled. "I was afraid you would say that."

"Let's not talk about it," Heather said. "Not today. Let's just say you were right about Amadora. It was always about the money."

"I know."

"Kitty says you don't come to town anymore," Heather said. "She said all your old women friends think you've died."

"I'm done with women. Never was good at it, anyway."

"You use every excuse in the book to keep from being good at it."

Luke picked up a pebble and tossed it into the deepest part of the fishing hole. "You never answered my calls or my letters."

"I read your letters."

"And you never sent a reply."

"You chose woodpeckers over me."

"I never knew I had a choice."

"Would it have made a difference?"

Luke didn't answer.

"You want to know something funny?" Heather asked.

"Tell me."

"I dream about the woodpeckers all the time. It's so simple for the woodpeckers. Why do our lives have to be so complicated?"

Luke looked into her eyes. "Do you think it's possible for us to start over?"

"Do you?"

"Yes, do you?"

"So, there's a chance?"

"Maybe."

"That means yes."

"No, that means maybe."

Luke started to speak, but Heather placed her finger to his lips and stopped him. "Let's not talk about it right now." Heather stood. "There's lots more to talk about."

She walked away, and just before she was gone, she turned back and shouted, "I'll be at the Slater House. You can call me. If you want."

"Maybe I will," Luke shouted back.

"You will," Heather replied.

She stopped at the big house and greeted Grace and Lula, still on the porch with their lemonade and cookies. She gazed at each corner of the big white house like she was seeing it for the first time. Then she turned and looked back at the green grass on the lawn and the pink azaleas that lined the driveway. She smiled at Grace. "Has it changed much?" she asked.

"It was something to see in its day," Grace replied. "It's much quieter than it used to be, and not so many people in and out."

"Maybe all that will change when your grandson is born," Heather said. She slowly rubbed the tiny bump in her tummy.

Grace and Lula stopped rocking their chairs. Their mouths fell open. After several long seconds, they smiled. "Will we be seeing more of you?" Grace asked.

"Maybe." A moment passed. "Yes, I'm sure you will."

Heather turned and walked slowly down the steps. When she reached the last step, the wind whispered, and a feather fell like a snowflake and danced slowly to the ground. Heather turned back to the ladies. "It's the will of the wind."

ACKNOWLEDGEMENTS

There are many people who helped with the content of this book. Some knew they were helping while others provided information and insight in a casual setting over dinner, riding horses in the field, hunting quail, or walking through the South Georgia piney woods. Others took the manuscript in hand and read early versions which brings to mind a quote from Ernest Hemingway, "The first draft of anything is shit."

Among those who I would like to thank for edits and on the early version are Laura Albritton, Lori Medders, John Wagner, Geoffrey Young, Kathleen Kelly, Rozzie Davis, EJ Morrow, Sara Morrow, Van Middleton, Bob Ireland, and Emily Eckles. I would also like to thank Warren Bicknell and Ebe Walter for their wisdom and insights into the history of the Red Hills Region during our early morning walks in the woods.

Most importantly, I would like to thank my wife, Rebecca, who provided support and insights, even when I knew she was thinking, *is he ever going to finish this book?*

Made in USA - North Chelmsford, MA
54701_9798988915409
01.09.2024 1449